CHILDREN OF EVER AFTER

Avery Yearwood

For all the mothers who love fiercely in an unrelenting world

CONTENTS

PART ONE

Chapter One

Rebecca

"Do you have children?"

Rebecca took a deep breath, trying to swallow the pain in her chest. *No, she didn't have children, damn it.*

The woman, a visiting professor of sociology, looked at her with idle curiosity.

"No, no, I don't," Rebecca sputtered, raising her voice, as if increased volume might move the conversation off in a less depressing direction.

The woman's pale lower lip protruded from her wrinkled face, and as she shifted, her breasts swayed slightly underneath her blouse. "I'm childless by choice, too."

"No," Rebecca corrected. "I want children."

The woman raised her eyebrows. "How old are you?"

Rebecca glanced around the party for her husband. Will was standing in a circle of professors, pouring generous glasses of wine. A white linen handkerchief fanned out of his breast pocket. Four years ago, after his first bestseller, he had started wearing designer clothes. She still hadn't adjusted to it. She missed his scuffed shoes and thinning khakis.

She turned back to the woman. "I'm thirty-nine."

The woman nodded with a smile, her upper lip shrinking into a thin line. Her bony finger tapped the face of her watch.

Rebecca squeezed the appetizer in her hand. She could feel the oily salmon on her palm and the cracker breaking.

The woman couldn't have known Rebecca had been trying to have a child for years. Will was in a perpetual state of almost. *We will have children*, he assured her, his light blue eyes shiny behind his glasses, his hand on her thigh, *just give me a few more months*. All the months, somehow, had avalanched into years.

The woman took a sip of her wine, her eyes flittering around the room. "I have to applaud your husband. *Conservative Netpression* is a brilliant idea."

Rebecca nodded. Will's book about conservatives using technology to oppress women and minorities was coasting at the top of *The New York Times Bestseller* list. She secretly thought his book was a shallow jumble of anecdotes and misrepresentations. They had hosted dozens of dinner parties in the book's honor, and for a long time, she was afraid, tipsy with red wine, she would accidentally reveal her true thoughts. But she gradually realized people weren't that interested in the content of the book. Maybe they hadn't even read it.

"I bet the Koch brothers masterminded the strategy," the woman opined. She turned to Rebecca, her eyes narrowed. "You're a professor, aren't you? Have you written a book?"

"Yes," Rebecca said, softening. Her book had only been purchased by 93 people, and its remnants were languishing on the basement shelves of university libraries.

"It was about the women of the African tribe Nobuso, a truly independent society of women—"

"Oh, Africa," the woman said, dismissively, as if there was nothing left of interest to say on that continent. "You know what's popular right now? China and the Middle East."

Rebecca retreated a few inches, as if the woman had poked her in the chest. "Excuse me," she said, not bothering to blunt her tone.

Rebecca walked a few feet and saw Will. He had been cornered by Phillip, an ambitious young professor that had recently joined Will's department from Harvard. Phillip was leaning in enthusiastically as he spoke, his lips close to Will's cheek.

"Professor Hamilton, your book is incredible. I'm actually basing my next article on your work. I was wondering if you've considered the impact of memes on conservative netpression?"

Will tilted his head, about to respond, but Phillip barreled on, barely pausing for breath. "I've been analyzing meme circulation patterns on Reddit. The data is fascinating! Did you know that cat memes spike every time there's a major US political event?"

The sides of Will's mouth flickered, suppressing a laugh. A group of professors and journalists interrupted the pair, circling around Will. Rebecca let herself be gently pushed backward, outside the throng.

Will smiled graciously and started talking about the time he had been on *Wake Up America*, and the guest after him was there with a bunch of exotic animals, and how a parrot had kept interrupting him, randomly repeating, "Wake up America!" Then Will had started sharing the lessons from the book in a way that they were lessons for America so he and the parrot had become a duet.

The crowd laughed. Rebecca had heard the story dozens of times before and she eyed him from the outskirts of the overly eager fans, waiting for him to acknowledge her presence, to see she was there.

They had not had sex in seven months. Watching him, his confident grin, she felt a rush of pent up desire. She wanted his slender body, his strong jaw, his wide mouth. But she was so resentful he was *always out there*, when he could be with her, having a child, that her desire was doused with anger, like if she reached out to touch him, they might both burst into flames.

As a young graduate student praised him, Will's cheeks flushed with joy. Rebecca turned in frustration and elbowed her way to the kitchen. The caterers were scurrying about, preparing fresh plates of hors d'oeuvres. Rebecca grabbed an open bottle of wine from the refrigerator. She walked back through the party, abruptly done with it.

It was only now that Will saw her. He threw her a

quick look of reprimand, his brows raised briefly with confused annoyance—*where do you think are you going, in the middle of hosting our party?*—but she kept walking. She couldn't stand all the parties, so consuming they left no room for little children.

She glided up the stairs, and the sounds of people talking and laughing receded. She closed the door to the master bathroom.

She sat on the toilet and chugged from the bottle of wine, wiping her mouth with the back of her hand. A gray box of condoms sat high on one of the open shelves. It was her daily reminder Will wasn't ready to have a child.

She reached for the box, studying it. The letters were embossed in silver. *Lubricated for her pleasure.*

She laughed bitterly. Condoms were for prom nights and bar dwellers and married men in roadside motels. Not for a woman in her late thirties, hoping for a child.

The wine bottle clanked on the floor, spilling, and the condom box tore easily in her fingers. She ripped open a packet. The condom was light, insubstantial, and she brought it to her mouth, catching her face in the mirror. There was the smooth oval shape, the straight, Grecian nose, the large blue eyes. As a child, her features had been too large for her face. She had been all nose and horse teeth.

So when her features settled out in her early twenties, her teeth fixed by five years of braces, her cheekbones appearing to make her nose seem prominent but no longer large, she noticed the difference in how people treated her. Her newfound beauty conjured up millions of small conveniences and appreciative smiles and looks of admiration.

Though she would never admit this to anyone she knew, these little indulgences had, for a long time, cheered her, left her feeling almost invincible, like the whole world, from cabbies to street cleaners to presidents of universities to book publishers, approved of her. But when she studied herself in the mirror now, she felt a cold sense of failure spread through her bones. Wasn't having a child, on some biological level, the whole point of beauty? Yet here she was, approaching middle age, with an empty womb.

She blew the condom into a balloon, watching the latex grow thin and taut. When it was about to burst, she pinched the end and tugged the rubbery band until it formed an unbreakable knot. She tossed the misshapen slug against the wall and it bounced a few times before settling next to the toilet.

She reached for another packet, and then another. She began to feel slightly woozy, and her mouth tasted like rubber and oil. She imagined Will watching her, shaking his head in disapproval, a piece of hair falling over his forehead, thinking she was juvenile. She ripped the packets faster and tied the knots tighter.

The bathroom floor was soon covered with thirty-six yellowish balloons. Some of them were round and stubby. One was bulbous, threatening to break, as if it were filled with small but expanding tumors.

Rebecca's tongue was waxy and dry, and surveying her handiwork, she laughed.

She needed to flee, leave this house, with all its empty bedrooms. Why did they even have five bedrooms? For what?

On the staircase, the clamor of the party, plates and forks tinkling, dozens of people chattering, washed over her. Her husband's laughter, with its distinctive loud bark, rang out.

She ran down the stairs, and almost collided with Peter, a law professor and one of their best friends. He was talking on his cell phone and he lifted his hand in a wave. She nodded. He didn't know anything about her desire for a child, and Will's refusal. They hadn't told any of their friends.

Outside, a cool breeze drifted over her bare arms. Her low heels clacked on the pathway. She started the car, and drove away, uncertain of where she was headed. The Victorian mansions on her block quickly transformed to apartment buildings and retail shops. She pulled over in front of a bar, annoyingly, called BAR (REL).

The narrow space was packed with twentysomethings in

skinny jeans, large key chains dangling from their belts, their feet in Converse sneakers or black boots, their phones glowing in their hands.

She found an empty stool near the garbage can. Punk music throbbed out of black speakers.

"Hey," someone said loudly. Perched on the next stool was a skinny young man with a scruffy beard and a Save the Earth shirt. He was drinking a Pabst Blue Ribbon out of a can. He reminded her of an article she had read in *Time Magazine*, about hipsters, and she laughed.

He smiled. "Alright, alright, you got a sense of humor. I like that."

She smiled, and then turned away, facing the bar. She hadn't been in a bar like this, loud and malodorous and dark, since graduate school. She and Will had gone to dinky bars with their friends, drinking and laughing until closing time. Then he had hoisted her on his shoulders, and they had stumbled home together, on the icy Cambridge streets. Wobbling precariously, her fingers clutching his head, Will shouted the Irish tunes from his childhood, the tunes his father had sung as he fixed their rickety farmhouse. "Oh," Will bellowed, "I first set my eyes on sweet Molly Malone, as she WHEELED her WHEELbarrow," and then Will laughed, and they had tumbled into mountains of snow, his lips surprisingly warm as he kissed her mouth, their friends cheering.

"I've never seen you here before," the young man shouted, his breath crossing her ear.

"I've never been," she said, raising her voice, to be heard over the blaring music.

He smiled at her wryly, and she suddenly couldn't bear the thought of a conversation about who she was, and why she was here, so she reached over the bar and grabbed a cherry, popping it in her mouth. It tasted treacly and artificial.

He was still watching her, with amusement.

"You want a smoke?" he yelled. He pulled a green pack of cigarettes out of his back jean pocket.

She shook her head, taken aback that anyone smoked anymore.

The man shrugged, and drifted into the amorphous throng of people.

The bartender appeared in front of her. His dark hair was shaved into a mohawk, but he was older, in his mid-thirties. The bare bones on his skull seemed soft, as if she might be able to compress them with her fingers.

"What can I get you?" he mouthed.

She ordered a double whiskey, and he nodded cheerfully, scooping up an empty glass. His body, broad-shouldered and tall, with slender limbs and large hands, reminded her of Will's.

He slid the whiskey over. He leaned on the bar, his hairy forearms flexed against the wood, and he stared at her with such naked interest, she thought, for a moment, he was going to kiss her. But then he simply wiped something off the shoulder of her silk dress, his fingers long and gentle.

She took a drink, not particularly enjoying the taste, but wanting to obliterate something, even if it was only the coherency of her own thoughts.

Seven months of abstinence had left her feeling bereft. Even as a child, she had been surprisingly tactile, hanging onto her father's leg and nuzzling against her mother's stomach and breasts. "Our little monkey," her parents would remark, sharing a look that she had sensed, even then, wasn't entirely free of a patrician disdain for flesh touching flesh.

By seven or eight, she understood she would have to look elsewhere for affection. There were her private school girlfriends, but when she wrapped her skinny arms around them, they giggled uncomfortably, their bodies rigid in plaid skirts and button-up shirts. So she was left with her menagerie of stuffed animals and baby dolls. She carried them tied to her chest and back, enjoying their weight pressed against her body. "I am your mother and I love you," she would whisper, cuddling their bodies against her stomach, stroking their heads, squeezing them until their seams frayed.

9

She and Will still touched, but there was a newfound hesitancy, a hovering. It was the feel, she imagined, of a phantom limb, there, but not quite. Occasionally, they would relinquish control, and grope each other like teenagers, dry humping on the couch, her underwear soaked, her fingers scratching his back, her chest trying to break into his.

But that happened less and less frequently, as it always ended with the same intolerable frustration: she wouldn't use a condom, and he wouldn't not use a condom. It was like some kind of twisted logic problem, but no matter how she phrased the words, they came out the same way: null, impossible, void. No way out.

He wasn't ready to have a child yet. She was. *But why*, she wondered, futilely recalling their premarital counseling (which they had completed to get married in his parents' church, something she had found awkward and strange, but had done for Will, to make him happy.) In front of the priest, they had reflexively agreed they would have two children, and maybe a dog, and a rambling house. She saw that life, and she had been happy.

"You want another?" the bartender asked, a questioning look in his eyes, as if he were impressed and surprised by her ability to drink.

She looked down. Her glass was empty. She was feeling unmoored, and it crossed her mind to move behind the bar and kiss the bartender, her fingers feeling the smoothness of his scalp, her lips parting. But the thought also sickened her.

She slid the twenty-dollar bill to the bartender. He didn't move for it. He just leaned over the bar, cocking his eyebrow. She could almost feel the hollow release of kissing him.

She pushed her way through the crowd and out of the bar. On the street, she shivered in her thin dress, pulling out her keys. A black cat darted out from underneath her car, startling her. The cat paused in the middle of the road and looked back at her. He - the arrogant way the cat moved made her feel like it was a he - glared at her, his yellow eyes reflecting the moonlight as he hissed. She scrambled into her car.

She drove home slowly, fiddling with the heat, wondering if she was over the legal limit, wondering if she would get pulled over. Maybe she would crash into a tree; maybe this would be her adolescent moment. As a teenager, she had never gotten into trouble. Her excitement had come from staying up late at the dining room table, drinking decaf coffee and discussing *Ulysses* and *The Feminine Mystique* and *Anna Karenina* with her parents. Both her parents were professors, and she could still remember the proud way they had glanced at each other, their eyes glowing, their lips slightly upturned, whenever she had proffered an eloquent or interesting idea.

They didn't always approve of her theories; sometimes they frowned or even laughed. But maybe she had known they wouldn't crush her; in their own way, they had been prodding and encouraging, coming down on her just hard enough. She wanted to do that for her own child.

She felt light-headed from the whiskey. As she drove up to the house, she saw the downstairs' lights were on.

She parked the car in the garage, and went in through the backdoor. The kitchen was cluttered with gnawed food and dirty glasses and dinner plates and trash bags. She could hear Will stomping around upstairs, and her heart fluttered in anticipation, knowing they would fight, but wanting to see him anyway. A bottle of opened wine sat on the counter, and she grabbed it by the neck, walking into the living room.

Someone had left a blue scarf strewn across the armchair, and she looped it around her neck. The scarf was soft, and scented with vanilla. She sat down on the white couch. Above the fireplace, there was a framed photograph of six Nobuso women at dusk. They were standing in front of a roaring fire, facing away from the camera, the muscles in their back long and lean. She had taken the photograph herself, thinking how beautiful the women were, how strong.

She closed her eyes, and remembered when she first arrived in the Nobuso lands, a wild stretch expanding across

Tanzania and Kenya; she had been awed and afraid. Afraid disease or violence would befall her, afraid the Nobuso would turn her away, destroying her chance at tenure, afraid she would lose her courage to live in a culture so different than her own. Far in the distance, the yellowed fields rose up to touch the pale blue sky. The hoofs of large animals thundered beneath her feet. Dark women pattered in a language she could not yet decipher, their tones light and musical.

Wondrous and terrible things seemed equally possible. And she remembered this feeling because she felt something similar about her marriage, that it might blossom or disintegrate.

"Why did you leave like that?"

Rebecca turned, startled at the sound of Will's voice. He was standing at the foot of the stairs, in his gray pants and white button up shirt, a black trash bag in his hand. He was staring at her intently, as if he knew her, but wasn't quite sure who she was any longer. The way her grandfather had looked at her when he was experiencing dementia. She took a swig of wine. Her mouth was gummy and dry.

He walked over, and stood with his knees touching hers. She wanted to reach up and clasp her fingers around his neck. *I am losing it because I love you*, she wanted to explain, *and I want your child.* But she had explained this before, dozens of times, and he had only cringed, his eyes misty and apologetic.

"This," he said, holding up the trash bag, waving it around, "was pretty ridiculous. What was the point of blowing up all these condoms?"

She laughed, feeling drunk. "The point *is* I want to have a child. I'm sick of putting it off so you can have more stupid parties to discuss your stupid book."

His face darkened, and he lifted the trash bag and shook it violently over her lap. The blown-up condoms, dozens of them, drifted over her legs, and onto the couch and the floor. She picked one up and threw it at him. It bounced off his chest.

She stood, and shoved his chest, hard. He stumbled

backward, breathing heavy, looking like he very much wanted to hit her.

"Go ahead," she taunted.

He moved at her quickly, and she flinched, surprised. He tackled her, landing them both on the couch. Condoms burst with a *pop, pop, pop*.

His body was warm and hard against hers, suffocating, and her heart swung, back and forth, over the line that divided love disappointed and hate.

"Goddamnit, Rebecca," he groaned, grabbing a chunk of her hair and pulling it. She could feel the tension in her roots, a dull pain on her scalp, and somehow, this was a relief.

She remembered when they were young, untenured professors, passed out after a party. They burrowed under the covers, his arm and leg wrapped around her body, his chest solid against her back. He had whispered in her ear, his breath smelling of wine, quoting James Joyce. *And then I asked him with my eyes to ask again yes and then he asked me would I yes and his heart was going like mad and yes I said yes I will yes.* She had smiled, and squeezed his hand, and whispered *yes I will yes.*

She reached up and lost her fingers in his dark brown hair, bringing his mouth to her own. She bared her teeth and sucked on his tongue, as if she could suck something essential out of him, the thing that was tearing them apart, preventing them from having a family.

He pulled his head back sharply, letting go of her hair. "Rebecca." His cheeks were flushed and he studied her face, the same way he studied his books, with an intense curiosity. "You have to stop this. We can wait."

"No," she replied, her voice rising, even though she knew loudness wouldn't make him hear better, wouldn't make him understand. "You can't possibly believe that. I'm almost forty."

His body went limp, and then he rose, dragging her with him, untangling their legs, so they were sitting, side by side. He picked up his glasses and rubbed them with shirt before carefully putting them back on. "What about the women of

13

Nobuso? You should write a sequel. It's important work. I think you'll breakthrough on the next one."

He squeezed her thigh firmly, his eyes wide and encouraging. He had loved her book, believed it was beautiful and interesting, even if few others had read it. She swept her hair out of her face.

"You won't be able to go back with a child. And you were happy there."

Part of her did long to return to the freedom she had felt in a land where no one had any expectation of her; she had been allowed, simply, to exist, her feet bare in the fields and her hands digging in the dirt.

But the children, intrigued by her presence, had tumbled on top of her, and held her hand, and climbed on her back, and she had reveled in these touches. The Nobuso women shifted seamlessly from working to mothering, carrying the children on their backs, pushing the toddlers to collect wood for the fires, teaching the older girls to sew. Rebecca had mothered the children, too, feeding the babies and toddlers, running with the boys in the morning to collect water, herding them back to the camp. *This, mothering,* she had thought, *feels right.*

And she had explained this to Will, but he had forgotten, or never heard her in the first place.

"I was surrounded by children there."

"OK," he acknowledged. "But you have to look at this from my perspective. I've worked my whole damn life to be this successful, to have this much influence. Now's not a good time to take off."

"I understand that's how you feel," she said bitterly. "How you think it is."

Ever since a conservative Supreme Court Justice had cited Will's first book *The Women and the Law* as the paragon of dangerous liberal thought, propelling the book to the top of the bestseller list, he had become a regular on *CNN* and *Good Morning America*, and this seemed to enlargen him. He stayed up late to respond to fan mail and internet commentators, happy to travel, on a moment's notice, to book fairs and book clubs and local TV interviews, and write endless pieces for newspapers and magazines. He had become an entity *out there*. There wasn't enough of him left *here*.

She often wondered how different their lives would have been, if that Justice had never mentioned his book.

"But it's not an either/or! You can have children and a career."

"I have momentum here, Rebecca. The public is fickle. I am still making a name for myself."

"Lots of successful people have children," she snapped. Her sister Elizabeth was a partner at a law firm in New York, and had three children. "Like my sister."

"True. But those children go days without seeing their parents. Is that what you want?"

"Nothing's ideal at this point, Will. But I have flexibility. I will take care of the children," she promised, feeling the fragility of this kind of bargain even as she offered it.

His face softened, and he laid his hand gently on her thigh. He seemed touched by this sentiment, her willingness to sacrifice for his career, but his eyes were narrowed skeptically.

What was he afraid of? She thought of Will's younger brother Seamus, who had fallen out of a tree as a boy, and was stuck, forevermore, at a mental age of eleven. Will's mother, a wan woman with a braid of long gray hair, still cared for him, day in and day out.

"Are you worried we'll have a child like Seamus?"

"No," he said quickly. "I love Seamus. He's my brother."

"Of course you do. But…" Rebecca wanted to tell Will their lives would be different, that they wouldn't be worn down by having a child, even one like Seamus. Not with their flexible jobs and salaries. But she couldn't respond to a fear he refused to articulate.

"Just trust me," she said finally, laying her hand atop his, feeling the familiar knots of his knuckles and the muscles in his fingers. "Your career will be fine. We can do this."

He closed his eyes, breathing slowly, and then anger washed over his face. "I'm sorry. I'm not ready to have a child. I don't know what to tell you."

The sounds in the room—her sharp breathing, his foot tapping the wood floor—suddenly seemed oppressive.

She could feel, pressed against her, all the hours she poured over her friends' baby photos and celebrity baby photos, desiring to become another woman, one with a baby nestled on her hip, the sweet breath in her ear. A woman who had children to curl underneath her arms as she told them fairytales and stroked their hair, and to run in the backyard with, squealing as the sprinkler went off.

She wanted to be obligated; she wanted to be tied down by all the needs and wants of little children, their gummy hands sticking to hers, demanding her attention.

"I'm going to leave, then," she said.

And once she said this, she realized her patience, her willingness to accommodate Will, had fled like the warblers at the dawn of winter.

"What?" he said. She had never once mentioned leaving; their marriage, having lasted for over a decade, had taken on the quality of permanence.

"I'm going to leave," she repeated.

The scarf was heavy and thick on her neck and she pulled it off. Will leaned back and stared at the ceiling. Flecks of gray dotted his dark hair.

It occurred to her that something had stopped her from finishing the sentence, from saying "I'm going to leave *you*." "I'm going to leave," theoretically, could have meant anything. I'm going to leave this house. This city. This country.

She rested her head against his shoulder, feeling the crispness of his shirt and the bony muscles underneath. She wanted to kiss him, and punch him, force him to choose her.

He turned, and touched her chin with his finger. Then his eyes fell, like he had seen, in her expression, she was done. If they were to continue, he would have to bend.

16

"God damn it," he said, exasperated. He swatted a condom away, and then curled his fingers into a fist. "But I still love you," he protested. "You're irreplaceable to me."

Rebecca resisted her urge to say something bitter, to give into her desire to blame him, to make things easy in that way. Because the truth was, even if he had told her, in their twenties, he didn't want children, she would have married him anyway. She would have risked it. She loved him that much.

He looked down at his hands, and then back at her. "Columbia offered me a visiting professorship next year. Maybe I should take it."

"Alright," she said bleakly, imagining him in New York, with its intellectuals and art galleries and fine restaurants, with its infinite supply of childfree women.

His hands gripped her neck, and her chestnut hair poured over his wrists and forearms. He kissed her, and there was resentment in it, a disappointment. His hands were on her breasts and her hips.

"You never know," he whispered, tugging at her hair. "Maybe," he continued, his breath on her earlobe. "You'll change your mind. Maybe I will."

She said nothing, annoyed by his refusal to acknowledge reality, even now. It was like he didn't want to admit he was losing her to keep his life free of obligations. She bit his lip and dug her nails into his back.

He tilted her head backwards, and thrust his tongue in her mouth, and she was hot and overwhelmed and distracted. She climbed on his lap, and peeled off her dress and tossed it on the couch. She wrapped her bra around his neck and his mouth twitched.

He ran his fingers along her back, and then he pushed her flat on the couch. He squeezed her breast, a ponderous look on his face she could not read. How strange it was you could be with someone for over a decade and still not know their every expression.

He unzipped his pants and he entered her quickly. Her

legs wrapped around him, not wanting to let him go. She still wanted a child. She still wanted *his* child, a child with his light blue eyes, with his widow's peak, with his curiosity about the world.

"Will," she breathed, softly.

It's me, she wanted to say, *it's us.* But she didn't say anything other than his name.

He gripped her arms, and she was waiting for him to retreat, to demand protection. *Don't,* she pled, closing her legs tighter, *I will raise this child.*

He kept moving, his eyes sad and focused, and then he came inside of her with a grunt. She searched his face for an explanation. He stared at her for a moment, breathing heavy, but his face was again unreadable, some vague mix of sheepish and regretful.

"I shouldn't have done that. I can't have a child right now," he said softly. He looked at the ceiling. "But I will always want you. And maybe I'm wrong about everything. Maybe everyone knowing my name and being on TV all the time isn't going to get me what I want."

He rose off her, and walked into the bathroom.

She raised her knees in the air, wondering, if the child was conceived, would it only be hers? No, that wasn't true. Will would love his child if they were born. If they were real and noisy and warm, demanding his attention with sticky fingers. The bathroom light and the faucet went on, and the water hitting the sink sounded angry.

She plumped a pillow, careful to keep her body straight. She cupped her stomach protectively, and tried to focus on the possibility of a child, of a little girl in her arms. Squeezing her eyes shut, she shook her head, trying to discard the dark thoughts that were like mosquitos flying around her, thoughts of being alone at forty, thoughts of being without the only life partner she had ever known.

Chapter Two

Brittney was tired. When she leaned over a certain way to pick up one of her children, a sharp pain radiated out from her lower back. Her knees, if they were straightened too quickly, cracked. But Chris waved these complaints away. He had blunt cheekbones and amber brown eyes and a masculine jaw. He stroked her cheek, and pressed his chest against her breasts and whispered he wanted one more baby.

"Three's the perfect number," he insisted, his breath warm on her neck, "and I love it when you carrying my child. I never seen a more beautiful sight."

She closed her eyes and smiled at this sweetness, allowing him to stroke her breast, pretending, for a moment, another child was possible.

His erect penis pressed against her thigh urgently, and he climbed on top of her. "We make great children, Brit. They're the best things I ever done."

She was so sleepy, after a day of playing with Ethan and soothing Madison's teething pains. Chris rarely made it home before they'd been put to bed. She shook her head. "I told you, Chris, I can't. I'm twenty-two, and I feel like an old woman."

But she didn't stop him when he yanked down her underwear and pulled up her t-shirt, bunching the cotton around her neck. He pushed inside her, moving back and forth.

"You don't feel old," he panted.

She laughed.

He smelled like liquor and body odor and smokes and the metallic of the police station, and her hips rose reflexively. He was the only man she had ever had sex with and whenever she thought of sex, she thought of him.

Terror buzzed on the edge of her consciousness—a fear of her body being beaten down by another pregnancy, of her mind being scrambled by more sleep deprivation—but she did not draw this terror close.

She allowed it to remain in the distance, a hazy shadow, so she could succumb to the pleasure in front of her, to Chris. His skin was inside hers, no barrier between them, and she liked the security of this, of knowing he was safe and accounted for and *present*.

The firm weight of Chris's body crushed against hers, and the darkness exploded with a kind of vibrating light.

Stay with me, she thought wildly, clutching his back, wanting to press his body deeper inside of her own. It felt so good to have him here, in her arms. She kissed the soft skin on his chest.

His moans grew louder, guttural, and her hips rose faster and faster and faster, wanting to be with him, make him feel good.

A cold breeze drifted over her ribs and neck. She shivered, and this discomfort brought her back to herself. She was being ridiculous. She couldn't have another child right now.

"Chris, we can't ..."

She pushed him away with a great deal of force. Her slender fingers spread like webs across his chest, and his chest rose up, peeling off her.

But it was too late. He came with a grunt, his eyelids closed, his hulky body rising in the night air.

He gasped, a childish gasp of delight that annoyed her, reminded her of his irresponsibility. *Damn it*, she thought.

He pulled his penis out of her, and the sudden emptiness felt like a slap. He tumbled to the side.

The striations in his back seemed to glimmer, and she wanted to reach over with her fists and beat his back, screaming *I told you, I ain't ready for another child!*

But she didn't. He had already closed his eyes, and he would snap at her, angry, if she woke him. Her body felt cold and damp.

She tugged her t-shirt down over her stomach and brought the covers up to her neck.

Outside the window, the moon glowed, round and white. She remembered being a child, sitting on the porch steps, her head against her mother's bony knees, waiting for her older brothers to come home. "Full moon's bad luck," her mother would say nervously, her breath smelling of beer and cigarettes, her wary eyes on the empty street as she played with Brittney's hair.

Brittney closed her eyes, blocking out the glow of the moon, listening to Chris's congested breathing. For months, Chris had been coming back from the bars, his words slurring as he cajoled her to have unprotected sex. She had let it go on because she feared she was losing him, slowly, and his hands on her hips, his pleading breath in her ears, reminded her, no, he was still here.

She gingerly climbed out of bed and searched for a piece of paper. She grabbed the envelope from the PECO bill and a pen. She scribbled I CANT HAVE ANOTHER CHILD RIGHT NOW!

On paper, the sentiment seemed reasonable, prudent even. In the bathroom, the moonlight illuminated the yellowed tiles and the porcelain sink. She triple underlined her words for emphasis. Then she laid the envelope on top of the toilet seat. It was for him, but maybe for herself too.

Chris had pulled all the covers over his giant body. She wished she could close the window, but the warped wood would scrape against the frame, waking Chris. She sighed and pushed up against his back for warmth, tugging a little piece of the covers over her legs. The position was cold and her head was tilted in an awkward angle. But she was exhausted, and the minor pains drifted away as she succumbed to sleep.

~*~

The sun woke her, its rays streaming in through the open window. Brittney stretched her legs on the empty bed. The TV was on in the living room, and she could hear Ethan asking Chris about the show. "What that mean? What that mean?"

She laughed, pleased Chris was home for once. She wrapped the comforter around her body. Breakfast had to be cooked, and Madison's diaper would need to be changed. It was easier to stay in the warm bed.

She closed her eyes, and then the door swung open, and Chris walked in. He pulled back the covers. "Come on, sleepyhead, I'm takin' you and the kids to breakfast."

Brittney smiled. She crawled out of bed and threw on jeans and an old Police Academy sweatshirt.

In the living room, Madison clapped her hands. "Ma! Ma!"

Brittney leaned down and scooped her up, kissing her cheeks. She herded Ethan into the bedroom.

Brittney rested Madison on the changing table, and handed her the fake keys. They had been Ethan's, and they were crusted with food, the pink paint chipping off to reveal a clear plastic.

"Put some pants on," Brittney said, glancing over her shoulder at Ethan. He obediently looked in his closet, searching for a good pair of pants. He was a tidy boy, and after he pulled out his khakis, he straightened the creases with his hands.

As they walked to the diner, Ethan held onto his father's hand. "Daddy, why do cars have four tires?" he asked.

Chris laughed. "If they only had three, they would be out of balance. That wouldn't get very far."

"Oh."

"Also, there's a Big Bad Auto Mechanic that haunts cars without four tires," Chris said, winking at Brittney.

Ethan laughed. "Ghosts aren't real, Daddy!"

"Oh, they aren't? Are you sure?" Chris asked, leaning down and tickling Ethan, chasing him up the stairs to the diner.

They piled into a back booth, and ordered pancakes and bacon and orange juice.

Aaron, one of Chris's friends from the police force walked in, his blue uniform tight across his chest. He smiled at Brittney and the children, and then kneeled down near Chris, talking quietly. Their faces were drawn and furtive.

"OK, man, I know," Aaron said somberly, standing up. "I'll see what I can do. Brittney," he said, nodding, and then he drifted off to the counter, to order take out.

Chris returned to his stack of pancakes. His eyes seemed darker. But she said nothing. Whenever she asked about work these days, he only grunted.

She sighed and took a sip of her orange juice, leaning back in the red booth. She loved being waited on. This was rare; she could not remember the last time they had gone out. Money was always short. It was impossible to hold on to, the moment Chris got paid, it blew off, to bills and food and rent and clothes.

The pancakes were dry but she lingered over them, dragging them in syrup. They were delicious because she hadn't been the one to pour the flour and crack the eggs and mix the batter and stand over the old stove.

The waitress refilled her water, and Brittney nodded gratefully. She offered Madison a piece of bacon, and her little mouth opened eagerly, like a blowfish's. Brittney and Chris laughed.

"She's got my appetite," Chris noted.

After their piles of pancakes were gone, Chris signaled the waitress and she dropped off the check. Chris examined the slip, checking each item, and Brittney smiled, thinking how pragmatic he was. She had moved out of her mother's house at eighteen, oblivious to what was required to run an adult life. Chris was the one who had gotten them cell phone plans, and set up their utilities, and negotiated their rent.

Chris pulled out his wallet, counting the bills and throwing them down next to the receipt. Brittney used a wet napkin to wipe Madison and Ethan. Their little hands and chins were sticky with maple syrup.

Outside, the sun was shining brightly. Chris lifted Ethan on his shoulders. Brittney winked at her little boy, her firstborn, struck, as she often was, that he was, somehow, no longer her baby, that his limbs were no longer pudgy and soft, that his cheeks were no longer so round.

Brittney's friend Nevaeh walked past with her one-year-old son, hunched over her stroller. She nodded at Brittney, her puffy eyes flitting warily to Chris.

Brittney beamed with pride. Who would have thought Brittney would be the one whose relationship had lasted? In high school, boys buzzed around Nevaeh, offering her rides and joints and shiny trinkets. But those boys were still driving their flashy cars, hitting on younger girls, while Nevaeh took care of her son alone.

Nevaeh rolled her eyes at Brittney, and kept walking.

Brittney reached for Chris, and he engulfed her hand in his. His grip was firm and comfortable.

In the beginning, she had yelled over his late night absences, telling him it wasn't fair. She needed a break too. He wasn't a bachelor anymore. But he hadn't responded; he had simply stormed out of the apartment, slamming the door, leaving her alone. She could still hear the sound of the door clattering on its hinges. And each time, her protests got quieter, her voice growing weaker with his indifference. Until she said nothing. She let him go out at all hours, without a word. She hated herself for this, but she didn't know what else to do. She could tell if she pushed, he would just leave for good.

Chris opened the door to the apartment building, and effortlessly swung Ethan to the ground. Ethan laughed and ran up the stairs.

Brittney smiled, caught up in the joy of the day, in Chris. Admiring his long, muscular back, the way his body glided up the stairs, she remembered the night before, and her heart sunk. She wondered if she should get the morning after pill.

Inside, Brittney sat on the couch, stiffly. Madison was trying to walk, her steps tentative and loose, and she clung to the coffee table.

Chris came out of the bedroom in his shorts and a black t-shirt. The sleeves of his shirt were cut off and his biceps seemed sinewy and large.

"I'm going out," he announced. He leaned over and kissed Brittney on the cheek, his breath a fog of cigarette smoke. "You need anything?"

She said nothing, her face locked with an anger she didn't want to release. Her anger would only give him an excuse to be gone.

"Whatever," Chris said, abruptly pulling away, "later."

The door rattled on its hinges.

She walked into the bathroom. The PECO envelope was in the trash can, on top of used cotton swabs, their ends yellowed with earwax. She unraveled the envelope, flattening it with her hand. In the fluorescent bathroom light, the triple underlines seemed childish.

She laid the envelope back on the toilet. Madison was only nine months old. Chris didn't understand how exhausting two small children were. He played with them for an hour here and there, blowing on their bellies and pushing them in the swings, and thought that was what it was like to watch over them all day, every day. He didn't have any idea of what it was like to be woken up multiple times a night and change a dozen diapers a day and potty train an unwilling child and brush teeth in mouths sealed shut and cook food that would be thrown on the floor. And to worry—constantly worry—a fever or rash or cough might balloon into something worse.

No matter what Chris wanted, there could be no more children. Two were enough. She didn't like the idea of hiding something from Chris, but she didn't want to fight about it anymore. It would be easier to let him think he had won, and to take birth control pills, burying the little pink container underneath her t-shirts, keeping them a secret.

She reached into the back of her closet and grabbed the shoebox with her emergency stash of money. She took a deep breath and opened the lid. Thirty dollars lay on top of her personal papers. She rummaged around the old drawings from when she was a teenager and some notes from her grandmother, but there was no more cash.

Had it always been so little? That wouldn't even cover the morning after pill.

It was only one time, she decided. You couldn't really get pregnant from just one time. It had taken her months with her other kids. She would just get birth control pills at the free clinic.

~*~

Brittney slid boxes of pasta into the cupboard, yawning. Madison was teething, and they had both not slept more than two hours the last few nights. Chris hadn't been home, which Brittney resented but was also grateful for. He got so angry when the kids cried at night and woke him up, sometimes shouting and stomping and slamming the door to go outside and smoke, which only made Madison cry louder. Ethan just kept his eyes shut, and when it got really bad, put his pillow over his head.

Her phone rang from inside her purse, and she grabbed it, wondering if it was Chris and if he would tell her where he was. She knew he wasn't at work all these days. She didn't recognize the number on the caller ID.

"Yes?" she said nervously.

"Is this Brittney Williams?"

"Yesss."

"This is Dr. McNaren. You came in for birth control the other day?"

"Oh, uh-huh. Can I pick it up now?" Brittney said, putting a can of black beans on the shelf.

"Well, actually, I got your test results back."

"Uh-huh."

"And you're already pregnant."

Brittney closed her eyes, her left palm flat on the counter, not seeing how that was possible. "You sure? How it is that? It was just only one time we didn't use protections."

"Sometimes that's all it takes. There are options, you know, if you don't want to keep it...."

"Right. OK."

Brittney took a deep breath and disconnected. She leaned against the refrigerator. She noticed a slight discomfort around her ribs. Her bra strap was a bit too tight, her breasts overflowing from their cups. That had been the same with Madison and Ethan. She slid down, her back against the refrigerator, and sobbed silently, not wanting to scare the children.

A tiny creature was monopolizing her body again. She would be nauseous for months, her stomach swaying back and forth, as if she were out to sea. Her moods would grow erratic, their edges sharp and pointed as they appeared and disappeared. How could she do that now?

"Mama, come look at the blocks," Ethan urged, his slender body standing in the doorway, his little hand on the frame. His skin had a natural tan to it, darker than hers and Chris's, and the kitchen light reflected off his nose and cheekbones in streaks.

He walked over to her. He had just turned four, and his steps no longer toddled.

"What wrong, Mama?" he asked, his head cocked thoughtfully.

His hand was soft on her cheek.

She mustered up a smile. She stood and took his hand, squeezing reassuringly, trying to press down her sense of dread. He was a sweet and serious boy, and she kissed him, her lips pressing against the soft tendrils of his hair.

"Knock knock," he said.

"Who's there?"

"Letters."

"Letters who?"

"Letters in!"

Brittney unexpectedly laughed, squeezing his hand, wondering where he came up with such things. How could she get rid of a child like him? It didn't seem right to her, though she knew it wasn't a child yet. She didn't know what it was. She remembered her first ultrasound, how he had looked like a little bean on the screen, not like a baby. But she had heard his heartbeat, and it sounded as clear as her own.

Days and then weeks unfurled, streaming by in a fog, but she couldn't bring herself to tell anyone, even Chris, about the pregnancy. It was the logic of wishful thinking: she thought if she could keep it to herself, the pregnancy might, somehow, stop existing on its own, relieving her of making a decision.

At night, when Chris was out drinking and the children were asleep, she ran up and down the stairs of her building. Each time she reached the top, she thought of missing a step and tumbling to the bottom, hitting her stomach over and over. Her toes dangled in the air, hesitating.

At this moment, she became aware of a live being, its tiny heart beating, its alien form flexing and growing, and she shook her head. She could not bring herself to play God and decide who lived and who died.

But as she charged down the stairs, she was angry. She did not want this baby. It was too much. More than she could handle. Why had God let this happen to her? Hadn't her childhood been enough? Why was her new family falling apart, too?

She returned to the apartment and grabbed one of Chris's beers from the refrigerator. She guzzled the beer, the fizz tickling her throat, the cold liquid spilling on her t-shirt. She tossed the empty can in the recycling bin. Back outside the apartment, she charged down the stairs faster.

Her feet still connected with the concrete.

As she vomited on the middle landing, Chris appeared at the bottom of the stairs in his police uniform, jiggling his keys. His starchy blue shirt was ruffled.

"What the fuck, Brit?" he asked, pointing to the watery vomit. He had never become immune to bodily fluids like she had, after cleaning up thousands of baby spit-ups and vomits and splattered feces.

She laughed at his squeamishness and leaned against the railing. It was too late. The pregnancy wasn't going to disappear without her help.

"I'm pregnant."

His face underwent a quick series of transformations, from shock, to pride, to fear. There it settled. He walked past her, his breath smelling of cheap beer.

Her heart beat rapidly. He was the one who wanted this, not her; he was the one who had practically forced it upon her. A burst of resentment roiled through her. Regurgitated food lingered in her mouth, and she spit it out.

The spit landed on her shirt. She wiped it off with the back of her hand, and trudged after him.

Chris had settled in front of the TV, drinking a beer. His gun, compact and black, was sitting on the coffee table. Brittney looked at it warily. One of her brothers had been shot on Woodlawn Avenue, his calf torn to pieces. At twenty-seven, he walked with a cane.

She turned down the volume on the TV.

"You gonna wake the kids," she chided.

Brittney considered throwing a vase at the TV, shattering the screen. Or picking up the gun and pointing it at Chris, demanding he stop hurting her.

"You were the one who wanted another baby."

Chris took another chug of his beer, his eyes glued to the TV. Two women were dancing in bikinis.

"Chris, why are you doing this?"

"For goodness sakes, Brit, stop hasslin' me."

Brittney began to cry—her moods were blowing easily from one extreme to the next—and her sobs softened the expression on Chris's face.

"Just come here," he said, stretching out his arm. She

burrowed in the crook, and he pulled her close. "Everything will be alright, OK? Don't worry so much. We'll figure it out."

She studied his hand. It was large and muscular, almost twice the size of her own. His hulking body—he was almost six and a half feet tall—made her feel safe, like his fists could destroy anything bad in the world.

She still remembered the first time she had seen him, when she was fifteen. He had walked into the apartment party, and she sensed a shift in the energy of the room. He dwarfed the other boys, and his wide smile—full lips and straight white teeth—was brilliant. Someone tossed him a beer and he yanked it out of the air, graceful and quick.

She snuck out to the fire escape, painfully aware her nostrils were too wide and her eyes were a little bulbous and her skin was broken out. She smoked a joint, inhaling until she felt light-hearted and warm, her self-consciousness peeled away.

She tied her shirt in a knot, exposing her small, smooth waist.

"Hi," she said, calmly, her face tilted up.

They had laughed and talked and drunk more beers, and, somehow, at the end of the night, Chris had offered to walk her home. It was dark and cold and quiet. She felt safe next to his large frame. On the street, size was a kind of currency, a warning. He was a man, not a boy, and he informed her he was taking classes at the community college. Still a sophomore in high school, she was impressed with his ambition.

They reached her steps, and she stopped and pointed. He glanced at her house, and heat rose on her cheeks. Half the roof was dangling off. Her brothers were supposed to fix it but they were too busy with sports and parties and girls. Chris didn't even blink. *He's above such things*, she thought. Her fifteen-year-old heart was beating rapidly and she wondered, crazily, if he would rescue her from the dank house where nothing got done unless Brittney did it. She had been cleaning and cooking since she was seven years old.

Maybe Chris would be her Prince Charming. He lifted her

up as if she weighed nothing, and placed her on the second stair. They were almost eye level. He cupped her chin, studying her face. She looked down the street shyly.

"You a good girl, Brittney, I can tell."

She glanced back at him. He was serious. Was she a good girl? Mostly, she felt tired, tired from studying and taking care of her mother and brothers. He leaned down and kissed her, and her knees went wobbly and heat gathered between her legs. She had been kissed before, but nothing like this.

"I need a good girl. I'm done with all the whores," he whispered, his breath warm and boozy.

The word was like a slap and she froze. It reminded her of some of the drunk men her mom had brought home. Men who had scared her, leading her to lock the door she shared with her brother. But then she felt the warmth of his arm around her and she nodded, remembering he said she was a good girl. She studied his hand, its muscles and veins and bones. She couldn't believe it was so large. The size seemed like such a powerful thing. *This hand could do anything,* she thought.

And she still did. His hand was calloused on the palm, and there were a few scars on his knuckles, but otherwise, it looked the same as it did seven years ago. She quelled her fears that he was changing, that the man who, in the end, had saved her from her mother's house was being lost to something she didn't understand.

He glanced over at her, and seeing her face, pleading and plaintive, he sighed. He squeezed her hand, and his eyes seemed unfocussed. *Whatever it is, I still love you,* she thought. *I love you so much.* He kissed her, and his lips were soft and adamant.

She pulled his hand down to her stomach, to remind him of the baby. It was hard to believe, someday, the peanut would be a little child like Ethan and Madison.

His hand rested there, against the softness of her belly. She remembered her first pregnancy, one neither of them expected. They had been reckless, never using protection, but they hadn't been trying. She had trusted him so much, thinking

31

because he didn't say anything about it, it must, somehow, be safe.

They often made love drunk, underneath her high school's bleachers. The stands had vibrated with noise, and she had been paranoid someone would see them, but she didn't tell him to stop. She didn't want him to stop. Maybe part of her thought, *if we have a child together, he won't never leave me.* Her whole life, people were leaving—her father taking off, her beloved grandmother dying, her brothers moving in and out. She couldn't imagine losing Chris; Chris, who encouraged her love of sewing, and understood her complaints about her alcoholic mother; Chris, who played the guitar, his large fingers strumming as he fashioned her love songs; Chris, who attended community college so he could become a police officer, his bright eyes intent and serious as he hunched over his textbooks, a yellow highlighter in his hand.

There was loud music beating and people cheering and bright lights high above them and Chris's hard body crushing against hers. The mud and grass were soft on her back, and she thought, with him inside her, they could never be any closer. She could never be any happier.

But after she skipped two periods in a row, she panicked. She was only seventeen. She had planned on college, to study fashion design. Her friends with babies hadn't even finished high school. Their boyfriends kept partying, occasionally bringing a package of pampers or taking the baby out for an afternoon. Brittney couldn't allow herself to believe Chris would be any better—she still couldn't quite believe Chris, this handsome and charismatic man, was with *her* (who was she? what was so special about her?)—but when she told him she was pregnant, stress on her brow, he smiled softly and assured her he would be a good father.

"You not gonna leave?" she asked, her lower lip trembling.

"Are you kidding? I ain't gonna be like my deadbeat dad."

Brittney had cried, the tension flowing from her body. She was crying because, inadvertently, she had gotten what she really wanted: to keep Chris, and to get out of her mother's house.

They moved into a one-bedroom apartment with a tiny stove and leaking toilet. It wasn't that large, but the apartment seemed vast. There were no mothers drunk and rambling or annoying siblings blasting the stereo. Brittney, still skinny except for her basketball-shaped stomach, happily swept and cleaned and painted the walls while Chris was at work. She pinned the sonogram pictures on the buzzing refrigerator. She was anxious about the baby. But she was also excited. Everything felt new, and possible.

Her anxiety now was heavier. She was worn out from her last two pregnancies, and she could feel Chris unburdening himself of them all. She could feel him leaving.

Maybe the new baby would change everything. Maybe things would go back to how they used to be, when he came home right after his shifts, his breath smelling like his lunch instead of beer.

Her racing thoughts circled around her head, in a closed maze, and she clutched Chris, as if she could pin him down, as if she could make him stay.

"Chris," she said, her voice soft, tentative, "now that another baby's coming ... could you be home more?"

His jaw raised itself defensively, like a rising ship. "What do you mean?"

"You been gone so much lately."

He pulled away from her, disentangling himself. "I'm sick to death of you hasslin' me, Brittney! Always askin' me where I am, what I'm doing. I don't have to account to you. I'm a grown man."

Brittney was startled, and shifted back against the armrest. "You don't got to get mad at me. They're your kids, too."

He chewed his lower lip, and balled his fists in frustration. "I know! Goddamnit, I know they are. I'm sorry."

He closed his eyes and gripped the sides of his head. "The truth is I'm losing my job."

A ball of panic coiled inside her stomach. How would they pay for everything? And what about her babies? She didn't want to drop them off at one of those kiddy mills with barred windows.

"What did you do?" she cried.

"Really, Brittney? You just gonna blame me?"

"Chris," she tried again. "Please. Just talk to me. It's *me*. Tell me what happened."

He looked at her, and pleading and fear stretched his mouth and brows. His eyes were glistening, and, for a moment, her anger, her desperation, lifted. She reached her hand out.

"Oh, Chris. I'm sorry. I know you love being a cop. I know that's what you always wanted to do."

He stared at her extended hand, suspended and waiting, and his tenderness morphed to anger, as if her hand were something threatening, like a knife. He rubbed his brows with his thumbs, and then stood up. He grabbed his gun, and walked toward their bedroom.

She was tired of chasing after him. But she had no choice. She needed his help. She couldn't do all this alone.

In the bedroom, he was throwing clothes and shoes into a large duffel bag.

"What are you doin'?" she screeched. She wanted to scream at him, a primal incoherent scream, demand that he stay.

He glanced over at her, and his eyes flickered with guilt. "You a good mom, Brittney. I know you'll work it all out, just like the other moms do."

"How can you say that? You just gonna leave your children like your father?"

He kept packing, quietly.

"How can you do this to your own children?"

He pulled a Phillies baseball cap down over his eyes. "I'm losing my job, Brittney. Ain't nothin' I can do for you right now. What do you expect me to do? You want me to stay home and play with the kids all day?"

"Be real," he pled. "That's no kind of life."

"I am being real. They're your kids, too."

"There's nothin' I can do! I'm losing my job. Steven was just waiting for an excuse to get rid of me and he found one. He never liked me, not from day one."

"So you got to leave your family, too?"

"I'm not going to sit here all day and change diapers, Brit. Do you know any men who do that?"

"But—"

"Nah, you don't. Look, you'll be fine without me hangin' around, and so will the kids. You raisin' 'em right."

"Chris," she pled, reaching for his arm.

But he moved, nimbly, past her. "I'm sorry," he said. "I can't just sit around and do nothing like that. Look, I'll try to get myself something else so I can send you some money. But I'm not doing so well right now. This was what I wanted to do. And yeah I fucked it up, I couldn't handle the stress, never knowing if a stop was going to turn violent. We ain't trained to handle all that. It's bad out there now. I needed a way to not be so anxious and then I failed a drug test."

Then he was walking out and slamming the door.

She stood still for a moment, stunned. This couldn't be happening. She had to go after him, convince him to come back where he belonged. Tell him his family loved him no matter what. He could find something else.

She rummaged in her closet until she found her lucky shirt, a green V-neck with soft blue feathers circling the waist. Slipping it over her head, she fingered the frayed feathers, trying to call up the feeling of wonder the shirt had once given her. The feathers had come from a box left on the street, buried under half-used spools of thread and swatches of fabric. For hours, she had sat in her bedroom, carefully stitching, watching as an ordinary t-shirt became an object of beauty, by her own hands.

That was before the children, when she'd had time for sewing.

She grabbed her black coat and cell phone, and locked up the apartment, telling the children, silently, she would be right back.

The night was quiet. The sky was dark, almost black, and she wondered if it was supposed to rain.

She walked to The Lounge, the neighborhood bar. It had been years since she had been in a bar, before Ethan was born, when she'd gone with her brother and his friends, pretending to be twenty-one.

Christmas lights lined the walls. A few young men, boys she remembered from high school, were drinking at the bar, and they nodded, interest in their eyes. She nodded back, and kept moving. A couple was dancing, their bodies grinding against one another.

Chris wasn't there. She sat at a table in the corner, and ordered a beer.

She stared at her phone, with its pink lining, and then chugged her beer. It was lukewarm and dry. She had no idea where Chris was.

He could be anywhere in the dark grime of the city.

She tossed cash on the table, and walked out, ignoring the catcalls. Her head was fuzzy, but she didn't want to go home. She was sick of the cramped apartment, with its chipping paint and noisy radiators, of taking care of the children all by herself.

She wanted to keep walking, deeper and deeper into the city, shedding her obligations. Consider other paths. Maybe she could enroll at the Art Institute, like her cousin Trinity. She could see herself with the sketchpads, and the stubby charcoal, her finger growing calloused as she drew. There would be dozens of fabric spools to choose from, with vivid flower prints and geometric patterns, her fingers tugging and sewing and cutting, forming the material into beautiful dresses and shirts. That was the life she had planned on, before Chris, before her children.

But she knew this was impossible.

She opened the apartment door, and walked through the kitchen, ignoring the dirty plates and glasses. The living room was empty.

She put the TV on low. Two girls were arguing on a

beach, their voices shrill. Their bodies were too thin. Their hair, though, was beautiful: waves of shimmering blonde. Brittney's own hair used to be blonde, but it had darkened to a dishwater color, and it was limp and greasy. She tugged at the split ends. There hadn't been time to get it cut, and now there would be no money.

She couldn't believe Chris was getting fired from the police force. Except, after she thought about it, maybe it wasn't that surprising. He was the only one in his family to go to community college, to try to get a steady job. And there was an anger in him, a rage. She wasn't sure why, but it was there. And it took less and less for this anger to come out.

A year ago, a man had tried to mug her and Chris. He was big and dumb and kept his feet planted, flashing his Swiss Army knife. They'd only had five dollars with them and Brittney was ready to hand over the money.

But Chris had cackled and gone furious, grabbing the man's wrist and twisting. There was a popping noise and the knife clattered to the sidewalk. Brittney was shocked by the limpness of the man's hand, the unnatural angle of the wrist, and the look in Chris's eye when he had done it. The look had been unhinged, crazy.

There had been other fights over the years—in bars, on the street—all in defense of something or other. Chris wasn't a bully. He had never raised a hand to her or the children. He had thrown things in the apartment, but never touched them. But it didn't matter. You couldn't fight people over every little thing. You couldn't walk around like a live wire.

She called his cell phone, and it rang and rang and rang.

"This is Chris. Leave a message."

"Please come home … we can figure it out." Doubt seeped into her voice, and her words sounded wobbly and uncertain even to her.

~*~

The days became long and heavy in Chris's absence, almost as if the nature of time had expanded. Fatigued from pregnancy, Brittney couldn't gather the children's coats and wipes and diapers and water and snacks and haul them to the playground or her friends' apartments. They stayed inside, the TV playing cartoons, the children climbing on the furniture and bringing pots and pans out of the cabinets.

Ethan started asking about his father, a heartbreaking little chant, "Where daddy? Where daddy? Where daddy?"

Brittney closed her eyes. "I don't know," she said, softly.

Ethan stared at her, his face dark and unmoving, like a still lake. The light danced off the amber in his eyes. She felt his rebuke, but she couldn't entirely suppress her annoyance. She didn't want to be reminded, again and again, Chris was gone.

She sat on the couch and called everyone she could, but his family had stopped answering her calls and none of her friends had seen Chris. The rent was due in a week and she didn't know if he would pay it.

The TV show, some cheesy family sitcom, ended. Ethan stood up, and put his hand on Brittney's knee.

"I want my daddy," he said, his voice level and even.

Brittney pushed her fingernails into her palms. "I know you do honey. But it's time for bed."

"I want my daddy to tuck me in."

"Sorry," Brittney said softly, moving around her son. She picked Madison up off the floor, and took her into the bedroom. Madison smiled happily, her pudgy hands reaching for Brittney's hair and cheeks.

Brittney could hear the sound of plates cracking in the kitchen.

"Goodnight, baby," she said, placing Madison in the crib,

and kissing her on the forehead.

Ethan was standing on the kitchen table, throwing plates to the floor, watching them shatter, a blend of anger and curiosity on his face.

"What do you think you doin'?"

He looked at her plainly, his fingers curled around another plate.

She reached out and held his face in her hands. "I don't know where he's at, Ethan, or when he's coming back. He didn't tell me that."

He pushed her away and jumped down from the table.

He yelped, and blood splashed across the tiles. He clutched at his foot, his eyes wild. She stepped over the broken plates and pulled his foot into her lap. A white shard of ceramic was inserted in the pad.

"I gotta pull this real quick," she explained.

She yanked it out and blood sluiced over her fingers and palm. The sight of it flipped her stomach.

She leapt up, and grabbed a wad of paper towels. She pressed this against his foot, waiting for the blood to slow. Her fingers felt sticky.

"It's gonna leave a scar," she said, his foot cradled in her hands.

He stared at his foot morosely. "Did you make him go?"

"I don't know," she said, wondering if he would still be there if she had cooked better meals, or if she had taken better care of herself and the apartment. Maybe he would. "But he loves you."

She heaved her son up in her arms, carrying him like an infant. His body relented, and he pressed his face against her chest.

In his bed, she rocked him, trying to be gentle, trying to suppress the anger she felt on his behalf, the fury.

His narrow, straight nose was the same shape as his father's. How could Chris leave a piece, all these pieces, of himself behind?

"What did one burger say to another?" she whispered.

He blinked, waiting.

"We meat again."

He smiled, and then closed his eyes.

She kissed his forehead and turned out the light, and closed the door. The apartment looked like it had been ransacked: toys, broken plates, chip bags, empty bottles, pots, and clothes cluttered the surfaces. But she was not motivated to clean it up. She hadn't even bothered to give Madison a bath in four days.

She had been paralyzed, waiting for Chris to walk back in and apologize. But the days of silence had spread, like an abscess, into weeks of silence, and her certainty was dissolving.

She lay down on the couch. She was sick of talking to her friends on the phone because she could hear *I told you so* lurking in their comments. Her cousin Trinity had paused and said, as if to explain it all, "He *is* a man." *No*, she had wanted to protest, *he's not **a** man, he's **my** man, he's Chris.*

She hadn't seen her own father in ten years, except for a handful of times they had passed on the street. Dressed in his SEPTA uniform, he nodded in her direction, as if she were a casual acquaintance. Once, she had almost yelled, "I'm your daughter, motherfucker!" but because Ethan was with her, she had swallowed this sudden burst of rage.

The rage she felt now couldn't be swallowed. Chris has passed his rage to her. And now it was spreading, like cancer, through her bones.

Chapter Three

Rebecca

Their three-story Victorian was too quiet, almost eerie, without Will bounding through, leaving his books and papers strewn about, rambling about his latest ideas, banging pots and pans as he cooked gourmet dinners, always leaving the mess for her to clean up.

Will hadn't waited to find out if Rebecca was pregnant to move out. He had packed up the day after the party, taking his clothes and books, smiling at her apologetically, frustration on his brows. Maybe he had seen the odds were similar to a lottery ticket for Rebecca and a car wreck for him, neither very likely.

Rebecca had sat on the living room couch, half reading, watching him and Peter haul out box after box, and it had felt as if she weren't even there, that somehow she was floating outside herself, watching her life fall apart. Weeks later, she had felt the blood in her underpants and she had sobbed in the bathroom, not realizing, until that very moment, how much she had believed she would get pregnant.

The silence of their house somehow drew attention to the absence of the noises she most wanted: a child running through the hallways with stampeding feet and laughter and the jangling clatter of toys.

But she had never thought about *how* she could have a child without her husband. Years ago, at an Amherst conference on Western Women in the 21st Century, Hannah Lyle-Stevenson had advocated sperm donation as a way for women to foster independence from the patriarchy. Rebecca had been impressed with her arguments and voiced her agreement, even writing an essay on the advantages of "single motherhood by choice" for *The Atlantic*. But of course then the stakes had been abstract. When the commenters and trolls had called her frigid and a cat lady, she had assumed, with smugness that now mortified her, that she and her professor husband would conceive two children naturally.

As the spring unfolded into summer, Will continued to reach out to her, calling and texting with meaningless updates about his life. Rebecca could neither bring herself to answer his many phone calls nor make an appointment at a fertility clinic. It was like she was paralyzed in the face of two unpleasant options, unable to move back or forward.

During the summer months, the throngs of undergraduates were gone, and the Penn campus felt still and unmoving, like a movie on pause. The air was slick with humidity.

Rebecca stopped off at her office, for the office hours that none of her summer students ever came to. In her seminar on "Women in America," there were two gangly basketball players, who rarely did the readings, and three girls who strolled in late, clutching Starbucks coffees and wearing yoga pants. They folded their lithe bodies into the plastic green chairs. The discussions devolved into platitudes about women's "objectification" and "subordination," the boys grinning as they spoke, their eyes intent on the girls, as if their words were a come on.

Normally, Rebecca wouldn't have tolerated such superficial dialogues, but she was distracted by her thoughts of having a baby, and she let the class wander aimlessly.

Rebecca turned on her computer, and scanned her emails. There was one from her sister, with the contact information of Adriana Green, a colleague of hers who had used a sperm donor. *She'll help you. Her daughter is lovely*, Elizabeth wrote, *you would never even know.*

Rebecca cringed at the implication, that her child's origin story would be something to be hidden.

She opened the Stanley, Weiss website, her sister's law firm, and clicked on the profile for 'Adriana Green.' Adriana was in her late forties with whitish-blonde hair. She was attractive, but her beauty had a rubbery sheen to it: her skin was stretched taut and her lips formed a gelatinous round bubble.

Rebecca reflectively touched her own lips, which were still full, but had thinned and paled the last couple years, in a subtle way no one would notice but her. She emailed Adriana, inquiring about the service she used.

Adriana's reply was instantaneous:

Hi Rebecca, Elizabeth mentioned you were looking. I used Elite Spermatozoon. HIGHLY RECOMMENDED. You can use my user ID (corporatelawyer3956) and password (lookingchildone26578!) to explore the database. The sperm was top-notch. AG

Rebecca couldn't quite imagine a stranger's sperm inside of her, gestating and growing. At least not yet.

Maybe she was still hoping, against all the evidence, that Will would appear on their doorstep and declare he had made a terrible mistake. Her heart had yet to grasp it, but in her mind, she knew if Will ever had a child, it would be years from now with a younger woman. Her life wasn't a Hollywood rom-com.

She closed her email.

She searched the internet for sperm donation, and scrolled through pages of sperm banks, their websites announcing donor requirements: *You must be at least 5'9. You must have a college degree. You must be healthy.*

On the fourth page, there was a forum for SINGLE MOTHERS OVER 40. One of the threads was titled, "I'm finally pregnant!!! So excited!!!" and Rebecca was momentarily jealous of this anonymous Internet stranger. What was she afraid of? Maybe she was afraid that, at her age, even after she conceived, she would lose her baby to miscarriage.

She shut her computer off, and walked to the train station. From inside her purse, her phone beeped. Perhaps because she hadn't returned any of his calls, Will had been texting her every day. Rebecca thought texts were cryptic, leaving so much unsaid and unexplained, and for that reason, were almost more frustrating than silence. Texting was for college students, who pecked in the back of class, their faces simultaneously illuminated and dulled by their glowing screens.

On board the train, her purse in her lap, she opened his message, and her heart fluttered with the possibility, however remote, that he would say something important rather than sharing the minutiae of his day.

Saw a 60s movie poster exhibit last night. U would like it.

She leaned into the window as the train jerked to a start. The train came above ground, and she watched the mass of cars on the highway, stuck in bumper-to-bumper traffic. She could text Will back, but what was the point? She didn't want to be his *friend.*

The train chugged along, and empty land whipped by. A woman began talking loudly on her cell phone.

It was strange to live in Philadelphia without Will. In the evening, she curled up on the porch and read Hemingway. He was Will's favorite writer, and she thought, if she read all his novels and stories, she might learn something important about Will, about a way to undo their separation. But so far, she could only see, in their essence, a swift brutality and a lust for adventure. These were hardly the qualities of a good father.

Sometimes, sitting on the porch, she just watched the passing cars. Once, a purple Cadillac with silver balls dangling from its rear bumper had sped by, its engine roaring. She had laughed until her eyes were tearing. She didn't really know why she found it so funny; there was something so ridiculous and ostentatious about it. Maybe she figured Will had become like that, only in a more sophisticated form. *Look at me, world, look at my big smart balls.*

At night, Rebecca wrapped their paisley comforter and sheets around her body, trying to fool herself into believing she wasn't alone. But no matter how tightly she was cocooned, inhaling the lemony laundry detergent, her cheeks growing warm, she would eventually shift, her leg kicking out or her shoulder rolling, and she would feel the expanse of unoccupied space.

Rebecca pulled *The Old Man and the Sea* out of her bag. She started reading, and she found herself rereading paragraphs, struggling to care about the old fisherman. But then she was struck by a line. *It is silly not to hope.*

The train conductor walked down the aisle, announcing the next stop was Penn Station. Rebecca rose from her seat, and gathered her things. The train chugged to a stop, and she was swept up in the stream of commuters headed to the subway, and she wondered if this was true, that it was silly not to hope. She was hoping Will would change back to the man he once was, or the man she thought he had been; she was hoping she would find some way to get pregnant and have a healthy child. Her hopes were so large they felt like burdens. To be without sounded freeing.

She emerged with a gaggle of professionals on the Upper West Side. She paused against the wall of a grocery store, taking in the miles of looming buildings.

She walked toward the river. Will's sublet—he had texted her the address a month ago, inviting her to stop by—was only a few blocks from her sister's apartment. She wasn't sure if he had done that on purpose, or if it was just close to Columbia. At the last minute, for a reason she couldn't discern, she veered toward his sublet.

The building was modern and glassy. The doorman was helping a woman unload her luggage, and Rebecca glided past, into the lobby, as if she belonged there.

She rode the elevator to the seventh floor, and knocked on

the door. No one answered.

For a moment, she was disappointed, even though she wasn't sure what she was doing here, what she wanted from him. Then she remembered, despite her protests, Will leaving their house key underneath a flower pot on their front porch. To her annoyance, he'd always been misplacing or forgetting his keys. She lifted the tan Welcome mat, and there was a gold key.

The apartment was dark with vacancy. She flipped on the lights, leaving her suitcase near the door. The living room had a view of the Hudson, and she stood in front of the window, watching the water swell in the wind, wondering where Will was. She hadn't seen him in months, since he and Peter had moved his books and clothes out of their house, hauling them away in a rented truck.

Her stomach rumbled and she walked into the kitchen and opened the refrigerator. Two bottles of wine, a six-pack of beer, a soft cheese, and a carton of eggs. It was the refrigerator of someone who ate out all the time. She grabbed the wine and rummaged in the drawer for the wine opener. She popped it open and poured herself a tall glass.

She wandered into Will's office, drinking her wine. She lazily clicked his mouse. His Penn email was open on the screen. She glanced behind her, and then slid into the black leather office chair.

She knew she had no right to be here, in his apartment, let alone read his emails. But she scanned his emails, anyway.

A "Lola Esperanza" popped up frequently, and Rebecca took another sip of wine, debating whether to click on one of her messages. Maybe it was an invasion of his privacy, but they had been married for twelve years. That had to count for something.

After another gulp of wine, she opened the latest message from Lola. It was a reminder about a party tonight, at her friend's apartment in the Village. So that's where he was.

Her face flushed with a warm heat. Lola's signature identified her as a professor in Latin American politics at Columbia. Rebecca typed her name into Google, but her finger

46

lingered over the enter key. Once she saw the woman's picture, she would be stuck with the image. That would make it too real.

She returned to his Inbox and read through the threads of their correspondence. Their exchanges were witty, lobbed back and forth with urgency. Some of the emails were sent at two or three in the morning, and they buzzed with electronic winks, referencing shared dinners and art openings.

Rebecca finished the rest of her wine and returned to the kitchen for more. She drank a few gulps and then parked herself in front of the window. The wine on an empty stomach had gone to her head. The world seemed hazy. As the sunlight disappeared from the sky, the last of the orange glow eaten by darkness, her image was reflected in the window. Her mouth looked tired and sad.

She remembered the moments in Africa when she had become aware of the paleness of her skin, the ease at which it burned and flaked off in the sun, and the trembling insufficiency of her muscles as she had tried to accompany the Nobuso women in their daily tasks. *I am weak,* she would think, rubbing the sweat from her brow.

Those moments had been fleeting; the women had smiled kindly, seeing her as a struggling child, and she had allowed them to lighten her load, reminding herself she was only a guest, that she would soon return to her own lands, where her physical fragility was, if anything, a virtue.

But, now, there was no other culture to escape to. Her nose looked too narrow, her skin seemed dull, and the wrinkles flanking her eyes looked like the thin fault lines on the surface of a cracked seashell, threatening to multiply and burst. The older she got, the more she could see herself either way—beautiful or unattractive, depending on her mood.

She turned away, knowing it was just a distraction. Being beautiful had never ensured a good life. It was better to be strong, like the Nobuso women.

She left the wine bottle in the sink, and closed the door to the apartment, slipping the key back under the mat.

Walking to her sister's, she thought about how far she and Will had diverged. It was hard to believe they had ever been so close she hadn't been sure where his ideas started and hers began. Her first book and his first few articles might as well have been co-authored by both of them; everything they wrote had been discussed between them endlessly before finding its way to the page. There had been no firm distinction between her mind and his mind. But, at some point, she had grown tired of *talking*.

She wanted to *live*, to travel overseas, to give birth to a baby, to raise a child. And now she could. Just not with him.

She opened her sister's apartment with her spare key. It was quiet, and she was grateful to find her sister sitting in the kitchen, alone.

"The kids are in bed?"

Elizabeth glanced up from her Blackberry, and smiled. "Maricel is putting them down."

Rebecca sat at the table. "I think Will is dating another professor," she said, even though she wasn't quite sure. It might have been an exaggeration.

"Already?"

"I think so. And yet he still texts me all the time, asking me to come visit him."

Elizabeth laughed. "Will's always been childish. That's part of his charm."

"I suppose."

"Remember when you were engaged, you discovered he had ten thousand dollars in credit card debt from a vacation he took to France?"

Had he? Yes, that was right. She had stumbled upon his statement while leafing through magazines on his coffee table. She had run out of his apartment barefoot, needing to breathe. She had tripped on the stone path, landing on her knees and hands. She stretched out to lay on the ground, unmoving, feeling the cold stone on her cheek and her stinging knees and wondering what other secrets he was hiding. For weeks they fought, their relationship suddenly precarious. He assured her it was a youthful indiscretion, a once-in-a-lifetime excursion of irresponsibility. He would pay it all back. And he had. Or they had, anyway.

"That was ages ago," she said, drawing a figure eight on the glass table.

"I know. But he never changed. If Will was going to be a father, he was going to be the fun dad, the guy that doesn't change diapers, and riles the children up before bedtime and lets them eat chocolate sundaes for breakfast."

"You're right. He would have been a royal pain."

Rebecca laughed. It had the dark ring of truth. "I can't believe I ended up here. I've always wanted a family. The whole cheesy thing—the two kids, the minivan, the yard, the picket fence."

"There are benefits to doing it on your own, you know. You get to make all the decisions."

It *was* how Elizabeth would feel. Even as a child, Elizabeth had been bossy. She had argued and wheedled her way to class valedictorian. The teachers seemed slightly afraid of her, timid smiles on their faces as they shuffled papers and considered her demand for a new grade.

Rebecca had been enthralled and a little scared of her younger sister's moxie. Rebecca had been more of a daydreamer.

But she had seen the women of Nobuso raise their children without men. So maybe she could too.

"I guess you're right."

"You'll make a good mother. You were made for it."

"Thank you."

"Get a sperm donor. It's the easiest way," Elizabeth said, rising from her seat. She kissed Rebecca on the top of her head. "More work to do. I will see you in the morning."

Rebecca nodded, watching her sister retreat to her office. Rebecca climbed the stairs to the guest bedroom. It had a King-sized bed, with a magenta canopy. She unzipped her suitcase and pulled out her pajamas. She changed, and then opened her laptop on the bed.

She scrolled back in her Inbox until she found the information for the Elite Spermatozoon website. Their homepage was white. Centered on the screen were small black letters. "ELITE SPERMATOZOON. Only the Best Sperm. You Cannot Afford Anything Less."

Really, Rebecca thought, logging in.

Welcome, Adriana. We hope you can find what you are looking for in our database. Every donor is vetted by our experienced staff. Medical records are required. Educational degrees and transcripts are reviewed. At least three recommenders are interviewed.

The sperm may cost more than other companies, but ... it's worth it.

Rebecca ran her fingers through her hair, and grabbed a rubber band out of her suitcase. She put her hair in a ponytail. The subtext of Elite Spermatozoon's spiel reminded her of the eugenicists of the forties and fifties. Children should be the smartest, the most beautiful, the most White.

The database offered a wide array of characteristics to search by. There were the physical, the cognitive, the emotional, as well as "areas of excellence" and a seemingly endless list of "personal quirks."

Rebecca began plugging in characteristics, picking traits without much thought.

When she was done, the database returned twenty-nine results. Was it that easy? Was Will that replaceable?

She scanned the thumbnail photographs. The men's teeth were white; their skin was smooth; their hair was full. They had the shiny gloss of youth.

As she read their profiles, she thought they seemed like actors on TV, their identities and resumes fabricated by a group of writers sitting around a table, tossing paper airplanes at one another as they brainstormed new characters.

It struck her that you couldn't *know* a person from a

profile. The points of reference were too abstract.

She undid the search and scrolled through the photographs. The strong jaws, the light blue eyes, and the straight noses blended together in a seamless run of masculine beauty. The expressions were the same. The bank must have coached them, telling them to half-smile and stare directly into the camera.

Finally, after scrolling through seven pages, a Persian man caught her interest. Maybe it was just because he provided some color in the expanse of whiteness. But he seemed to have a wise glint in his eye, a sense this was a bit absurd.

She clicked on his profile, and, after perusing the basic stats (six feet tall, engineering Ph.D. student), she played his video. He had long, dark hair and beautiful brown eyes. A woman's chirpy off-screen voice asked him inane questions ("What's your favorite memory? What is your biggest goal?") He smirked a little every time she finished speaking, but not in an unkind way. As he spoke, he glanced down at his folded hands, as if he were trying to check his watch. Discomfort and resignation fought for prominence around his wide mouth. She supposed he wanted to forget he had ever sold his sperm.

Rebecca leaned back. On the top right of Ramin S.'s page, she noticed an exorbitant price tag ($3,995 per vial) and realized maybe that was the reason he had sold his sperm. Maybe he had a sick mother, or even a child of his own he could not afford to send to daycare.

She closed the profile, and stared at the dozens of model-like headshots. She didn't doubt their sperm would make beautiful, intelligent offspring. But she couldn't see having a child with a stranger. Ramin might bully his students or plagiarize his papers, for all she knew. Maybe he was cold and sociopathic. No matter how appealing he seemed, she didn't know him.

She didn't know any of them.

She walked to the window. They were on the twelfth floor. West End Avenue was lit up below, a steady stream of cars passing by.

"So, then," she whispered, her fingers gripping the window curtain. No one would inherit her full chestnut hair, or the ever so slight bump in her nose, or her flat feet, or her love of books. She would not look in her child's face and see remnants of her own.

But that was OK. There were so many children who needed homes. She would save a child, and a child would save her. It would be an equal balance in the universe's ledger.

She thought of the view from her own house, the sprawling wood porch and the green lawn and the giant beech trees. The porch swing that swayed gently in the breeze. That swing was the first piece of furniture she and Will had purchased for the house. She had assumed one day she and Will would sit in the swing with their child, the child's head nestled underneath their arms.

She could still imagine a child there, only it was just her and the child, swinging gently. Her shoulders were weighed down with responsibility, and her back was aching. But there was a particular closeness, too. The two of them would have their own private world in their rambling house, their own routines and special touches and jokes and imaginary words.

She could almost feel this small child sitting on her lap, clinging to her neck, as she kissed them with a love that felt infinite. Hope ballooned in her chest and it was so strong that she felt certain she was no longer running from Will and his endless maybes, but running toward the child who was already hers.

Chapter Four

Brittney

Brittney sat Madison and Ethan in front of her cousin Trinity's TV, and rode the bus for hours, submitting dozens of job applications to restaurants, daycares, and stores.

The managers, mostly men in their thirties and forties, were brusque. "Not hiring right now." "Sorry, we need someone with experience." Even the women managing the daycares were harried and distracted, throwing her meticulously filled-out application into a bin behind the counter. "We'll call you if we need you. *Please*, don't call us." Somehow, in their slightly turned faces, it was clear they wouldn't be calling her.

When she returned to Trinity's apartment, her hands freezing and her eyes dried out, she was frustrated. She lingered in the hallway, gathering her energy, telling herself it would work out if she just kept trying. She couldn't give up because of a few obstacles. She remembered a glass magnet on her grandmother's refrigerator, the letters shiny and blue. *With God, All Things Are Possible.*

Could that really be true? She opened the door. Trinity was sitting on the couch, in a shimmery blue blouse. Magazines and CDs and textbooks—previously stacked neatly on the coffee table—were scattered across the living room floor.

"Hey," Trinity grinned. "Madison's a busy girl these days."

Brittney smiled, and crashed on the couch. Madison climbed up in Brittney's lap, and Brittney hugged her soft body, rubbing her round belly, kissing her neck, inhaling her scent.

Trinity squeezed her shoulder. "I have to get changed. I got a *date*."

Brittney nodded and watched her cousin walk to her bedroom. Trinity was a year older, but she was childless and slim hipped, and she seemed younger. When they were girls, Brittney's mother had often dumped Brittney at Trinity's house, before she went off to the bar and who knows where else. Brittney had slept with Trinity in her twin bed, their legs pressed up against one another. They had bundled under the covers with a pink flashlight and dreamt of owning a loft downtown, and designing clothes for Cheryl Thompson, the NBC Philadelphia anchor.

Never, she thought, did they fantasize about being unemployed single mothers.

Brittney leaned down and started packing up the children's cups and toys and diapers. The truth was she loved being a mother; it was the best thing she had ever done. Teaching her kids, tending to their scrapes, singing them to sleep, it made her feel so valuable, like for the first time in her life, she really mattered in this world. She was proud of how her kids were growing under her care, becoming little people better than she ever was.

Trinity strutted out of the bedroom, her slender body clothed in a slinky red dress with chunky black stripes. She twirled, and Madison clapped from the couch. Even Ethan, glued to the TV, glanced at her new outfit, transfixed with the stark geometry.

"What do you think, babe?"

"It's pretty. Nice shape and color contrast. Where'd you get it?"

"I made it. My instructor *loved* the design, said it was hip."

Brittney studied the dress. Looking closer, the stitches were larger than normal; the black cotton material peeled off the red dress at the edges. Still, it was more beautiful than the dresses they had stitched together as teenagers, using the fabric from clothes they bought for a dollar at the thrift store. The last dress Brittney had sewn was pale blue with a white lace collar and an empire waist. She had stitched it when she was pregnant with Ethan, resting the fabric on her bump. It was hanging in the back of her closet, unworn.

"I thought you got it at a store, for sure. Who you going on a date with?"

"A guy from Drexel asked me out. He's taking me downtown. Drexel, baby, Drexel."

Brittney laughed. It was a very good school. Trinity slipped on black high heels, and moved to the living room mirror, to apply her makeup.

Brittney remembered when she was preening in front of the mirror just like Trinity, waiting for Chris to pick her up. She had been filled, then, with a sense of possibility. Chris, she thought, would carry her off to a better life.

And for a long time, she reminded herself, he had. She threw the rest of the toys in her giant cloth bag, and then heaved Madison on her hip, and pushed Ethan out the door. She thanked her cousin for watching her kids, kissing her on the cheek.

On the bus ride home, Ethan kicked the seat in front of them, his little sneaker WHAPPING against the blue plastic. WHAP. WHAP. WHAP. Brittney held Madison close, and pointed out the window, labeling the houses and trees and cars. Madison nodded, mouthing the words in interest. She was a learner, and Brittney was grateful for that because it was satisfying to teach her new things. It made her feel like a good mother. Like she was doing something right.

And if Madison did well in school, then she could get a nice job. Maybe as a teacher or a nurse. Brittney would tell her to make her own money, and never depend on a man to take care of her, no matter how reliable he seemed.

At home, Brittney discovered another RENT OVERDUE notice in the mail. She tore the letter up in tiny pieces, burying it in the trash.

She had borrowed all the money she could from her

friends and brothers. She couldn't believe no one would hire her. She was willing and able to work. Wasn't that enough?

Her phone rang, and she looked at it hopefully. It was her brother's girlfriend.

"Hi, Angel."

"I got you a job at the Call Center."

"You did?"

"The job sucks, though. The supervisors listen to all your calls, and customers just bitch."

"I don't mind. Chris ain't givin' me any money. I'll take any job I can get right now."

"It's twelve bucks an hour. Training starts on Monday, eight in the morning."

"Thank you, Angel. This means a lot to me."

"Whatever. You won't like it. The shifts are always changing, but I'm sure I'll see you sometimes. We can complain together," she laughed.

Brittney smiled, thrilled at the opportunity. Her chest felt like it was going to burst with happiness. She would be able to take care of her kids now.

She called around, asking her brothers and friends about daycares. It turned out, even the cheap ones, with the barred windows and pot-smoking workers, cost more per hour than she would be making. Ask your mother to watch them, her friends insisted, that's free. Brittney considered this. Her mother loved Ethan and Madison, pulling them onto her bony lap and peppering them with questions. But she had the rusty smell of illness, and she often fell asleep while they were visiting, her bottle of Olde English falling from her hand, her mouth open as she breathed heavily. The children wouldn't be safe there for ten hours.

Brittney kept calling around, to friends of friends and acquaintances she hadn't spoken to since high school. Finally, a friend of a friend called her from her neighbor Justice's apartment. Justice came on the line, and told Brittney she watched a swarm of little children in her apartment, and she had room for two more. As they talked, Brittney could hear children screeching in the background, and the sound of the TV blaring.

"It would be one hundred dollars a week, flexible hours," Justice announced. The environment sounded chaotic, and Brittney hesitated. A hard pressure filled her head.

She couldn't afford anything else. She needed money and she needed it soon.

"OK," she said finally. "I will be there on Monday. Can I talk to Eva again?"

"Yeah, sure."

"Hey, girl," Eva said.

"Are you *sure* it's safe over there?"

"Yep. Don't worry. It's not the nicest but Justice is cool."

"OK. Thanks," Brittney said, and part of the pressure dissipated. She trusted Eva because even though she didn't know her, she knew Eva worked as a nurse's aid and had always been a mousy, responsible girl, the type not to stay out too late or do drugs.

On Monday morning, before seven, she and the children arrived at Justice's apartment. Justice swung the door open. In the living room, there was a beige couch and a large screen TV. There were a couple puzzles and a ball on the floor. A sickly three-year-old was lying on the carpet, a worn teddy bear in his arms, the whites of his eyes wide and yellowed. Brittney didn't know what was wrong with him, but she hoped it wasn't contagious.

Brittney ushered the children in, and looked around. In the corner of the living room, there was a dead mouse, his small body closed in a trap. A baby was sitting near it, a grape soda in her hand. Brittney swallowed. She told herself it wasn't that bad.

She crouched down near Ethan, and whispered to him. "Look out for Madison, baby. Don't let her touch that boy on the floor, or climb anything, or eat other people's food, or go in the kitchen, or play with the blinds or the mouse traps or the cabinets."

He nodded somberly, his new blue backpack on his

stooped shoulders. He clung to her arm, pulling her closer.

"Please don't leave us here, Mommy," he whispered. "I don't like it."

He rarely asked her for anything. But someone had to pay the rent and buy their food so she kissed him a dozen times, on his cheeks.

"I'm sorry, baby, we need the money," she breathed, softly, into his ear. "It's just for a while, till I find something better."

"Hey," she said, "what has four wheels and flies?"

He shrugged.

"A garbage truck."

He smiled, and she smiled back, kissing him on the forehead one more time as she rushed out the door, to catch the bus.

At the Call Center, she was nervous. She had taken care of her mother and brothers since she was young, but she had never worked a real job before. Seated in her cubicle, she followed a script that addressed customers' problems and complaints about their internet and phone service.

In the afternoon, they started giving her real customers. Her voice shook slightly on the first call. The caller had a gentle, older voice that reminded Britney of her grandmother. Britnney was able to renew the woman's contract and the woman was grateful and told her to have a nice day.

Gradually, as she took more calls, her voice grew steadier, and more confident. She found herself chatting with customers, almost forgetting it was work. This wasn't so hard.

The first rude caller startled her and she swallowed anxiously, suddenly stumbling over her words. He yelled, "You're ripping me off! You're ripping me off! How can you raise the cost like this?" Overwhelmed, she pressed buttons on her console, patching him through to the manager, even though they weren't supposed to.

She took a deep breath, and reminded herself it wasn't her fault. Sometimes grown men acted like children. The next time someone got angry with her, she closed her eyes and took

a deep breath, waiting for him (it was almost always a man) to quiet down. Then, once he finished, she spoke in a monotone, explaining the available options.

She was too busy to think too much about her children, but when she went to the bathroom or or took her break, she missed them so intensely she had to pause in the hall and steady herself. She had never been apart from them this long. Worry ran through her veins, and she pictured the sick boy and Madison playing with the dead mouse.

When her shift ended, she ran as fast as she could to catch the bus.

The TV was still on at Justice's and new kids had appeared. The sick boy was gone, which was a relief. Ethan and Madison ran over to her, and Justice waved goodbye, not lifting her face from out of a magazine.

The kids seemed eager to leave, and cranky and exhausted as they walked to the bus stop to go home.

"How was it?" she asked Ethan, Madison squirming in her arms.

"I don't like it. She watches soap operas all day."

Brittney laughed. "I know it's bad, honey," she said, ruffling his soft hair, noticing it almost touched his shoulders. He needed a haircut. "It's not forever, I promise."

The first day she was paid, she bought sketch pads and markers and blocks at the Dollar Store, sliding them into Ethan's blue backpack. Brittney couldn't let herself think about how lonely he seemed at Justice's. Only occasionally did a child his age appear. Usually, it was toddlers and babies.

The days all jumbled together, composed of bus rides, Justice's apartment, and the call center. Soon, Brittany had fielded hundreds and then thousands of calls, and memorized all the service scripts. She took satisfaction in her work, how clear and straightforward it was. She was motivated to raise her number of calls and positive ratings, and she watched as the red numbers in the corner of her screen went up and up and up.

In her 60-day review, her supervisor Eric complimented

her patience and her high daily numbers and she felt proud. She was doing this. She hung her review on the refrigerator, right next to Ethan's drawing of a red car with huge wheels.

~*~

Brittney woke up disoriented, her back aching from the heavy weight of her belly. Her alarm clock was blaring. It was 9:50 a.m. She panicked. She was twenty minutes late. She lurched out of bed, pulling on her black pants and red polo.

She opened the door to the children's room. Ethan was sitting near the crib, showing Madison a book.

"We have to go," Brittney cried. "No time for breakfast."

She lifted Madison out of her crib, taking a deep breath as shooting pains ran down her back. Madison squirmed, kicking Brittney's belly.

"Careful of the baby, Madison," Brittney chided, setting her on the floor.

"Baby," Madison repeated, smiling, pointing to Brittney's belly. She toddled out to the living room. Brittney shoved extra diapers and granola bars in Ethan's backpack.

She rushed to Justice's as fast as she could, pushing Madison in the umbrella stroller, pestering Ethan to hurry.

"I'm hungry," he complained.

"Eat at Justice's. We're almost there."

At the apartment, Ethan climbed up on the couch, and leaned against the armrest. He seemed tired as he rooted around in his backpack. Justice's eyes were intent on a morning talk show; a perky woman was yapping about removing wine stains.

Madison had moved over to the window and was tugging at the cord to the blinds. Brittney closed her eyes, thinking this was not a safe place, but she had to get to her shift or they wouldn't be able to pay their rent and what else could she do. She opened her eyes and Madison was still tugging on the cord, and she told Ethan, sharply, that he needed to watch after his little sister.

Ethan sighed and bounced off the couch, and grabbed his sister's arm. "Come on, Madison, stay away."

Madison toddled with him to the couch, where she began playing with the glossy magazines on the floor.

Brittney stared at her son. His brown eyes with flecks of amber were back on the TV, and his legs were swinging in the air, up and down, as he munched on his granola bar. He was old enough to protect his sister and there was no one else to do it. But she was sorry she couldn't let him be a little boy, free from responsibility.

She kissed him on the forehead and his skin was warm.

"You're a good boy. I'm sorry I need you to watch your sister, but I really do."

He nodded slightly, his eyes blinking. She tapped his head lightly. "I love you, baby."

He gave her a half-smile.

"Please watch out for Madison."

"I will, mom. I promise."

Then she was running late and she hurried out of the apartment and down the stairs and up the street.

The bus was coming and she sprinted alongside it, even though it felt like climbing a steep mountain, her breath thin and raspy. The bus passed her. She couldn't miss it. Her supervisor Eric had told them they could be late twice, and then they would be fired.

She reached the bus exhausted, and banged on the glass doors. The bus driver glared at her, shaking his head. She stared back, her palm spread on the glass door, her eyes pleading with him. The doors opened and the driver grunted as she stepped onboard.

There were no seats and she stood in the middle of the aisle, clutching a pole as she tried to smooth down her hair. Her hair was thinned out and greasy. It fell out everywhere, in the shower, at work, on the bus. She didn't know why. Last time, that hadn't happened until after she had given birth.

She wore a black headband because she didn't think Eric

would approve of a scarf. During the training day, Eric had explained that all representatives must wear Call Center red polos with black pants and black shoes. "No 'ghetto' accessories either," he had added, his young face rigid in warning. A couple of the trainees laughed and muttered, "Dude, really?" and "Naw, he didn't," but she simply looked down, rubbing her shoe on the tile floor because she didn't really understand what he was trying to say. Eric looked like the type of person who had grown up in some leafy town with two well-off parents. What did he know about the "ghetto"?

An older woman, a boxy purse in her lap, gestured to Brittney, offering her seat. "You should sit, dear."

Brittney smiled; even though she was nine months pregnant, her belly large and swollen, people rarely offered her seats. "Thank you."

She admired the woman's eggshell blue suit. It was wide at the shoulders and tiny at the waist. The material was linen. Maybe one day Brittney would have money to stitch herself a suit. She missed sewing, missed the feeling she got from constructing something functional and beautiful out of plain sheets of fabric. It was empowering, to make something out of nothing.

Brittney switched buses at Broad Street, climbing up the steps to the number four. Even though she didn't mind her job, she hated the hour-long commute. After work, she ran, or waddled, the mile to the bus stop. The work day was over, then, so it no longer mattered if her forehead and nose glistened with oil or if her body odor was pungent. Her rubbery black shoes chafed against her ankles, splitting open the skin. Her back ached with the weight of her belly. But she didn't care; she needed to get back to her babies.

There had been days when the number four was late or she missed the first G bus, and then she had to run to work, too. She would start her shift disheveled, her lower back stinging with pain. She tried to avoid standing too close to Eric or her coworkers until she could scrub her armpits with the fluorescent pink soap in the worker bathroom. The soap emitted a chemical scent, burning her nose, and the brown paper towels chafed her skin.

She stood up and pulled the hanging cord to indicate she wanted to stop. A few other people followed her off, but they headed in the opposite direction. She was glad to be alone. The night before, she had risen to pee six times. The only position she could sleep in was on her side, a pillow tucked between her legs, the great expanse of her belly resting on the sofa cushions. The punctuated sleep was wearing her down, frying her concentration.

She walked quickly along the six-lane road. Her red polo was stretched tight, and its threads were starting to thin in the middle. The path edged along a park of grassy fields. Everything, even the sidewalk, was clean and tidy.

The Navy Yard was a giant office park, with dozens of buildings, and tourists often came by in shuttles, gawking at the boats and buildings.

Large gray ships were docked in the dark water. She didn't know if they were working ships. But the looming gray forms, ovoid and pointy, had a stark beauty. The June sky was clear and blue. She had a sudden sharp longing for her children. For years, day in and day out, small, warm bodies had tumbled on top of her or lay in her arms or grabbed her hands. Now, all these hours alone, her body felt cold, as if it had lost its ability to regulate itself.

Ethan would love the ships. She could hear his little boy's voice, "Wow." His soft hand tugging hers. Ever since Chris left, he oscillated between an eerie quiet and bursts of rage. Whenever Brittney could find some money to spare, she bought him small toys and treats from Dollar General, trying to bring him a little bit of happiness.

Madison was different. Maybe she was too young to miss her father. When Brittney was waddling to the bus, her chest burning, it was Madison she held in her mind. Madison squealing happily, Madison reaching out for an embrace.

The baby in Brittney's stomach kicked, and she rubbed the elevated spot on her stomach, wondering if it was a boy or a girl. She hadn't gone to the doctor in six months. Her work schedule was erratic, her shifts changing from week to week, and it was impossible to schedule a medical appointment. She hoped, though, the baby was a girl. She could see Ethan watching the men in the neighborhood, and her brothers, studying their deep voices and wide-leg stances, their casual bantering and cocky smiles. She knew as much as she could teach him, she could never show him how to be a man. Not really.

She had been telling herself Chris would come home before the baby was born. He just needed to run wild for a while, like a dog. He would tire out, lower his tail and return. But so far he had stayed gone. There had been no word from him for five months.

A few weeks ago, Trinity had spotted him in the neighborhood. When Trinity called to report this, her voice low, Brittney had been surprised. She had assumed Chris had taken off, to live with his cousin in North Philly or maybe even with his father in New York. How strange, she thought, that Chris had just kept on walking her city blocks, shopping at her corner stores, like a ghost.

Trinity had been riding the bus on Lindbergh when she glimpsed him trotting down the steps of an old row house, his hand resting casually on a girl's butt.

Brittney had called in sick the next morning, and walked over to this house, the children at her side.

A young woman opened the door in a large t-shirt. Her bare legs were long and shapely. Her face was round, like a child's.

She giggled when Brittney asked her about Chris.

"I know Chris. What's it to you?" she mused, examining her red nails in the sunlight. Her expression was haughty.

Brittney shifted Madison on her hip and calmly explained Chris had three kids by her and wasn't giving her any money.

The girl frowned, her full mouth tilting left. She flashed

her eyes and said, "That's not my problem, is it," and slammed the door.

Madison started crying, and Ethan was breathing heavily, looking like he was about to break something. Brittney lifted her fist in the air to knock again, to demand an answer, but Madison's cries were piercing. Brittney stroked her daughter's back, assuring her it would be alright. She hoped Chris would hear his little girl crying and come rushing out.

But inside the house, someone turned the stereo on full volume, blasting Mos Def.

Sex, love and money ...fun ...

Brittney wanted to scream. Life wasn't one big sex party. There were responsibilities. Children needed to be taken care of.

She knocked on the door, banging loudly, trying to be heard over the music. No one came, and Madison started whimpering, her hands covering her ears. Brittney peered in the window. A cat was sitting on a ratty couch, his green eyes unblinking. There was a flimsy coffee table with magazines and empty beer cans on top.

Ethan knocked on the glass, his little fist adamant.

"DAD, YOU IN THERE?" he shouted.

Brittney shook her head, although she thought, maybe he was in there, waiting for them to leave.

But what could she do about it? She pulled Ethan off the steps, and took the children to the gas station. With false cheer, she bought them chips and candy.

Trinity had stopped by the girl's house a week later, looking for Chris, and the girl had told her Chris was gone. "Are you happy now?" the girl had asked, petulantly. "No, bitch," Trinity had snapped, "we ain't."

"Morning, Brit. How's it going?"

Brittney slowed her quick pace, and took a deep breath. Her supervisor Eric was smiling at her, jangling his car keys near the entrance to the Call Center.

"Morning," she said. They walked up the steps of the Call Center, an old refurbished factory with only a few windows.

"You're late," he said, checking his watch.

She said nothing, a sense of panic tingling her arms and legs. This was her second time.

Eric held open the door. His chest was bony, almost concave. "But I'll tell you what. Your daily call numbers have been rocking. How about I erase this from the system and no one will be the wiser?"

"You'd do that?" She said, surprised at his kindness, feeling a warm rush of gratitude.

"Sure," he said, winking. "You do a good job here. Screw corporate rules." He smiled conspiratorially and he looked so boyish, she realized he was not much older than her.

"Thanks, Eric."

The ceiling of the Call Center was thirty or forty feet high and the overhead lights were bright. Rows and rows of cubicles were filled with customer service representatives in black pants and red polos.

Brittney said goodbye to Eric at the bathroom, and then checked in for her shift, swiping her card on the wall. She hustled to her cubicle. A picture of Ethan and Madison sat on her desk, one of the only ones she had, and she gave them a crooked smile.

She flipped on her computer screen and put on her headset. She took a breath, donned her persona of a happy company representative, and accepted her first customer call.

She had to take one call after another so there was no free time to worry about Ethan and Madison or the baby. She followed the script, answering the same questions, over and over again. When customers were rude, she waited, her lip in a tight line, trying to feel blank inside, as they fumed. She thought about how Eric had overrode her lateness and it gave her more patience. She wanted to do good for him.

As the clock neared 7 p.m., she noticed, with pride, her Daily Calls Number was far above the required minimum.

She stood up, stretching her arms in the air, and then swiped out on the wall. She headed to the locker room, and the helpful girl with the chipper voice slipped away from her, replaced by an anxious mother.

She grabbed her purse from her locker and then peed, listening to the chatter of some of the other girls. They were discussing how boring their college classes were.

She walked to the mirror, and the two girls—one skinny white girl with frizzy brown hair, one black girl—didn't pay her any mind.

She wanted to grab their collars and shake them and say, you have so much opportunity, so many choices.

But Brittney just turned away, and hustled to the bus stop. People were milling about, waiting. The bus was late. It didn't come for forty minutes. By the time she was back in Justice's neighborhood, it was after nine thirty. The blinds to Justice's apartment were drawn back, and the ceiling light was on. Nothing seemed amiss. But, still, she felt a rising sense of panic, worrying that Madison was hurt.

Brittney huffed up the stairs, and threw open the door. Madison was sucking an empty bottle of grape soda, and she tossed it aside and toddled over to Brittney, her arms open, smiling, "Ma ma ma."

Brittney hugged her, and then checked her scalp and back and legs for bruises or bumps. She was OK. Nothing was wrong. Ethan was sitting underneath the dining room table, drawing on his sketchpad, and he climbed out.

"You're late," he said.

"I know," Brittney said. "The bus was late. Come on." She turned to Justice, who was still sitting on the couch, as if she hadn't moved all day. "I'll drop them off at eight tomorrow."

Justice glanced up from her phone. "Yeah. But you can't be so late like that. I got things to do too."

"I'm sorry, the bus didn't come on time."

Justice raised her eyebrow, but she didn't look up from her phone, and it didn't seem like she really cared.

The five blocks to the bus stop seemed to take forever. Madison was whiny as it was way past her bedtime. When they got home, Brittney unlocked the apartment door and flipped the light. Roaches and mice darted into hiding, rustling in the trash. Stacks of dirty dishes filled the sink and counter and the table.

For months, she had been meaning to clean up, to buy Raid and mousetraps, but when she had a day off from work, she was so exhausted. She didn't have the energy. And now the mess in the apartment had grown so large, so crusted, the job of cleaning it seemed impossible.

She grabbed a can of cheesy ravioli from a bag on the counter. She rinsed a plastic spoon in the sink, and handed it and the can to Ethan. He looked disappointed, but said nothing as he retreated to the living room. The TV turned on, and Brittney opened the refrigerator and juggled Madison as she poured milk into a bottle.

In the children's room, she put Madison on the changing table. Her diaper was caked with dried poop and bright red splotches bloomed on her bottom, like patches of cauliflower. Brittney shook her head, trying not to cry, and rolled the diaper up and threw it in the trash. Brittney rubbed diaper ointment across her bottom. She had needed so much more since Justice's.

Brittney kissed Madison on the belly, and Madison laughed, her small hands brushing Brittney's cheeks.

Brittney collected Madison in her arms, and rocked her to sleep in the chair, singing softly, feeling her heartbeat against her own. Her body was warm and soft and crooked around Brittney's rounded belly, and, for a moment, Brittney felt perfectly content. Brittney closed her eyes even though she knew she should keep them open. Ethan was still awake. She had to eat dinner.

But she was too comfortable. It was hard doing everything by herself, being the mother and the father. She drifted to sleep, her fingers unrolled, Madison wedged between her belly and the side of the chair.

~*~

Brittney was startled awake by a sharp pain in her lower back.

Then, the pain settled, becoming softer, and she took a deep breath. She heaved Madison up as gently as she could, and laid her in the crib.

Ethan was asleep on the couch, cheesy ravioli smeared on his shirt and pants. The open can and dirty spoon were on the carpet. On the TV, an infomercial for gold necklaces was playing.

She quietly grabbed his blanket from his bed and draped it over him. She undid the Velcro on his shoes, and slid them off. He rustled, grabbing the blanket in his hands, rolling onto his side. She leaned down to kiss him on the cheek and a wave of pain shot out from her back, radiating through her body.

She stood up, breathing deeply, and went into her bathroom. She needed an aspirin, but the bottle was empty. *Of course it's empty*, she thought, tossing it on the floor. On the toilet, she sprawled out, her limbs askance. The pain was coming and going, wrapping itself around her belly. It occurred to her, then, the baby was on its way.

She washed her face, and changed her clothes, pulling on comfortable gray sweats. She phoned the Call Center and told them she was having a medical emergency and wouldn't be in tomorrow. The shift manager—a gruff, older man—told her she wasn't providing enough notice.

Brittney hung up. The least they could do was let her have her baby.

She stared at her phone. She had forgotten how bad the pain was. When the pain abated, she tried Chris's number, even though the number had ceased playing his message months ago. The phone beeped at her, and an automated woman listed the number, inviting her to leave a message, which she did.

How, she wondered, could Chris be cruising the city streets, shacking up with a girl, while she was here alone, about to give birth to his baby?

She collapsed on her bed, and curled up in the fetal

position. The pain clenched her stomach, and tore at her insides like knives scraping her intestines.

She leaned over the edge of the bed and vomited.

Another contraction passed, and she ground her teeth, waiting for the next one. Chris had been able to walk away, not once looking back, but she was stuck here.

She thought of the brightly lit hospital, and the doctor injecting the drugs in her spine, numbing her.

She clutched the phone, and pressed the speed dial for Trinity. The phone rang but then went to voicemail. She hung up, leaning over in pain, reciting part of the Lord's Prayer as her grandmother had to her, "Our Father… Thy Kingdom come; Thy will be done on earth as it is in Heaven."

She called Dave, the most reliable of her four brothers. He picked up, his voice groggy, and she cried out in relief.

"Dave, I'm havin' my baby and I need you to watch the kids."

"Huh? What's that?"

"The baby … my baby is coming …."

"Yeah, OK," he said, his voice fatigued, "I'll be there in a few."

"Thank you, Dave."

He grunted, and hung up, and she dropped the phone. She wanted her Grandma Frances, with all her padded softness. She wanted to curl up in her lap and stroke her Grandma's long hair, admiring how it was thick but still slipped through her fingers like water. She could see her face, her strong, wide nose, her pale skin, her droopy earlobes.

Her voice whispering in Brittney's ear, "You can be whoever you want. Your ancestors immigrated here from Ireland during a famine and have been surviving ever since. You have survivor's blood."

Brittney closed her eyes, remembering how it felt to be loved by someone who felt safe and steady.

There was a knock at the door and she walked over to open it.

Dave was wearing an Eagles baseball hat, slung low. He pushed past her.

"Damn, Brittney, it looks like shit in here."

She said nothing. She slipped on her sneakers and pulled her purse over her shoulder.

"Chris still in the wind?" he asked.

Brittney nodded.

"What an ass! If I see him, he'll be sorry, trust me." he said, punching the palm of his hand. "How are you feelin'? You want me to call you a cab?"

"I'll take the trolley," she whispered. She had so little money saved up. Cabs were too expensive.

She closed her eyes, and leaned against her brother, feeling the hardness of his chest. She didn't want to do this alone.

"You got this, Brit," he said, squeezing her back. "You can do it, mama."

"OK," she said, even though she didn't feel that way. She felt like she was made of hundreds of unraveling threads.

A breeze brushed over her face as she made her way to the trolley stop. She wondered, fleetingly, if the baby was a boy or a girl, if the child would be easy or hard.

A souped up car roared by, an angry rapper blasting from the stereo, and the noise was aggravating.

She sat on the curb, and this eased the pain. She took deep breaths, watching her belly rise and fall. Brittney felt no love for the baby inside. Not yet. All that seemed real was the imposition: the excruciating pain, the months of fatigue and back pain, the nausea. It had been her hardest pregnancy and the one she had thought the least about.

The trolley came into view, clinking on its tracks. It heaved to a stop in front of her.

Aboard, the fluorescent lights were jarring. A man was sitting in the front seat, his black garbage bag spilling into the aisle, and he smelled of unwashed skin. A group of young men were congregated in the last four rows, their hands clutching bottles in paper bags.

She closed her eyes, half-listening to the young men banter about a party downtown. The contractions were coming faster, and, instinctively, she squeezed her legs together, telling the baby not to leave, not yet.

The young men in the back laughed, and they seemed far away, their oval heads hazy, as if they were part of a dream. She looked out the window, searching for the hospital, and as her stop appeared in the distance, she walked to the front.

The boys' laughter echoed in her ears as she walked down the trolley's steps, gripping the sides. The baby was pushing down near the opening of her vagina. It was too late for an epidural, and this saddened her, that she would not have that moment of complete relief.

The street was empty. She wondered if the baby would drop out on the street, its head falling onto the concrete.

Would this baby disappearing be such a bad thing? she thought.

The glass doors of the ER parted, and once she stepped in, she crumpled to the ground. People shouted and ran. Brittney lolled back inside her head.

~*~

"It's a healthy baby girl."

Brittney was relieved, remembering all the appointments she had skipped, how little she had even had time to think about this baby, how deep down she had hoped it would just disappear.

"What's her name?" the doctor asked, his fingers clasping a pen.

Brittney didn't know. Naming the baby would have meant Chris wasn't coming home in time for the birth.

She closed her eyes, and waited. She remembered when she was pregnant with Ethan, even though Chris had never asked her to get married, she had fantasized about a wedding. She had imagined herself recreating one of Maggie Sottero's scarlet red dresses, an A-line with crystals decorating the empire waist. The thought of sewing it and then wearing it at her own wedding had made her feel invincible.

"Maggie," she said.

The doctor raised his eyebrows. "Margaret?"

"No. Maggie."

The doctor nodded, scribbled the name down and departed. The other doctors were stitching up her vagina, their heads lowered in concentration. One of them seemed even younger than Brittney.

Maybe in another life, one where Brittney's mother wasn't a drunk and her brothers weren't blasting N.W.A. all day and night, making it impossible for her to study, Brittney could have been a nurse. She wouldn't have minded delivering babies.

The nurse was rocking Maggie, waiting for them to finish with their stitches. Maggie looked frail and bony.

"How much does she weigh?" Brittney asked.

"Five pounds fifteen ounces."

"That's small."

"Small but healthy."

Brittney nodded slowly, wondering. Madison and Ethan had both been over eight pounds. The doctors at her feet stood up, announced they were finished, and moved their equipment and tray table out of the way. The nurse placed Maggie on Brittney's breast. She clamped right on, and Brittney stroked her flat cheek with her finger. Maggie looked sickly and wrinkled.

"You sure she's OK?"

The nurse nodded, cleaning up bloody clothes on the floor.

Brittney wanted to send Maggie to the nursery and sleep for a long time. Maybe then she could wake up refreshed, and be a good mother to this child she was already worn down by.

A different nurse came in the room, and explained they had to move rooms. Brittney nodded, gathering her things.

"Can you put her in the nursery?"

"If you want."

The nurse took Maggie in her arms and walked out of

the room. Brittney didn't feel any sadness at seeing them go. The truth was she needed Chris to look after Maggie while she recovered, but he wasn't here so strangers would have to do his job.

She thought of leaving Maggie here in the hospital for Chris to come collect. Or if not him, some childless couple. She could walk back to the tentative life she was building as a single mother. Things would be so much easier that way. She wasn't attached to Maggie yet.

Brittney hobbled to the assigned room, and she swallowed the pain medication and then curled up in the bed and fell asleep. Nurses came and went, handing her paperwork and checking her blood pressure and heart rate. Women chattered in the hall.

In the morning, she ate her breakfast, and then slept some more. She needed more sleep, but she had to get home, and this made her want to cry. At noon, she changed out of her paper gown and back into her regular clothes.

She sat on the edge of her bed, and when the nurse came to check on her, the questions rang loud in her mind. How can I adopt my baby out? There must be a loving couple who would take her, right? Do you know anyone? Do you want her?

But when she opened her mouth, all that came out was that she needed to check out now. She needed to go home.

The nurse argued with her, telling her she had to stay. Brittney yelled about needing to take care of her other children, and the nurse eventually relented, agreeing to release her, but not Maggie.

Brittney was annoyed, but then she thought, another night of uninterrupted sleep wouldn't be so bad. And Maggie would be well-tended in the nursery, where the rotating herds of attentive young women fed and bathed whole rows of tiny creatures.

Brittney signed the paperwork, streams of it, not even bothering to read, and promised to return the following evening for Maggie, and then she was suddenly out on the street again.

Her nether regions ached as she walked to the trolley stop. Each step was an agitation.

On the ride home, the firm plastic seat whacked against her like a paddle. She stared out the window, watching the green trees and row houses slide by. She would have to stop at the pharmacy, and buy a bottle of ibuprofen and laxatives. It would be her only chance. Tonight, she would sleep, but that was it. After that, she would be woken up every few hours, the piercing cry of newborn grating at her ears.

She tried to gear herself up for this, to say her prayers, to think of her Grandma, but she couldn't reach those things. They seemed dull and hallowed out. What was real was the task of caring for a newborn and two small children, alone.

She could feel the tenuousness of her situation—maybe she would get through it, maybe she wouldn't. As a child in the park, hiding under the jungle gym, she had ripped the empty chip bags into long, thin pieces, thinking, *God gonna save me, God ain't gonna save me, God gonna save me*. Until there was nothing left to shred. She fudged the answer, leaving a slightly larger piece intact if it landed on *God gonna save me*. Because when her mother called for her, ready to go home, she needed to believe it would all work out somehow, that God would watch over her and maybe even stop her mother from drinking so much.

But, for some reason, she couldn't bring herself to fudge anymore, to believe God was tending to her little piece of the world with a loving eye. She got off the trolley and walked toward the pharmacy. She had the distinct sense that it all might prove too much. Yet she couldn't bring herself to call the hospital and ask about giving Maggie away.

Chapter Five

Rebecca

Rebecca only knew one couple with adopted children. She drove to their large house in the suburbs and drank their green tea, feeling an unexpected formality without Will. Neil was a law professor, more Will's friend than hers.

Neil was happy to share his experiences—the adoption process had taken years, with multiple trips to China and new expenses and new rules cropping up daily—but the girls, who were one and three at adoption, had transitioned well to life in America.

The daughters ran into the living room while they were talking. Eight and ten now, the girls were petite, with high cheekbones and ivory skin. They wore blue jeans and t-shirts, and smiled politely at Rebecca, and folded their hands in a quasi-prayer position while they "pleeeeased" their mother Sandra for popsicles. Sandra nodded and headed to the kitchen, and the girls hovered around her happily as she retrieved two popsicles from the freezer.

Neil watched the three of them, his mouth lifted with pride. Rebecca's chest tightened. She would never have that—there would be no one looking on with joy as she mothered her child.

In the kitchen, Sandra was gently wiping the younger girl's cheek, and there was a tenderness in her gesture, a brightness in her face. Rebecca smiled, warmed by the reminder: she wouldn't need an audience.

The girls ran back outside, waving their popsicles and giggling to one another. Neil stood up, offering Rebecca a tour of the house, to highlight the Chinese artifacts and books they had purchased.

"Sure," she said, gathering her purse and slinging it over her shoulder.

He explained the various objects and paintings, and she murmured her approval even though she could not see the little girls stopping to admire the large bowl in the style of the Ming Dynasty, or read a tattered copy of the *I Ching*. Long scrolls of calligraphy hung in the dining room, and a miniature pagoda sat in the corner of the study. A shimmering silver blanket was draped over the pagoda. Neil's mouth twitched in an apologetic smile. "The girls like to use it as a podium."

"Why did you decide to adopt from China?"

He shrugged. "Honestly, it was quicker. In the US, there are a lot more parents who want to adopt than there are healthy infants."

"Really?"

"Yes. Adopting parents compete with one another with catchy profiles and glossy photographs. There's a whole cottage industry around it. It was strange."

"Oh."

"The other issue," Neil said, "is once a foreign adoption is done, it is done. Sandra read a lot of domestic horror stories, of a birthmother or birthfather suing to get the child back, months, or even years, later."

"I see."

"Also, you might want to consider," he continued, pausing and clearing his throat. "Well, we were told by a friend who was trying to adopt by herself that, domestically, it is very difficult for an ... older single woman to be chosen by the birthparents. That profile has difficulty competing with the young married couples."

Hearing this outloud felt like a slap, even though Rebecca had already read this herself. It was common knowledge in all the adoptive parent forums. Rebecca nodded, running her fingers through her hair. She knew she would have trouble adopting domestically, but she wasn't sure she wanted to adopt from another country. She thought of the Nobuso children, who she had lived with for years, off and on. She couldn't see them living in a city. It seemed wrong somehow, though she was not sure how exactly.

"Did you ever worry," she asked, "the girls would lose their culture?"

"We did—we do—worry about it. But ultimately we decided it was better for them to become American than to grow up in an orphanage. The truth is they don't remember China, and they aren't terribly interested in it, despite our efforts. They want to be like their friends."

"That makes sense. You're right, of course."

On the drive home, she knew what Neil had said was true, but for some reason, she still had a longing to adopt from Philadelphia, so the child could at least keep her birthplace, like a fish taken out of a lake, and thrown right back in. The decrepit old buildings and the clank of the trolley, the hundred-year-old trees and the smell of chlorine in the tap water, the drivers running red lights, the towering city hall and the greasy food carts. She and the child could have that much in common, at least.

But she was still heartened by meeting Neil's family. Their experience of adoption was good and they seemed happy. Happier than most families she knew.

Many women her age had adopted from the foster care system. The Department of Human Services (DHS) was desperate for more homes. Of course, almost all those children had undergone some form of trauma. It was riskier. Her child might have psychological problems, or, after a year in her care, be returned to the biological parents. Was that what she wanted? Was she willing to risk that loss?

She looked out her front window. The sky was thick with gray clouds. Maybe it wouldn't be easy, but adopting from foster care felt like a chance to do something good. She thought of her university friends, how they would ostensibly admire her, but also think a child adopted from the system would never compete with theirs, never go to the same colleges or display the same brilliance, and would, therefore, be inferior and less interesting.

For years, she had heard her colleagues flout their children's accomplishments. One child was reading at three, another was doing algebra at four, another won a prestigious violin competition. Some law professor had even written a bestselling book about this competitive way of parenting, *How We Raised Two Ivy League Kids*.

Rebecca was glad she wouldn't feel compelled to enter her adopted child, with her mysterious genes and mysterious experiences, into this kinder rat race. It didn't seem like the right way to raise children anyway.

OK, she decided, running her finger down the window, watching the tree branches shudder in the wind. *That's what I'll do. I will adopt from foster care.*

~*~

The Transitions Foster and Adopt Agency was in an Eastern-bloc chunk of concrete. The lobby had tattered olive carpets and a security guard at a flimsy table. He didn't look up from his phone as she signed his clipboard. The agency suite was at the end of the hall, and she could hear the light sound of children talking and laughing.

Women were sitting in plastic chairs, chatting or reading or scanning their phones. Children slept in strollers at their feet or chased each other around, their laughs light and giddy. They seemed normal, no different than any other group of children, and this was reassuring.

The harried receptionist took Rebecca's information and pointed her down the hall, to room 701. Boxes and binders cluttered the floor and Rebecca stepped over them. She knocked on the door.

A woman's voice told her she could come in. The room was a large closet, barely big enough for a desk and two chairs. A woman who looked fresh out of college was seated behind the desk, a phone cradled against her ear.

"I'm running late," she said, her hand over the phone. "Can you wait outside?"

"Of course," Rebecca said, closing the door. She sat on the floor. The carpet was gray and bunchy and Rebecca tugged at a loose thread. She thought about the other night, when she'd told her closest friends, two childless couples, about her decision. There had been a moment of silence, of shock, and then everyone had chimed in with their congratulations. Their approval had been at arm's length, though, as if she had announced she was moving to Arkansas to feed homeless veterans. Erica, a pediatrician, had exclaimed, "Wow, good for you, I could never take that on." After an awkward pause, Peter had changed the subject, to a visiting law professor. Apparently, he had been caught making out with one of his comely students.

Rebecca had smiled, allowing the conversation to drift away, but she had been disappointed. She had hoped her friends, even though they had no plans for children, would have been interested in hers.

Her mother, an ardent feminist and long taken with the idea of children raised free from the influence of a man, was more enthusiastic.

"Thanks, mother," Rebecca had responded, winking at her father, who smiled wryly.

Her father had cleared his throat, then. "This is an admirable thing to do, Rebecca. But are you sure such a child will fit into your lifestyle?"

"What lifestyle?"

"Oh, there might be someone else more familiar with these children's … backgrounds."

"Does that matter?"

"It might."

The way he said this indicated he didn't think it was the best decision. She hadn't pushed him, though. Arguing with her father could be like falling down a neverending rabbit hole; he was that clever and stubborn. She asked him about his students this year and, as she knew he would, he perked up. He told her about a boy from Cambridge, the offspring of two MIT mathematics professors.

"I was a little surprised he chose a history major," he pondered, clearly elated, and a little proud, the boy had selected his department, which was losing enrollees every year.

She felt a nostalgic wave of jealousy, remembering how she'd labored over her history books as a girl, hoping to catch his attention. Every year or two, there would be a new student under his wing. They were almost always boys, skinny and tall and bookish as they sat at their dining room table, eating the take-out her mother had ordered as fulfillment of her domestic duties.

Rebecca doubted her foster child would be a history prodigy, that the child would have that to share with her father. But there would be other things, she supposed. She stretched out her arms, grateful for her sister, who had been genuinely happy for her. Maybe it was just because Elizabeth's vast professional ambition meant she had no energy left for criticizing how people got or raised their children. But whatever the reason, Elizabeth had been supportive, asking her if she needed a lawyer, or extra money.

Will, too, had been supportive, when she had texted him her decision (she had been too cowardly to call, afraid hearing his voice would throw her back into paralysis) and he had offered to fast-track their divorce, and give her the house and half their savings.

His generosity had angered her, and she had written dozen of letters, filled with purple prose, her hand aching, her hard print leaving marks on her desk, asking him how he could still be so loving and still break her heart. But then she had crumpled the letters, and thrown them in the trash, and sent him a simple text: Thank you.

Two young women walked down the hall, oblivious to Rebecca as they continued their conversation.

"I, like, don't think she's qualified ...."

"Can we really afford to be that picky right now?"

"Can we afford not to be? What if something, you know, were to happen?"

"Like what?"

"I don't know, you know, like, I have a bad feeling ...."

The women turned the corner and their words turned indistinct then disappeared. They had sounded like adolescents, and this was surprising, that such young women were tasked with deciding who could, and could not, foster a child.

The door swung open behind Rebecca.

"Come on in," the woman called, inching her way back behind her desk.

Rebecca sat in the hard, plastic chair. The woman pulled out a folder with Rebecca's name on it, and rifled through it.

"So," she sighed, pushing back her buoyant hair. The gesture was jerky, impatient, as if the inevitably of her hair drifting back in front of her face made it barely worth the effort. "I'm Molly, your agency worker. We have to schedule a home study."

Molly turned back to her computer and pulled up a calendar, and she clicked through October, November, December and January. Rebecca felt her child receding farther and farther away from her.

"How's February third, at two p.m.?"

"Is that the soonest you have?"

"Yeah, we're really understaffed."

"Alright."

Molly handed her a folder with a checklist, littered with her wet fingerprints. "Here's a list of things you need to complete."

Rebecca scanned the bright yellow lettering: a criminal background check, a physical at a doctor's office, proof of completion of training, proof of income, proof of housing, a study of her home, a list of references, and a personal fact sheet.

So it would be a while before she would have a child.

"Any questions?"

"What is the timeline for everything?"

"It depends what you are willing to take on. If you're open to children of color, older children, sibling sets, disabilities, kids still on unification track—the placement could happen days or weeks after you're approved. To be honest, you never know. The system is kind of unpredictable."

Rebecca nodded, looping her purse around her shoulder. She knew fostering was a danger—you could take care of the child for a year and then lose her—but she had flipped through a book of children free for adoption without wait, and the book had depressed her. It had been filled with the hardened and angry looks of teenagers, and young children in wheelchairs, and on oxygen tanks, their eyes unfocused, their hands curled. Children Rebecca knew she wasn't capable of caring for. Not by herself.

"OK."

"Call if you have any questions."

Rebecca nodded, tucking the folder underneath her arm. There was more she wanted to know; she wanted to know everything about her child, and how her child would come to find her, but she couldn't formulate a sensible question. It was too vague.

"Thank you," she said instead.

Opening the door, she wondered if she should have tried harder to befriend Molly. Molly, with her cotton candy hair and adolescent pimples, would determine whether Rebecca ever became a mother.

~*~

It was a cold, snowy winter. The roads were icy, and

Rebecca bundled up in her heavy winter coat and trekked to school by foot. The undergraduates threw snowballs at one another, laughing and running across the lawn in their flimsy coats and sandals. Rebecca taught her two classes, supervised her three graduate students, and researched an article on equal pay for equal work the editor of *The Study of Women and Work* had solicited.

On the weekends, she went out to dinner with Peter and Erica or saw a movie at the Ritz. But as she was doing these things, her mind was occupied by waiting.

She often wondered where her child was at that very moment. Maybe the child was shivering in a filthy apartment without heat. Or, she was alone in a locked room, her belly empty; or a man, tall and looming, was yelling at her.

These scenes disturbed Rebecca, and she wished there was something she could do, somehow intervene before the child was hurt. But of course this was impossible; the hurt was the very reason the child would be taken away. No one could anticipate the abuse or neglect. But it didn't stop Rebecca from wishing it was so.

She thought, too, of the child being happy, the child laughing as she watched cartoons on television, or enjoying warm macaroni and cheese at a table. In her imagination, the child morphed from a girl to a boy, from a baby to a toddler, from black to white. Some things, though, stayed the same: the child was sweet; the child's house was rundown; the parental figure was repulsive. And, always, somehow, the child belonged to Rebecca. It was a kind of magical thinking, a magical thread connecting them from birth to death.

This was a risky game, as she knew very well even if a child were placed with her, the child could be sent back to the biological parents. She *knew* this but somehow *felt* it would not happen to her; she *felt* that once the child came, the child would remain.

Her foster care training was held at a church deep in West Philadelphia. Rebecca walked there on a Saturday morning, a mug of coffee in her gloved hand. As she left the comfort of her gentrified blocks, she was grateful for the icy cold that rendered the streets quiet. They seemed safer that way.

Many of the row homes were well-kept, the vinyl siding intact, the little yards tidy, a potted plant or chair on the porch. But those homes were often adjacent to abandoned properties, their windows and doors boarded-up, pieces of their roof dangling precariously.

The sidewalks were missing large chunks of concrete, and weeds and dirt grew in their place. A daycare's playground was wrapped in barbed wire.

The air, somehow, seemed alight with decay.

An old black man in a tattered coat rummaged through a trash can, mumbling about a man he was going to get. His fingers were bony and bare. Rebecca's impulse was to offer him money, or a cup of coffee, but his loud words were directed at an invisible interlocutor, and this scared her.

She turned onto 52nd Street, a retail strip. Two black men were smoking blunts in front of a restaurant that promised FISH CHICKEN BEEF PIZZA HOAGIES BEER BREAKFAST.

The church was a storefront, directly next to a windowless MR. JAMES EXOTIC GIRLS EVERY NIGHT.

Rebecca reached the door at the same time as a young couple. They were both wearing cashmere coats.

"Are you here for the training?" the woman beamed, revealing a set of blindingly white teeth. A gold cross dangled from her slender neck.

Rebecca nodded, and part of her was relieved that she was no longer alone, walking through a neighborhood that seemed to have fallen into disarray.

"I'm Martha and this is David."

"Rebecca."

The woman circled her arm around Rebecca's, and jumped up with excitement. She smelled like vanilla, and reminded Rebecca of a yapping show dog. David opened the door, and held it as Martha pulled Rebecca in. The heat was dry and overwhelming. Folding chairs were arranged in a circle, and another white couple was already there, seated.

"Bill! Natalie!" Martha squealed.

The other couple smiled, equally beatific. They piled into the adjacent seats, separating by gender. The men started talking about the Eagles, and the women looked at Rebecca expectantly.

"So," Martha smiled, "is your husband coming?"

"No. It's just me."

Martha's expression flagged, confusion in her eyes, but this was immediately blinked away. "Are you hoping to adopt?"

Rebecca nodded.

"We want to adopt, too. We both felt God calling us to help children in need."

Natalie nodded. "We are open to whatever comes, whatever God wants."

Rebecca smiled vaguely. It had been years since Rebecca had heard people talk in this manner. Except for her wedding ceremony and holidays with Will's parents, she had lived a thoroughly secular life.

More people were streaming into the room. A lesbian couple, one woman boxy with a crew cut, the other curvy, and a thirtysomething black woman were followed by a twenty-something in a puffy coat carrying two cloth bags and a pencil in her mouth.

The woman plopped her bags on a table, and began pulling out workbooks and pens. "I'm Viv, everyone," she said, "your instructor for the day."

Viv wore boxy black glasses over her square face, giving her an angled appearance. She started handing out workbooks.

Another woman opened the door and walked in. She noisily removed her coat. She must have been close to fifty, but she wore a plunging v-neck and black stretchy pants. The fabric of the pants was translucent, and Rebecca could see the cellulite dimpling her butt and thighs.

Viv handed the woman a workbook. The woman took it,

and then dropped it loudly on the floor.

"OK," Viv announced, her voice uneven. Splotches were forming on her pale neck. She leaned against the table, and picked up one of the workbooks. In a monotone, she began reading. "Foster parents are individuals who provide temporary care to children or youth who are removed from their parent's care and …."

The content was basic and repetitive, a Foster Care for Dummies type book. As Viv proceeded to Chapter Three ("How to Support the Child in Your Care") even Martha's encouraging smile seemed to flag.

Rebecca surveyed the circle, and noticed there were three middle aged black women who, like her, appeared to have come alone. One of them was wearing business casual and listening intently, her hands folded in her lap. Another occasionally yawned.

Rebecca wondered if she would be the last person in the room to receive a child. Two women would be better than one, right? As for the single black women, the majority of children in Philadelphia's system were of color. Would this matter? This wasn't something she dared ask.

She leafed through the workbook—it didn't provide any details on how the children were placed; it only stated, mysteriously, "The social worker will place a child based on the home's particular strengths and capabilities."

Viv's monologue abruptly ended and she tossed her workbook on the table.

"Almost 9,000," she said, jumping on the table and swinging her legs back and forth. "That's how many children were under our supervision last year in Philadelphia. We do need more foster homes. But it's our priority to make sure everyone knows what they are getting into."

Viv took off her glasses, and rubbed the lenses with her ratty sweater. The tan wool was stained and unraveling. "We have to remember that all the children have experienced a trauma—the trauma of neglect or abuse, and the trauma of leaving the only home they have known."

"Yeah, trauma inflicted by DHS," the older woman in the tights muttered, crossing her arms over her chest.

Viv inched back on her table, looking at the ceiling. "We're going to do a thought exercise. I want everyone to visualize the following ... an eleven-month-old boy is placed with you. After an initial period of upset, he bonds with you. He is very affectionate. He calls you 'mama' and 'papa.' He wakes up happy to see you. Soon, the mother stops coming to the visitations.

"Eight months pass, and the boy seems to have forgotten about his mother. He is happy. You are happy. He is walking and talking. He tells you he 'wuvs you.' You start to think the boy is going to be your son. The worker begins preparing you for adoption. You celebrate his second birthday with all your friends and family.

"All is well.

"And then, suddenly, the mother is back. The visits start up again, and the boy is upset by them—he cries a lot before and after. He is confused, doesn't understand what is going on. After a few months, the worker tells you the visits are going to be longer. Soon they are unsupervised. The boy becomes defiant. He starts hitting and biting. His speech regresses. Still, the visits get more frequent, and a plan is made to return him to his home.

"At thirty-two months, he is returned to his mother. The mother decides not to keep contact with you. You have no right to see him. You have no right to know what is happening to him. Your boy is gone, just like that."

Rebecca took a deep breath. How ... unbearable. She knew, but didn't want to know, this was the risk she was taking.

"This is a true story," Viv added.

"What happened to the little boy?" someone called, softly.

Viv took off her glasses. Her face seemed rounder, less harsh. "He was with his mother for two years, but she couldn't control her addiction, and he was put back in care. Unfortunately, his previous family had moved away.

"Remember, reunification with the birth family is the first

goal. How many of you are interested in adopting?"

Half the people in the circle raised their hands.

The older woman shook her head, her arms across her large chest. "Ain't right. That's stealin'. They ain't your babies."

The woman stared at Viv aggressively, disdain clouding her eyes.

Viv nodded. "I understand you're upset, but we only place children out of the home as a last resort."

The woman snorted. "My sista's baby was stolen. I'm here listenin' to this crap so you can 'approve' me to watch my own goddamn niece."

Viv leaned against the table and stared at the floor. "I can't comment on individual cases, but all removals must be approved by a judge."

The woman scoffed and narrowed her eyes and pinched her mouth. She said nothing further, staring at the wall.

Rebecca was skeptical of a middle-aged woman dressed like a teenager. She had to think DHS or the courts would undo mistaken removals before it was too late.

Viv checked her watch. "Any other questions?"

The circle was silent, and Viv nodded. She thanked everyone for coming. People burrowed into their coats and headed out the door, glad the hours were over.

On the sidewalk, Martha grabbed Rebecca's arm. Martha asked for her number so they could all get together later, with their children. Rebecca recited it, appreciating Martha's bright blue eyes and quick smile, even though her perpetual cheeriness seemed almost unbelievable.

Rebecca walked toward her house, dangling her empty mug in the air. As she reached the intersection of Pine and 52nd, she realized one of the middle aged black women from the training was standing there, waiting for the light to change.

The woman's hair was straightened and cut to a bob.

"Hi," Rebecca said.

The woman turned, her face wary. Seeing Rebecca, she smiled. Her two front teeth overlapped slightly. "Whadcha you think?"

"It wasn't terribly useful."

The woman shook her head as the light turned and they crossed the street. "No kidding. DHS is all about wasting people's time, one way or another. My time would be better spent with my girls."

"You already have foster children?"

"Yep, two girls. They're four and seven."

That sounded nice. "Is it just you?"

"Uh-huh. I got sick of waiting around for the mythical man who wants to get married and can keep a job."

Rebecca laughed. "I just got divorced. He had a job, but he didn't want to grow up," Rebecca said, indulging her lingering frustration Will only ever called to chat, not to say he had changed his mind.

The woman nodded knowingly. "I'm Yvonne."

"Rebecca. Do you think you'll adopt the girls?"

Yvonne shrugged. "I hope so, but you never know. She was right about that."

The ancient trees in Malcolm X Park were large and imposing, their thick branches covered in ice. The two colorful playgrounds were abandoned, the silver slides scuffed with mud, the benches scrawled with graffiti tags.

Yvonne stopped in front of a row home. It was a small two-story, and the front siding was worn vinyl. Two children's bikes were chained to the porch fence.

"This is me," she said, reaching into her purse and pulling out a business card.

Rebecca smiled and took the card. *Yvonne Jackson, Bank of America, Customer Service Representative.*

She rummaged in her purse, and slid one of her business cards out of their holder. She rarely used them. Yvonne plucked the card out of her hand and read it. Her mouth turned down with disappointment.

"You don't like Penn?"

Yvonne shrugged. "In my experience, university folk got

an attitude, think they're better than everyone else around here."

Rebecca nodded sympathetically. Penn *had* gentrified the area around the campus, paying its faculty and staff to purchase houses, subsidizing the local public school, and financing community service officers to diligently patrol the streets.

"We're not all bad, though," Rebecca said, tucking her left hand in her pocket.

"Yeah, I know," Yvonne said. "Anthropology, that sounds interesting. I took one of those classes at PCC, on a Native American Indian tribe. Amazing how different their lives were than ours."

"Exactly. That's what I have always loved about anthropology."

She pointed to her door. "My mom's waiting. Good luck with DHS."

"OK," Rebecca called, watching Yvonne walk up the few stairs to her house. Rusty bars covered the only window on the first floor. The green paint on the concrete porch was chipping. But the red door had a festive twig wreath.

Rebecca lived four blocks from Yvonne, and as she walked, the houses grew larger, and then separated to twins and then to singles. The materials shifted from vinyl and concrete to brick and slate and wood. The sidewalks became smoother, and dilapidated homes, with their boarded-up windows and doors, vanished.

She walked up the path to her Victorian, grateful for its paneled windows and slate roof and solid frame, but she also felt a twinge of guilt, and she wondered if her child would find the house imposing and strange.

~*~

Rebecca baby-proofed her home, locking the medicine cabinets, dulling the coffee table's sharp edges, securing unsteady bookcases, installing more fire detectors. She bought a crib and assembled it in the room next to her own, hoping she would eventually receive a baby. She painted the walls a warm yellow, and hung wood-framed giraffes and elephants and bears.

She lost herself in the tasks, imbued with purpose. The last time she had done so much with her body was when she had lived with the Nobuso women. She had forgotten how good it felt to be physically capable.

Over a long weekend, she drove to Manhattan and loaded her sister's barely used goods—a trove of clothes and toys—into her car. Boxes filled the trunk and the backseat and the passenger seat. She drove cautiously, checking her side mirrors, content to be surrounded by the bright colors of children's things.

She placed the blue bouncer in the living room, nestled near her favorite armchair. She would often look up from her research on the childrearing practices of Mormons in the 19th Century, imagining her baby in the bouncer, laughing.

When she went to bed, she would stop in the nursery and turn on the nightlight. She smiled at the teddy bear with the yellow bowtie, sitting in the rocking chair, and ran her finger over the baby socks, each barely bigger than her thumb.

And then she waited. The home study appointment— the final element of her certification—was scheduled, canceled, rescheduled and canceled again. Molly apologized for the delays, but she never offered an explanation and her light tone suggested unreliability was to be expected. There were corruption charges pending in the mayor's office and Rebecca began to suspect the city, including DHS, was incompetent. She asked a professor at the school of social work, and he told her DHS was a bureaucratic nightmare, staffed by incompetently trained caseworkers.

The summer brought more slick humidity, and Rebecca taught three different summer classes, determined to keep busy. She didn't want to think about the child she might never have, or how she still missed Will, and struggled to delete his texts

- which now arrived every other month or so - unread. In moments of weakness, she would write long replies, eight or nine paragraphs, but then somehow, she would manage to find the willpower to delete them, saving herself from reopening the scar on her heart that was still healing.

In August, a fourteen-year-old girl with cerebral palsy was found dead in her West Philadelphia home, weighing only forty-two pounds. The open bedsores on her back were infested with maggots. The family had been under DHS supervision for years, but DHS was refusing to comment.

Rebecca lost her breath, for a moment, worrying her own child was languishing in a dilapidated row home, praying for someone to come save her. But her sister had already spoken to a lawyer. Rebecca had no rights. There was nothing she could do but wait.

On the day of her rescheduled home study, Rebecca canceled her classes again. She baked banana bread so the house would smell warm and comforting.

"Any interview advice?" she asked her mother, cradling the phone in her ear as she wiped the counters.

"Just be yourself. They'll be thrilled to have someone like you."

"You think?"

"Of course. A lot of foster parents are low income. They do it for the money."

"Hmm," Rebecca said, vaguely skeptical that it was true.

"Did you put the book out I sent you?"

"I forgot. I will." She walked into the office, grabbed Dr. Spock's *Baby and Child Care* from the desk and then put it on the coffee table in the living room.

"Mom," she asked, her voice cracking, "do you think I'll ever actually have a child?"

"Yes, you will. Just be patient. It hasn't been that long."

"It feels like I have been waiting forever. Wanting forever."

"I know, but it will happen before you know it."

There was a burnt smell in the air, and Rebecca rushed

back to the kitchen.

"I have to go, mom. The bread is burning."

"Spray some perfume."

"OK."

The loaf was blackened and dry, and Rebecca tossed it in the trash, pushing it to the bottom. She retrieved her perfume from her bathroom, and sprayed it in the kitchen. It smelled like burnt flowers. She laughed.

She scrubbed the pan and put it in the drying rack. She carried her empty wine bottles out to the curb, and dumped them into her neighbor's recycling bins.

After a hot shower, she slid on zipper-less khaki pants and a short-sleeved white blouse. She wasn't sure what a paragon mother looked like, but this was her best guess. She brushed her hair until it was soft and wavy.

The house was spotless, and up to code. She sat in her armchair and waited. It was five and then ten minutes past the assigned time.

The doorbell rang, and Rebecca smiled in relief. The burnt smell of banana bread still lingered in the air, and Rebecca waved her hands quickly, as if that might diffuse it.

She swung open the door, taking a deep breath.

A black woman stood on her front porch, a briefcase in her hand. Tight cornrows snaked along her scalp and down her back. Large silver earrings dangled from her ears.

"Rebecca?"

"Yes," Rebecca said, moving away from the door. The woman walked in and looked around skeptically.

"I'm Leona Dwabe," she announced, and put her briefcase on the entryway table. She pulled out a clipboard with a bunch of pages on it, and slammed the briefcase closed. "Let's take a tour of the house, and then we can talk."

Rebecca nodded, intimidated by her brusque demeanor. She led Leona into the living room. Leona walked around perfunctorily. She leaned down and checked the plugs on the outlets. She tugged at the rubber on the coffee table's edges.

In the kitchen, she checked the cabinets and the refrigerator.

"Is something burning?" she asked, wrinkling her nose.

"Oh, that was some bread."

"Hmm," Leona said, scribbling something down on her paper.

"It was just burnt on the edges. Still edible," Rebecca clarified.

"Uh-huh," Leona said, opening the back door. They toured the garage and the backyard, Leona never saying a word as she checked possible hazards and scrawled notes on her sheets of paper.

Rebecca knew she had complied with all the requirements, but Leona's silence was driving her to doubt herself.

On the second floor, they walked through the three bedrooms and bathroom, Leona stepping out onto the fire escape and giving it a rattle. On the third floor, she paused in the nursery and checked her files.

"This room is for a foster child?"

Rebecca, standing near the door, nodded.

Leona opened the closet doors and studied the designer baby dresses and Burberry coats and leather shoes Elizabeth had given her, and laughed. It was clear she was laughing *at* Rebecca, at how ridiculous she was, but Rebecca wasn't sure why. Was it ludicrous to offer foster children nice things? It wasn't as if she had bought those herself.

Leona inspected the crib, inquiring about the purchase date, and then they proceeded to the master bedroom. Leona surveyed the sprawling room, and shook her head dismissively. The bathroom cabinets were child-proofed, and Leona undid the clasps and searched through them. She pulled out a bottle of pills.

"What are these?" she asked, her eyebrows raised.

Rebecca grabbed the bottle and read the label. "These are my ex-husband's. He had a hernia surgery a few years ago."

Leona smiled and made notes on her sheet, and Rebecca panicked, wondering if she was writing *drug addict*. Rebecca leaned down and opened the cabinet beneath the sink, and put them in the trash, letting the bottle clack loudly.

"They're expired anyway."

Leona said nothing. She inspected the non-skid pads Rebecca had applied to the bathtub, her limber body leaning over the side. The cornrows whipped through the air as she raised her head.

"Is there another floor?"

Rebecca shook her head.

"OK. Let's go back downstairs and do the interview."

As they walked down the staircase, Rebecca reminded herself she was a successful woman, that she had published a book and a dozen articles. That was a professor at an Ivy League university. But her hands were clammy as they sat down at the dining room table. The stakes were so high and this woman was hard to read. She didn't seem to like her.

"Would you like something to drink?" she offered.

Leona glanced up from her papers. "I'll have a glass of water."

Rebecca was glad to leave the room. In the kitchen, she tried to calm herself. She took her time pouring two large glasses of water from the pitcher. Leona reminded her of a colleague in the women's studies department, a tall, regal woman who said little but seemed perpetually disappointed in other people.

Rebecca returned to the dining room, and placed the glasses on the table. Water sloshed onto the table. Leona frowned.

"Anyway," she said, holding her clipboard at an angle.

Leona asked her dozens of questions—about her parenting philosophy, her religion, her dating plans, her social and familial support, her finances, her openness to racial minorities and special needs children—and as Rebecca spoke, Leona stared back at her coldly.

What? What's wrong with my answers? She thought,

panicking. She took more gulps of water, and tucked her hair behind her ears. She rambled about how much she wanted to be a mother.

Leona's mouth and eyebrows were tipped up with impatience, and she checked her watch, flipped her papers over, and stood up. "OK. Thank you for your time. I have all I need."

Leona walked to the entryway, her cornrows bouncing on her back. Her arms were slender and muscular as she placed her clipboard back in her briefcase.

She opened the front door and walked out, pulling the door shut so firmly it rattled against the doorframe. Rebecca watched her from the window, annoyed she couldn't be bothered to give her an indication about her application.

Leona crossed the street quickly, opening the door of a blue Honda. Sitting in the driver's seat, she applied lipstick in the rearview mirror. Rebecca wanted to run over to her car and pound on the window. *I'll be a good mother. Isn't that what matters?*

Leona put the key in the ignition and as she checked her blind spot, she saw Rebecca in the window. Rebecca searched her face for answers, but at this distance, she could see nothing. Or maybe there was nothing to see, only blankness.

Rebecca wished she hadn't dumped the rest of her wine in the sink. She couldn't see the situation clearly anymore. She wanted a child too badly. But she had done all she could for the adoption. Even though Leona had seemed to—inexplicably—dislike her, there was no reason to reject the application. She had to believe the certification would go through, and then a child, her child, would be placed with her.

Chapter Six

Brittney would discover the white envelopes lying on the floor, half-wedged under the scuffed *Welcome Home* mat. There were no names or addresses written on the front. Inside, a page torn out of the *Philly Weekly* or the *City Paper* was wrapped around a stack of twenties. Sometimes the twenties added up to four hundred dollars; other times, it was one hundred and eighty; the highest was six hundred and sixty. The envelopes appeared at odd intervals, but they came frequently enough that she began relying on them.

The first time she found one of the envelopes, on her way to her mother's house, newborn Maggie strapped to her chest, Madison toddling by her side as Ethan ran ahead, happy to be out of the musty apartment, she had cried in relief, thinking the money meant Chris would be coming home soon, or least stopping by.

But he hadn't. He had never met, or even asked about, his youngest child.

Maggie was a terrible baby. She cried all the time, her little back arching in anger. Brittney had tried everything to stop it. She rocked Maggie for over an hour, until her ears were burning from the noise, and her back and hips were aching. She sung lullabies and blasted a fan for its swooshing white noise. She read children's books, her voice a soothing whisper. She positioned Maggie in front of the TV. She rubbed Maggie's scrawny limbs with lotion; she burned vanilla incense; she gave her homeopathic drops from the pharmacy.

Maggie was oblivious to it all. She just kept crying and crying, the same high-pitched yowl, her tiny mouth sprawled open for hours at a time.

Every time Maggie cried, even though Brittney knew there was nothing she could do to calm her, Brittney tensed up, her blood pressure rose, adrenaline coursed through her veins, and somewhere, in the recesses of her mind, a voice shouted, *the baby needs you, the baby needs you, the baby needs you.*

And the message kept screaming until Maggie exhausted herself into a slumber, her bony hands scrunched. Then it took a half an hour for Brittney's pulse to calm, for her mind to relax, for her body to fall back asleep.

Out of desperation, Brittney took her to the doctor. In the free clinic waiting room, Maggie screamed discontentedly while the other patients grumbled about the racket. Brittney wanted to tell them, if Maggie was your baby, you wouldn't be doing any better. She wasn't a normal child.

After two hours, Brittney was led to a patient room, and the harried doctor examined Maggie. The doctor wiped her hands and shrugged.

"It's just colic. She'll grow out of it."

"What do you do for colic?" Brittney asked, raising her voice over Maggie's cries.

The doctor smiled ruefully. "There's nothing to do. Colic is unexplained and persistent crying."

"That's it?"

"Sorry," the doctor said, printing a piece of paper, and handing it to Brittney. "Good luck."

Brittney folded up the sheet with the useless diagnosis, slipping it in her giant bag. The doctor was rushing out of the room, and Brittney wanted to call her back, demand a solution, but she was too tired to argue. Besides, what could she say?

The door closed firmly, announcing there would be no

relief. Brittney was stunned as she rode the bus to her mother's house. It had been three and a half months of constant crying; she couldn't take it much longer. She was losing her mind.

Maggie finally fell asleep as Brittney unlocked the door to her mother's house. In the living room, the TV was on, and her mother was sleeping on the couch, a bottle of Olde English cradled to her chest. She could hear Ethan and Madison prattling, and she found them in the kitchen.

Ethan was standing on a chair, next to the stove. Two of the burners were on, and the plastic bread bag was melting.

"What are you doin', Ethan?"

"Making grill cheesed sandwiches. We're hungry."

"Hungry," Madison repeated.

"You're too little to use the stove," Brittney said, and anger and fear leaked into her voice. "You know better."

She walked over to him, and grabbed the spatula. "Here, I'll do it."

Ethan shrugged and climbed down from the chair. "There wasn't anythin' to eat, and Grandma fell asleep."

"Yeah, I know she did," Brittney said, taking the chunk of cheese and bread slices out of the pan. She arranged them into sandwiches. She should have known better than to leave her children with her mother.

"Hey, mom," Ethan said, leaning against her leg. "What did one wall say to the other?"

"I don't know, what?"

"I'll meet you in the corner!"

Brittney smiled. "That's a good one. Why do birds fly south in the winter?"

Ethan was quiet as Brittney served up their sandwiches, putting them plates and then laying them on the small kitchen table.

"I know!" Ethan exclaimed. "Because it's too far to walk."

Brittney rubbed his unruly hair, which was down to his chin. "How'd you know that?"

Ethan shrugged, a grin on his face, and took a big bite of

his sandwich. Madison laughed, fidgeting in her seat, and waved. Brittney waved back.

"Hey, pretty girl."

On the walk home, Maggie woke up with a long screech, and Brittney walked faster, to try to lull her back to sleep.

"She's so loud!" Ethan said, running ahead.

"Mama, ears hurt," Madison whimpered from her stroller.

"I know, baby, mine do, too. Mine do, too."

In the apartment, Brittney turned up the TV to block out Maggie's shrieking cries. Ethan touched her on the knee.

"Hey, Mom, can we take Maggie back to the hospital? I really think she's broken and maybe they can fix her there," he said.

"No, baby," Brittney replied, rubbing his head. "She's here to stay." She said this very gently and sadly, because the truth was she too longed to send Maggie away.

At night, without the sunlight streaming in through the windows, Brittney's mind was occupied by a thick, dark fog. Her body ached, demanding to be shut down. She had always been an early riser, and it seemed unnatural to be awake at 2 a.m., night after night.

Maggie's bassinet was in the far corner of Brittney's bedroom. Brittney had moved to the couch, burying her head in soft pillows, fighting any signs of consciousness. But, from behind the closed door, Maggie's piercing screams would accost her. Without sleep, Brittney's mind was slowly degenerating; it was blanking out on her, unable to retrieve basic words, like *milk* or *rent*, or perform simple calculations without paper; her emotions were dulled and erratic; her muscles were heavy. And the worst part was Maggie roused her, but she didn't seem to need or even want her. Nothing Brittney did could stop her terrible screaming.

Eric, her old supervisor, had called about an opening on the night shift, and Trinity had agreed, reluctantly, to watch the children overnight. Brittney was looking forward to it. She needed time away from the relentless screeching, to think her own thoughts.

The first night at work, Brittney was tired—she had only slept two hours, from 8 p.m until 10 p.m—but the ten hours were so wonderfully quiet, and she knew the scripts by heart, and she didn't need to be fully awake to recite them.

In the morning, after talking to other adults all night, she felt more like a person, more like herself. She found Trinity curled up on the bed, facing the wall, as Maggie cried in her bassinet. She stared at the slender curve of her cousin's body, and she was overwhelmed with gratitude. *Thank you for helping me*, she thought.

Trinity rolled toward Brittney, her eyes wide and spastic over puffed skin, and she croaked, "I'm sorry, babe, I can't do this."

The air, abruptly, seemed stale and thick. Brittney's chest tightened, and her breath grew shallow.

"Are you sure?" she whispered, and her tone sounded pathetic.

"I'm really sorry," Trinity repeated. "But I have school and my job at the coffee shop. I can't be up all night. Maggie doesn't sleep."

Brittney collapsed on the bed. Trinity kissed her on the cheek and then padded into the bathroom to wash her face.

"Do you think somethin's wrong with her?" Trinity asked, her face wet, her hand on the doorframe. Trinity looked older than she had the night before. Maggie whimpered, a sign she was about to fall asleep.

"Yes," Brittney said, closing her eyes. "I do."

Trinity kissed Brittney on the cheek again.

Brittney nodded and squeezed Trinity's bicep, to tell her she understood. The gesture felt empty, though. Forced.

"I can still watch them in the evenings so you can do your errands."

"OK."

Trinity changed her clothes and grabbed her bag and left the apartment. She was late for class. Madison was talking in her crib, and Brittney knew she should change her diaper, and feed her breakfast, but she couldn't rouse herself from the bed.

It was Maggie's cries, an hour later, that forced her up.

She brought Maggie's bassinet in the kitchen, and began brewing a pot of coffee. The morning light streamed in from the window. She had started drinking coffee after the birth, the coffeemaker a gift from Trinity, and, at first, she had tossed it down quickly, swallowing it like a bitter drug. But she had grown to love the taste, and lingered over each cup, even if it made her fingers tremble and her mind buzz from scattered thought to scattered thought.

She could hear Madison and Ethan chatting in their room. "This is a circle, Madison, and this is a triangle," Ethan announced. Brittney smiled, grateful to her son. He had started taking care of Madison at Justice's apartment and he had never really stopped. He even changed her diapers, his little boy face intent and methodical. And he was trying to teach her to use the potty.

It was wrong to let him do so much, she knew, but she was too tired to stop him.

She poured a cup of coffee and sipped it at the kitchen table. Maggie was watching her from the bassinet, her eyes large and blinking. Brittney smiled, and, to her surprise, Maggie smiled back, a huge, toothless grin.

Brittney kept smiling, afraid any change would provoke more of Maggie's screams.

After a while, though, her face felt frozen, and she returned to her coffee, waving her fingers at Maggie. Maggie studied this with interest, and Brittney burst into a smile again, thinking, maybe, there would be an end to the constant crying.

Maybe things would be OK. Brittney fiddled with her cell phone, and dreaded calling the Center, telling them she wouldn't be able to take the night shift after all. Eric had pulled strings to get her the job back. But Trinity had quit and her mother had shaken her head when Brittney had asked her to watch the children, claiming she was "way too old for a baby cryin' at me

103

like that all night long."

She knew there were child care subsidies she could apply for, and she had gone into the office when she was pregnant and the agency had told her she would need to take Chris to court first. Even if she could locate Chris, find out where he was living, she wasn't really ready to take him to court, to use the law against him.

She couldn't afford to send Maggie to a real daycare, which she supposed was the only kind that would tolerate the colic. She took another sip of coffee and considered leaving the children by themselves. Ethan and Madison rarely woke up during the night, and the neighbors were accustomed to Maggie's cries. Several had complained. Brittney had laughed incredulously, telling them if they knew of a safe way to quiet the baby, she would gladly do it. Of course they had only stared at her, shifting their feet in annoyance as they repeated their request to keep the screeching down, as if it were as easy as turning down a TV.

Why did she need to be here at night, really? Sure, it was possible something terrible could happen while she was gone, a crazed intruder or a building fire, but that was unlikely. Should she give up on a good job, a job that would pay their rent and for food and diapers, for things that were so unlikely to happen?

But as she finished her third cup of coffee, her mood grew darker. The Call Center shift and the commute lasted over ten hours, and, the longer she was gone, the more she would worry. Besides, if she worked at night and watched the children during the day, when would she sleep? She had never thought that part through.

She moved Maggie to the living room, and let Ethan and Madison out of their room. Madison's diaper was droopy, but she was unbothered by it, toddling happily through the floor full of toys.

Ethan asked for the remote and she handed it to him, hugging her mug of coffee. She gave Ethan two breakfast bars from a box she kept underneath the coffee table. He diligently opened one and gave it to his sister before plopping down in front of the TV.

She called Eric in the afternoon, and he sounded disappointed, but he said he understood. When they hung up, she knew she would never see him or her job again. She was so sick of the apartment, with its pale yellow walls with chipping paint, and the clutter of toys and trash and plastic bags and cups and plates and discarded clothes and dirty diapers. Everything smelled musty, like it was dying or dead.

~*~

She ran her errands at night because it was easier to shop without Maggie screaming and squirming in her arms. Usually, Trinity came by to babysit, working on her latest dress designs at the kitchen table, the dirty dishes moved to the counter, the stack growing perilously tall. Before she left, Brittney would admire Trinity's sketches, the sleek lines and the feminine curves, briefly remembering a time when she had the energy to think that way—in shapes and bodies and fabrics.

Sometimes, Dave volunteered to babysit, and when he came, he sprawled out on the couch to watch TV, asking her when she was going to clean up this dump. She shrugged, irrationally angry, as if it was him, not Chris, that had deserted her.

She lingered at the Save-A-Lot, walking up and down the bright aisles, searching for sales. She was living off the envelopes, knowing she needed to apply for welfare, but putting it off. Welfare required streams of documentation and appointments where Maggie would scream as the agency worker frowned at her disapprovingly, thinking she was a bad mother.

Maybe the agency worker would even report her to DHS. There would be more appointments and more paperwork: applying for jobs and childcare and suing Chris for child support. She chucked cans of beans and collard greens and store brand cereals into her cart, trying to keep track of the running total, but having to start the calculation over each time she placed a new item in the cart.

The truth was the envelopes were adding up to as much as a welfare payment, without the hassle. But she wondered where Chris was getting so much cash. How could he be doing that legally? And she knew they might just stop one day.

In the drug aisle, she grabbed more aspirin for her headaches, and then she noticed a box of Aspirin PM. Smiling moons covered the front of the blue box. What if the pills caused a sleep so deep she wouldn't be woken by a baby's cries? Maybe she could sleep for a whole night. Maggie was five months. She was old enough to go seven hours without formula.

She tossed the Aspirin PM in her cart.

At the front of the store, she pushed her cart into an empty lane. The clerk was a young man, and he nodded at her as he rang up the items. She wanted to chat with him—she was starved for adult conversation—but he was handsome, and she couldn't think of anything to say. Words came to her but then disappeared into the warrens of her mind.

"Slow night?" finally popped into her head.

He glanced over, a subtle smile on his lips, and nodded. "People don't usually come in now."

"You like the quiet shifts?"

He shrugged. He was long and slender. "Gets boring, but better than the crazy busy ones where everyone's yellin' atcha."

"Yeah, I know whatcha mean. I used to work at the Call Center."

"Props. My brotha worked there. I heard some whack shit goes on."

Brittney laughed.

"It's eighty oh two."

She counted off five twenties and rooted around in her bag for change. She handed him the money.

"Seventeen cents?" he asked.

"Oops, sorry."

He handed her a twenty and a nickel and a dime back, winking at her, and she was flustered, annoyed with her mind for malfunctioning yet again. She couldn't keep anything straight. She collected three grocery bags in each hand, smiling at him awkwardly.

Outside, the air had a late fall chill to it, and she walked faster than she would have liked to stay warm. It was just as well, though, if she was gone too long, her brother would never offer to babysit again. That had happened with a couple of her friends. They had babysat once, but then, when she'd asked again, they had one excuse after another. So she had stopped asking, too proud for more rejection.

Her other brothers hadn't even volunteered. Mark was out dealing drugs in his ridiculous Escalade. The last time Brittney had seen him was when she was pregnant, at a cousin's birthday party. She had brought him a cold beer, thinking, at thirty-five, he was getting too old for gold chains. She asked him if he had heard anything about Chris. He had slowly shaken his head. Brittney sensed he was withholding some information, but she closed her eyes and changed the subject because she didn't have the energy to argue.

Her brother William was wild when he was younger, too, but after he was shot on the street, he cleaned himself up. He worked long hours advocating against street violence, and Brittney and Chris used to have dinner with him and his girlfriend and their two children. But now he was in a protracted custody battle with his girlfriend and he rarely found the time to see Brittney, let alone watch her children.

Benny was just Benny, off in his own world of talking voices and collecting soda cans and sleeping on street corners. They had all tried to help him, but he wasn't interested. He liked the voices in his head or maybe he just felt like he had to listen to their orders.

Her family felt tenuous and fractured. She envied the families she saw on TV: even when they bickered, they were still together. They were still *there*. Her mother and brothers said they loved her, but she was struggling, alone, under the weight of a colicky baby and two small children. It seemed like she could disappear, or be killed in her apartment, and they wouldn't notice for weeks. No one would but her children.

At least Dave helped her when he could. That was something. It was the same as when they were children. After a family meal, their mother would retire to the couch, her bottle in hand, and William, Mark, and Benny would scatter to their rooms or outside. Dave, if he wasn't busy with football, would stay behind and help Brittney clear the table and wash the dishes. Dave turned the dishes into a game: he would wash, and Brittney would dry, and they would race to the finish. By the end, they were laughing and whipping each other with towels.

When Brittney reached her apartment building, she took a last breath of fresh air, trying to strengthen herself before heading inside. The apartment had a rank smell; it was no longer possible to discern where, exactly, the smell was coming from. It needed to be cleaned with gallons of bleach.

Another envelope was tucked underneath the welcome mat, and she slipped it in her bag, wanting to save it for later, hoping there might, finally, be a message inside, an inquiry about Maggie, an apology. The sad thing was, even after all this time, she knew she would take him back in a second. She was too tired and lonely not to.

Dave was on the couch and he glanced over, his red baseball cap low on his head. He shut off the TV with the remote. Maggie was crying, screeching angrily, from the bedroom.

Dave took the bags from her. "Something's gotta be wrong with her, Brit."

"I know. But the doctor said there ain't nothin' I can do now. Just got to wait it out. Colic."

Dave shrugged and put the grocery bags on the kitchen table, on top of the dirty plates.

"You need to clean this place. You got mice and roaches."

Brittney rubbed her forehead. She was embarrassed by the mess, and frustrated with him for drawing attention to it again. But through her fatigue, these emotions were dull and she hunched her shoulders. "As soon as Maggie grows out of her thing, I will. I'm just so tired all the time."

Dave stared, concern on his brow. "Come on, let's do the dishes together. Like old times."

Brittney smiled, grateful for the sentiment, but the plates and glasses and bowls were stacked high, crusted over with food and mold. She didn't have the energy to stand, let alone dry dozens of dishes.

"Next time, OK? I gotta feed Maggie and take a nap."

She remembered the sleeping pills in her bag and wondered if, for once, sleep would be more than a nap.

Dave's phone beeped, and he pulled it out of his pocket and glanced at the screen. "Angel," he announced, opening the text and reading it quickly. He sighed and slipped the phone back in his pocket. He walked over to Brittney and kissed her on the cheek. The stray hairs around his mouth grizzled her skin, and his smell was ruddy and masculine.

"Things will turn around soon, OK? I'll call you later."

She nodded, watching him go, wondering why Angel got her brother, and she got nobody. What was so special about Angel? What was wrong with her?

When he closed the door, she searched in her bag until she found the white envelope. It smelled like cigarettes. Inside, the *Philly Weekly* page was torn at a diagonal, and she turned it over, searching for any scrawls. But there was nothing, just the newspaper typeface, square and neat.

She put the money in the tin and then rooted out her sleeping pills. She popped two in her mouth and retreated to the couch. She remembered, after she had sunk into the cushions, she still needed to feed Maggie. Maggie didn't particularly enjoy drinking her formula—usually she fussed over it, shaking her head and throwing out her back, taking an hour to drink a few ounces—but Maggie needed the calories. She was still too slight. She looked more like a miniature child than a fat baby.

Brittney sighed and heaved herself off the couch. Her eyes were at half-mast as she returned to the kitchen and rummaged around for a bottle. Her limbs were clumsy and she knocked a plate to the ground.

"This too shall pass," she whispered, "this too shall pass."

She had uttered this so much since Maggie had been born that the words didn't seem to have meaning anymore. They were just soothing sounds, an infant's lullaby.

She dumped the powdered formula in the bottle and then ran the water and gently shook the bottle. Brittney felt mummified from the sleeping pills, like she was wrapped in a heavy gauze, and as she fed Maggie, instead of the usual piercing anxiety, she felt like she was watching a baby cry on a small TV.

Somehow, Brittney managed to feed her the rest of the bottle and then retreat to the couch. Her mind immediately went dark.

She dreamt of clothes swirling out from her fingers—a chiffon wedding gown, fuchsia silk scarves, a turquoise skirt composed of triangular cuts of cotton. The materials were textured, and beautiful, and they were everywhere.

~*~

The sleeping pills gave Brittney something to look forward to—a whole night of sleep—and she held off as long as she could, marking the days on a school calendar Trinity had given her. She didn't want to become addicted, and the pills put her in such a deep sleep, she worried her children would need her and she would just keep sleeping.

One night, while she was under, a loud banging inserted itself in her dreams. It persisted until she reluctantly opened her eyes.

The dank ceiling of her apartment hung over her, and someone was pounding on her door. Maggie was crying.

In the hall, a woman was yelling, "Brittney! Brittney!"

Brittney groggily pulled herself off the couch, glancing down at her stained sweatshirt as she stumbled to the door, tripping on plastic toys.

She flung open the door, confused.

For a moment, the woman was pleasantly surprised, but then the anger returned like a dark shadow falling across her face.

"Your baby's been cryin' all night. Ain't nobody can sleep through the racket!"

Brittney couldn't remember the woman's name. She had lived in the building for less than a year and her apartment was adjacent to Brittney's. The walls were papery thin, and Brittney had heard the woman's TV late at night. Brittney had also heard the woman having sex with a man who came and went. The man was rough during sex, and sometimes he called the woman a whore and a slut.

"I'm sorry," Brittney said, rubbing her forehead. "She got colic. The doctor said there's nothin' to do."

"I got to work tomorrow. I'm sick of the fuckin' cryin'! All night, all day!"

The woman's eyes bugged out as she shouted, and spittle fell on her chin. Brittney had seen her smile, once, when she was leaving with the man, his arm around her shoulders. She looked luminous. But with her features scrunched, she seemed ugly.

"What do you want me to do?" she asked.

"I don't fuckin' know! You're the mother. Figure somethin' or I am going to call the cops!"

Brittney laughed. The cops had better things to do than investigate a crying baby.

"You think it's fuckin' funny? See how funny it is when they takin' your kids away," she said, crossing her arms over her chest.

"I really have tried everything."

The woman's anger morphed into frustration and she closed her eyes and sighed. "Whatever," she screeched, "You gotta fix it! I need sleep."

Brittney nodded blankly, not because she could stop the crying, but because she wanted to go back to sleep, and there was nothing to say to this woman. She wasn't the only neighbor who had complained, but she was the pushiest.

The woman closed her eyes again and then turned on her heels and stomped back into her apartment, slamming her door.

Brittney looked down at the welcome mat, checking to see if there was a new envelope. The floor was scuffed and scattered with dried brown leaves. Maybe she should leave him a message, she thought, in an envelope of her own. She went back inside, and found the last envelope he'd left. She didn't have any paper so she ripped a piece off an empty cereal box. Carefully, she wrote:

Thank you for the money. Maggie got colic. She crying all the time. I can't take it. Can you gimme a break?

She debated whether to sign it "love." She didn't think she loved him anymore. Or, if she did, the feeling was so darkened by disappointment, it was no longer recognizable. She signed her name in cursive and then tucked the envelope under the mat, so only an inch was visible.

Back on the couch, she fantasized about Chris taking Maggie for a while. It would be so quiet. She could hear herself think.

A few days later, the envelope was gone. But it wasn't replaced by another. She wondered, anxiously, if Chris was judging her, thinking she was a failure as a mother. Which, she was. She didn't know how to be a good mother to Maggie.

She was annoyed, though, and mad at herself for sending him a message. For a long time, she had suppressed her anger; she had deluded herself into thinking that, by sending money, he was not a bad father.

She checked the welcome mat three times a day, waiting for another envelope, her anger at Chris growing, like the black mold in the tub.

Finally, the envelope lay there one evening, its edge scuffed with a footprint. She ripped it open in the doorway.

There was no message. The stack was thicker than normal, adding up to eight hundred dollars. Maybe giving her more money was all he was willing to do.

She returned inside, her blood pressure high, her fingers trembling.

Madison was squatting in the kitchen, smearing the green kitchen soap over a plastic train set. Brittney sighed, retreating to the couch. Ethan was watching a courtroom drama on TV as he drew skyscrapers on the back of a paper bag.

"Those are nice buildings," she said. He was talented.

"Thanks. It's New York. That's where *Law 57* is," he said, gesturing to the TV.

Brittney nodded, and then closed her eyes. Trinity was coming at eight, and she couldn't wait to get out. How could Chris not even acknowledge her request? She decided, before she went to the Save-A-Lot, she would stop at The Lounge and get a beer.

"Mama," Madison called, her hand on Brittney's knee.

Brittney looked down. Madison's pajamas were covered with green slime, and so was Madison's puckered mouth. Brittney laughed and leaned down and scooped her up.

"We're gonna clean this off."

They walked through the bedroom, where Maggie was tossing in her sleep. The bathroom was cluttered with children's toys and empty boxes of tampons and toothpaste and toilet paper rolls and shredded toilet paper.

Brittney leaned Madison over the sink, and washed her mouth out with water. Madison smiled at herself in the mirror, and Brittney smiled, too, thinking, even with her wild, untended hair and dirty face, her daughter was beautiful. She had high cheekbones, a small chin and full lips and large soulful eyes. There was something reassuring about this, that her beauty had not been marred.

"Mama, bath?"

Brittney nodded, and closed the drain and turned on the tub water. The black scum was multiplying, crawling up the sides of the tub, and Brittney was careful not to touch it. Madison picked up a ball and tossed it to Brittney.

Brittney caught it, and was suddenly overcome with affection and she sat down on the floor and held out her arms.

"Gimme a hug."

Madison obediently climbed in Brittney's lap, and put her small arms around Brittney's neck. She smelled like urine and dish soap.

Madison giggled and leapt off her mother, turning to the tub and running her hand through the water. Brittney helped her take off her pajamas—she had worn them all day, maybe she had worn them for days, Brittney wasn't sure—and then plopped her in the tub.

Brittney noticed brown spots of grime behind Madison's ears and around her knees and ankles, and she scrubbed Madison's legs with a washcloth. Madison fidgeted. "Don't like that," she pouted, and her lower lip trembled, threatening to cry.

Brittney lifted the washcloth off Madison. She couldn't stand any more crying. Instead, she lathered soap onto the washcloth and scrubbed at the black mold on the side of the tub. She pressed as hard as she could, rubbing fervently, her muscles aching. It wasn't coming off.

"Damnit," she cursed, scrubbing harder, pushing against the porcelain, trying to scrape it with her fingernails. "Come on!"

"Mama?" Madison said tentatively. "You mad?"

Brittney closed her eyes, and pulled her hand away. What was the point?

"No, baby," she said, kissing her on the forehead. "Not mad. I'm going to get your brother, OK?"

Madison nodded, her face serious, and then she turned away, splashing the water coming from the faucet.

She left Madison in the tub, and walked into the living room, telling Ethan he needed to take a bath. He refused, entranced by a detective grilling a suspect on the TV. Maggie was crying now, her screeches in full bloom, and Brittney's head throbbed in response.

"Oh, fine, be dirty," she snapped at Ethan. She returned to the bedroom, offering Maggie her pacifier. Maggie took it and then threw it across the floor.

Brittney went in the bathroom and closed the door. Madison looked scared.

"Why she cry?"

"She unhappy."

"You make it better?"

"I don't know how. I wish I did."

"Oh.

"Mama, I love you."

"I love you, too, pumpkin." Brittney petted her daughter's head. Her hair needed to be brushed. It was long, down to her waist. It was knotted and matted in places. Brittney had tried to brush it at the kitchen table, like her grandmother had done for her, but Madison had grown antsy and whiny, and Brittney had given up. It somehow looked worse than before, with a few sections straight and the rest a knotted tangle.

After the water turned cold, Brittney dried Madison with a towel, ignoring the musty smell in its fibers. She couldn't remember the last time she had washed the towels. Going to the Laundromat, with Maggie screaming on her chest and Madison in the stroller and Ethan running off, seemed impossible.

Back in the living room, Brittney shifted Madison on her hip. "Time for bed," she told Ethan.

"That's not fair! My show's almost over."

"Off, Ethan."

The bedtime was one thing she would not compromise on. She needed time to rest, alone, without the children squealing and throwing things around the apartment.

Brittney turned off the TV and retreated to the children's bedroom, with Madison on her hip. She read Madison a story in the chair, and then lifted her into the crib.

"Night, baby."

"Night, Mama," she said, rolling over on her stomach, clutching her teddy bear.

115

Ethan had turned the TV back on, and it was playing a commercial. A family was standing in front of a house with a large lawn, announcing how much they loved their blue SUV. Brittney wondered, for a moment, what it would be like to be that mother, to live in that house, to have a loving husband who could afford to buy her an SUV. It seemed strange that some people lived like that, that they had lives that easy.

"Come on, Ethan," she said softly, "time for bed."

"I wanna watch the end of my show!" he cried.

Brittney nodded. "It's too late. Watch more tomorrow."

"It ain't on tomorrow!"

Brittney picked up the remote and clicked it off. "It's bedtime."

Ethan closed his eyes and groaned. "I'm sick of this place! Why don't we go out anymore?"

"Once Maggie's better, we're gonna."

"All she does is cry. I want her to go away from here and dad to come back."

Brittney crouched in front of him, and hugged him. He resisted at first but then succumbed, his face pressed against her breasts. She stroked his back.

"I know, baby. I know. But it's not her fault," she whispered. "She's sick. This will pass." Her voice rose in uncertainty. It seemed impossible that the crying would ever end.

He nodded against her. "OK."

She led him to his bed, and piled the blankets over his chest. She was about to leave when he grabbed her hand. His was warm and sticky. Pieces of food cleaved between his fingers and on his palm. Her once tidy boy no longer cared about those things.

He closed his eyes, and she sang to him, softly, about angels.

When his chest moved up and down in a steady rhythm, she took her hand back and crept out of the bedroom. Normally, she would have crashed on the couch, the long day behind her, the long night ahead, but Trinity was coming—she could finally leave the apartment—and she hurried to prepare Maggie's bottle.

As she fed Maggie, one hand cupping her bony ribs, she thought of Chris and the anger blossomed in her chest. Refusing to speak with her was childish. He left her money, but couldn't be bothered to ask about Maggie, his child he had never even met.

She needed help. Maggie was like a parasite, only demanding and taking, giving nothing back in return. Brittney was being smothered. She could barely remember what it was like to laugh with her girlfriends, and feel satisfaction at teaching Ethan and Madison about the world, and fantasize about different clothing designs, the shapes and colors forming in her mind.

Maggie gurgled and spit up her formula, the white cottage cheese spraying across them both. Brittney whispered, "It's OK, it's OK," even though she knew this was a lie. Maggie had never been OK. She removed Maggie's clothes, her ears burning. She piled new blankets in the bassinet.

She checked her watch. Trinity would be here any minute. Brittney offered the pacifier to Maggie, but Maggie ignored this, her eyes scrunched up as she cried. Brittney kissed her on the forehead, not because she felt love, but because she *wanted* to feel love. She *wanted* to do what was right. Maggie's forehead was dry and scaly.

Brittney stood up. She took off her own sweatshirt, throwing it in a pile of dirty clothes on the floor. She found a nice blue blouse in the back of her closet and pulled it on. She slid on her brown leather boots and closed the bedroom door.

In the kitchen, she applied her deodorant heavily, trying to mask the smell of not having taken a shower in days. She tied a turquoise scarf around her head. In her handheld mirror, she looked tired: bags drooped under her eyes, and her skin was flaky and wan. She considered venturing back in the bathroom to put on makeup, but decided it wasn't worth it. What did it matter what she looked like?

There was a loud knock, and she rushed to open it, relieved to get out of the apartment.

But it wasn't Trinity. It was the woman next door, her lips pursed. She was wearing tight black pants and a low-cut blouse. Her face was beautifully made up, and Brittney envied her this.

"Look," she said, "You gotta keep it down tonight."

Brittney was annoyed at this woman's persistence. "Do you want to see her? Do you want to see everything I have done?"

"Oh my god! Just stop it! I am so sick of this cryin'!" Her whiny voice was screechy and Brittney realized she was probably in her early twenties, maybe even a teenager.

"I've done everything I can," Brittney repeated.

The woman groaned and stomped off, slamming her door again. Brittney closed her own door softly and went inside. She rummaged around in the kitchen and found a bag of chips, which she took to the couch. She heard a man striding down the hall, his footsteps heavy. For a second, her heart fluttered, thinking it might be Chris. That he had decided to speak with her after all. But then the man knocked on the neighbor's door and the woman opened it right away. She laughed at something the man said. Brittney could hear them talking from inside her apartment—the deep tenor of his voice, and the light chipper of hers—but the words were garbled. She could have moved near the shared wall and listened to their conversation, but she didn't want to know. She didn't want to hear about their hatred of her and her baby. Nor did she want to hear them having sex. It had been so long since she had been touched in that way.

Her phone beeped, and she glanced down at it. Trinity had sent her a text.

So sorry, babe, can't get away – crazy project in the works. How bout next week? Love T

Brittney closed her eyes, willing herself not to cry. She had been looking forward to this for two weeks. It was her only time out of the apartment, away from the children. She rubbed her temples and then messaged her cousin back, assuring her it was OK. There was nothing else to say.

She heard moaning from next door, and grunting, and the man's voice *oh yeah you like this bitch dontcha.*

Brittney grabbed her coat and purse and stepped into the hallway. The noises were dulled, but she could still hear the man goading the woman, telling her she was a slut, and Maggie's cries, and so she walked to the edge of the concrete stairs.

One of the stairwell lights was out and the other was blinking noisily. Brittney walked down the stairs, clutching her purse, appreciating the descent into silence. She would walk around the block, get some fresh air, and come right back.

The November air was cold and crisp and she inhaled it into her lungs. She shoved her hands in her pockets. The trees were naked, their branches thin and spindly. It woke her up to be outside. She felt more like herself. She needed to come up with a plan. Maggie was six months old and her colic had not abated. There had to be something else wrong with her. She had to take her to a different doctor.

The red door to The Lounge was lit up with Christmas lights, and she considered going in. She desperately wanted adult company, someone who could talk to her like she was a person with her own opinions and feelings. For weeks, the only adult she had talked to was her complaining neighbor. She opened the red door halfway, peering inside.

She took an empty stool at the bar. A small paper turkey hung above the cash register, and Brittney laughed to herself. Thanksgiving hadn't even occurred to her. Usually, they had it at Chris's mother's house.

The bartender asked her if she wanted anything, and she blinked. "Sure. Budweiser."

Because of her mother, Brittney had never been much of a drinker, but abruptly she had a sharp longing to get drunk, to lose herself in alcohol.

A young man plopped on the stool next to her, smiling. He was comely in a nerdy way—his frame slender, his eyes shining

119

behind clear glasses.

"Hey. I'm Anton."

"Hey. I'm Bri—Trinity."

She knew it was silly to lie, but she wanted to forget who she was for just a few minutes. She took a long sip of her beer, and Anton laughed.

"Don't get ahead of me, now."

He flagged down the bartender, and ordered a whisky straight. Then he looked at Brittney, his glasses on the tip of his nose.

"So who is Trinity?" he inquired.

She laughed, and said, "I'm in school for fashion design. Sling coffee for a living."

"Interesting. You design clothes?"

"Yep, women's clothes."

"Very cool. I'm studying engineering. I deliver mail to pay the bills."

"Like a mailman?"

"Yep, Mailman Anton, that's me."

She finished her beer. "Dog ever bite you?"

"Not yet, but there's some gnarly pit bulls around here, let me tell you."

Anton ordered her another beer, and she eagerly took it. The beer gave her a burst of energy, and she gestured to the back of the bar.

"Want to get a booth?"

Anton grinned and picked up his whiskey, leading the way to the last booth. It was dark. They sat on the same side, and she could feel the warmth of his arm and leg pressed against hers. They both sipped their drinks, listening to the music.

"Ya know, the best thing about being a mailman is you invisible to everyone else. You wouldn't believe the shit I've heard. People yelling at one another about stupid shit. People having sex in their front room. It's made me realize people are just crazy."

She laughed, and after she finished her beer, he leaned

over and kissed her. His lips were soft and gentle, and his fingers were on her waist, and then her breasts. She could hear people talking and laughing and the music but it was faded, distant. It felt so good to be touched again, to have hands on her body, to have a mouth on her mouth. She wanted him on top of her, to feel her whole body weighed down by another body.

He pulled her out of the booth, and she let him drag her to the single person bathroom. Her mind was hazy with fatigue and alcohol. He looked at her with hunger, and she leaned up against the wall, and he grinded against her, his hands roving from her breasts to her crotch, where he clutched clumsily. She could feel the warmth of his penis pressed against her pants, and she sighed, tilting back her head. In her mind, she fell back on a feathery bed and spread her legs, letting him enter her. But the smell of feces and stale urine drifted to her nose. She squeezed her eyes closed, trying to block out the water stained ceiling and the fluorescent lights and the stink of the bathroom.

"What's wrong?" he breathed on her neck. "You want to go to my place, Trinity?"

She took a deep breath, catching herself, remembering she wasn't Trinity. The bathroom mirror was smeared with brown smudges, and her skin looked patchy, and Anton seemed small, his body barely the size of hers. Her urge to have sex fled as quickly as it had come.

"I'm sorry, I gotta go."

He looked disappointed. "Really?"

"Sorry," she repeated, fumbling with the door handle.

"Do you want to meet up later?"

"Sorry," she said once more, hurrying out of the bathroom. She was still hazy from the beer and she couldn't tell how much time had passed, but she knew she should get home. She wasn't Trinity, free to come and go as she pleased; she was Brittney, bound to her apartment.

The door clattered shut behind her, and she walked toward her apartment. She meant to go quickly, but once she was outside, in the quiet, she slowed down. It was a beautiful, clear night. A web of bright stars dotted the sky. She pulled her cell phone out of her pocket, and tried Chris's number. To tell him she didn't want him anymore. She just wanted him to help with the kids.

No one picked up. She shoved the phone back in her pocket, and, then, thought of Anton. It had been ridiculous, but fun. It made her realize, maybe, there would be a life for her after Chris. That he wasn't the only one she could be with.

The building was quiet, and as she went up the stairs, she braced herself for the sound of Maggie screeching. But it was worse than that: Madison was crying and Ethan was shouting. She ran up the last few stairs, and saw her door was open a few inches, and her heart clenched. An intruder? Chris?

There were two police officers and an older woman in a suit standing in the living room. The woman was rocking Maggie in her arms. They all turned to her, and a loathing crossed their faces.

She felt an incredible tightness in her chest, as if something unidentifiable and horrible was sucking all the oxygen out of the room.

Ethan and Madison ran to Brittney, each clinging to her leg, and she crouched down, and hugged them.

"Ma'am," one of the officers said, "these children are too young to be left alone."

Brittney nodded. "I just stepped outside for a moment. To get some air."

The officers looked at each other skeptically, and the older woman stepped forward, Maggie whining in her arms. She had a wide face, and her skin was pink and smooth underneath her sparse brown hair.

"We've been here for an hour, ma'am. We were just about to leave." Brittney noticed Madison and Ethan were wearing jeans and jackets, and Ethan had his little blue backpack on.

"I'm here," Brittney said, her voice shaky, "You can go."

The woman glanced at one of the officers, the taller, younger one. "Actually," she said, "we don't think this is a safe environment for the children. We'll need to take them for now, and, then, once we verify this is a safe environment, they can be returned to you."

"What do you mean take 'em? Take 'em where?"

"To a safe place where they will be well cared for."

"How can you do that? They are my kids! There ain't nothin' wrong with 'em."

Ethan started sobbing, clinging to Brittney.

"You can't take me! You can't take me!" he shouted.

Brittney's fingers trembled as she held her son. Madison's large eyes blinked nervously and she ducked her head underneath Brittney's arm.

"Ma'am," the woman said, firmly, "it will be easier for your children if you explain what's going to happen."

The officers looked uncomfortable but the older one nodded in agreement. Brittney felt like someone stabbed her in the chest. How long had she been gone? An hour? How could they take her children for that? They'd been sleeping in a locked apartment. What could have happened?

She looked down at Ethan, his round, somber face, and held his cheeks in her hands.

She whispered in his ear, "Baby, I'm sorry. They are gonna take you right now but I will come get you soon. I need you to look out for Madison and Maggie, OK?"

"I don't wanna go with 'em," he blubbered.

The woman interrupted, throwing her thin pleather bag over her shoulder. "We have to go now, ma'am."

The younger police officer picked Madison up, and Madison started crying, silently.

"How do I get 'em back?" Brittney demanded.

The woman rocked a screeching Maggie in her arms, and told her she could tell the judge her side of the case tomorrow.

"I'm not leaving!" Ethan shouted. "You can't take me!"

Brittney hunched down and pulled his slender body to her own. He clutched her back, and she tried to remember the way he smelled, the way his ribs felt under her fingers, the way his hair tickled her cheek.

"You got to go, baby," she whispered. "I need you to look out for your sisters."

"Ma'm, please," a woman's voice called.

Ethan wiped his nose on her neck and then he disentangled himself from her body. He followed the rest of them out of the apartment, glancing back, anger in his eyes.

The woman stared at Brittney and then pulled the door shut. The wood was splintered where they had broken the lock. Brittney stayed on her knees. She could hear them walking down the stairs. Maggie and Madison were crying. The police officers were talking to one another, their voices low and mumbling.

And then it was quiet. Except it was a terrible quiet, and Brittney sobbed loudly to fill the emptiness. It suddenly occurred to her why her children had been stolen and she ran out of her apartment and knocked on her neighbor's door. She pounded and pounded until her knuckles ached.

"How could you do this," she sobbed, and fell against the door. "How could you do this."

"My children are everything," she whispered.

She pulled the scarf out of her hair, and told herself it was all a misunderstanding. She would go to court tomorrow and the judge would see how ludicrous this was, and he would return her children, and she would never ever leave them alone again.

Chapter Seven

Rebecca

In November, Rebecca was in the yard, raking leaves. Her home study had been approved, and she was waiting for the agency to call her with a match. Her cell phone was heavy in her pocket. Every morning, she woke up with anticipation, a sense that today could be the day—her child could be coming home!

As the days had morphed into weeks and the weeks had morphed into months, her anticipation had become doubtful and then desperate. She had trouble falling asleep at night. She tried to remind herself of all the difficulties, of the lack of free time, the dirty diapers and the runny noses and the temper tantrums. But this didn't really work. She was ready for those things.

Weeks ago, she had bumped into Will in New York, on the street, his arm around a beautiful woman. Gray hairs seemed to have proliferated on his head. He had smiled at her, winking. He seemed genuinely happy.

This, surprisingly, had depressed her, left her feeling like she was the only person left behind at a busy station, watching as full trains pulled out on their tracks. He had invited her to come to dinner with them, and seemed disappointed when she had declined. "Call me," he mouthed as he walked away.

His laughter had echoed on the street, and the tiny, irrational part of her that still wanted him to realize she was more important than being childless, to realize he had made a mistake, was crushed.

Her phone vibrated in her pocket, rocking against her hip. It would likely be her sister or her mother or one of her colleagues, but still there was a little flip in her chest that said *maybe this is it, maybe this is the call about your child.*

The number was local, and her heart raced a little more, in anticipation.

"It's me, Molly. Look, this might be too much, but I need someone to take these kids today. It's a sibling set, a five-year-old boy, a two-year-old girl, and a six-month-old girl. What do you think? Are you interested?"

Rebecca's arms were light and airy, and her fingers were prickly. She couldn't believe her child—no, children—were finally here. Then she thought, no, three children were too much, how could she possibly handle that many children at once? It would be chaos.

But a baby, a six-month-old baby. This might be her only chance for a baby, to raise a child from infancy to adulthood.

"Do they have any special needs?"

"I don't know. They seem pretty normal except for the usual separation issues."

"I see."

She knew it was risky to take this many children, but she was sick of waiting and waiting and waiting, the phone a dead weight in her pocket. And she had often seen one Nobuso woman watch over a dozen children, her face patient and alert as she prodded and assured the herd of children, directing them to where they needed to go. Three would be easy, in comparison.

"OK. Yes."

"Do you have everything ready?"

"I can have it ready by tonight."

"OK, great. I'll give you a call on my way over."

Rebecca stared at her phone, dumbstruck. Three children were coming to her house. Three. All this time, she had been thinking of one child, but she should have known she would not be chosen for a single baby. She would only be called for the harder case, the one the coupled parents or single black women

126

turned down.

She laughed at the idea of herself with three children, and stood up. It felt good to have a purpose, to be put into action. She emailed her evening seminar, canceling it without explanation. It was a privilege of tenure, that no one would question her, at least not in a way that mattered. She had to buy a twin bed and some boy's clothes and toys.

It seemed weird to call her childless friends or her friends from the university. They might go but think it was a tedious interruption to their research. Martha and Natalie, she realized, would drop everything and happily assemble children's furniture.

She called them both, and they agreed to meet her at IKEA. Rebecca's fingers trembled as she drove on the highway. She didn't even mind all the traffic.

She waited near the entrance of IKEA, scanning the parking lot for their station wagon. She was full of energy, eager to buy the right things. She wanted the children to feel loved.

The silver station wagon pulled into the lot, and Rebecca inched forward. Martha got out of the driver's seat and then reached into the backseat. Natalie waited, her hands resting on her purse. Martha lifted Dyod, a nine-month-old boy, into her arms. He was black, and his soft, spongy hair lay against Martha's lavender coat as they walked toward Rebecca.

It looked strange, this large black baby curled up against the white Barbie. Rebecca felt a flash of guilt for thinking this, even though she wasn't even sure what she was supposed to think. Was she not supposed to notice their racial differences, or notice them, but think nothing of a white parent and a black child? She had read her colleague Samuel Davidson's articles on the "travesty" of middle class whites adopting poor black children, and she couldn't help but think of the articles when she saw Martha's pale white hand with its elegant gold watch gently petting the baby's Afro.

Molly hadn't informed her of the race of the children coming to her house. *My children* slipped into her thoughts, as she felt they were already hers, that they would never leave. But she pushed this terminology away, reminding herself they might only be with her for a few months, that she might have to give them back.

Martha kissed her on the cheek, and Rebecca congratulated her on the baby. Martha beamed, gushing that Dyod was "perfect." His mother was addicted to crack, she explained, her voice lowered and her eyebrows raised, as if the mother had made a kind of dinner party faux pas. Rebecca nodded, studying the boy's sleeping face for any sign of abnormality, and not finding any. He had long lashes and a wide nose and skin the color of milky tea.

Martha and Natalie were more than a decade younger than Rebecca, but they knew about babies and boys from friends at their church and they led her through the aisles of IKEA and then the Toys "R" Us, helping her fill her cart with sheets and jackets and car seats and pacifiers.

The total was fifteen hundred dollars. Crumpling the long receipts into her purse, Rebecca was heartened, as if the children would, somehow, feel more loved by the sheer volume of stuff.

They loaded everything into the two cars, and then drove back to her house. The whole time, Rebecca was jittery, careful to look in her rearview mirror when she changed lanes, afraid, in her excitement, she would sideswipe another car.

As they assembled the beds, Dyod played in the bouncer, his pudgy hands hitting the orange duck and three brown monkeys. When they were finally done—the Thomas the Tank Engine sheets and comforter on the mattress, the pillows cased and fluffed on the twin bed—they stretched out in exhaustion.

Rebecca brought up glasses of sparkling water and a box of ginger cookies. Smiling at how the room, with its trains and racecars, seemed appropriately boyish, she suddenly envied Martha and Natalie's knowledge of children, gleaned from their church community. In her circle, women were too overworked to build a community around mothering. Her own sister had three children, but wouldn't be able to advise Rebecca on eating issues or potty training or discipline. The nanny had taken care of all those things.

"Are you nervous?" Natalie asked.

"Yes," Rebecca responded immediately, and then laughed. "But mostly I'm excited."

"Maybe we should foster a sibling set. I always thought I'd just have one baby."

"You should wait until it feels right."

Natalie nodded, concern on her practical brows. She stroked Dyod's hair. "You'll be a good mom," she said softly.

"Thank you."

Martha stood up, pulling her cashmere coat on, a smile on her face. "We should get back. Ready, Nat?"

Dyod cried when Martha picked him up, and she shushed him, reminding him there were plenty of toys at home. He hugged her, his little arms squeezing her neck, and Rebecca smiled. Soon she would have her own baby.

Rebecca watched them walk down the pathway. She wished, for a moment, they could stay and help the children settle in. She pictured three children wailing in her living room, their eyes scrunched and their faces splotchy, as she stood by helplessly, not knowing what to do.

She sat on the couch and called her sister. She left a message to the effect that three children were coming. Yes, three, she laughed.

She picked up a pillow and hugged it to her chest. It occurred to her she had no idea what five-year-old boys were like. How much did they know at that age? What did they think about?

The doorbell rang, and she jumped, dropping the pillow.

She flipped on the lights as she walked to the front door. She felt like she might be meeting her children, the people she would love above all else, and the gravity of this made her slightly dizzy.

She swung open the door.

Molly stood on the steps, her black coat dotted with

crumbs and white threads. A chubby toddler was on her hip, facing the street. Her hair was a tangled bird's nest of curls and dreads and knots, springing in Molly's face.

A boy was standing a few feet behind, on the pathway. He had a blue backpack on his slender shoulders, and his hair, too, was long and unruly, as if it had never been combed.

They were real children. Here.

Molly called to the boy. "Come on in, Ethan."

Ethan turned away, facing the street. He was slender, his limbs long and elegant. The skin on his arms and legs was tan and ruddy with dirt.

Molly sighed and put the two-year-old girl down. The girl ran down the path and stood near her brother, tugging on his tan shorts. The boy picked her up in his skinny arms. For a moment, they were still, watching the cars passing by. Then he shifted toward the house.

"Where's my mom?" he asked Molly, accusingly.

"Mama?" the two-year-old said, her face lighting up as she looked in their direction.

Rebecca glimpsed the girl's face, and she was taken aback. Under the coiled springs of hair, she was a beautiful child. She had large brown eyes hooded by thick lashes, and her mouth was full.

Molly held out her hand. "Come here, Madison."

Madison smiled, and it was a lovely smile, broad and full of straight teeth. But she stayed in her brother's arms.

Another woman was walking up the path, a yowling baby in her arms.

Rebecca took a deep breath.

"I'm Katie," the woman called. Her blonde hair was in a messy bun on top of her head.

Rebecca nodded, but she wasn't paying attention to the woman. She was eying the tiny baby, small as a bag of flour.

Katie put her hand on Ethan's back and urged him forward. "Time to go inside."

Ethan set Madison down, and grabbed her hand. "Stay

near me, Madison," he warned. He trudged slowly toward the house, his eyes lowered.

Rebecca moved back, letting everybody in. Katie offered her the baby.

"This is Maggie."

Maggie was shrieking, her mouth open and wet. She was angular, her chin and cheekbones jutting. Rebecca took her, gently, and huddled her against her chest. Maggie's right arm flailed in discontent, and Rebecca held out her pinky. Maggie's tiny fingers latched onto it.

Rebecca rocked on her heels, thinking, it's okay, baby, my poor screaming baby. She kissed her on the forehead, and her skin was smooth and warm.

Katie and Molly were talking, and then Katie left, waving goodbye as she drifted out the door.

Molly looked around. "Where are Ethan and Madison?" she asked.

Rebecca realized they had gone from the room. She walked down the hall.

"Ethan? Madison?"

They were in the study, sitting in Will's leather chair.

"This house is big," Ethan said, stroking his sister's hair.

"It is. I'm Rebecca."

"Where is my mom at?" he asked, his voice breaking. Tears suddenly ran down his cheeks, and he wiped them away furiously, glaring.

"I don't know," she whispered, putting her hand on his shoulder. "I'm sorry."

He leapt out of the chair. "WE WANT OUR MOM! LEAVE US ALONE!"

Maggie shrieked, and Rebecca backed up, startled. She didn't know what to do. Molly pulled her out of the room.

"He's having adjustment issues. Just give him some space. I'll get Madison."

"OK."

Molly cajoled Madison down from the chair, and returned,

holding her hand.

"Than mad," Madison said, pointing, her mouth in a wary frown that seemed oddly adult.

"It's OK," Rebecca assured. "He ... will calm down," she said, even though she wasn't sure this was true.

Inside the study, Ethan was tossing books on the floor, the hardbacks hitting the wood with a clunk. Molly shook her head and checked her watch. Rebecca wondered if the boy would be more than she could handle. In preparation, she had read dozens of books on early childhood development, but in the face of an actual, angry child, all the advice she could recall, about patience and reward charts and gentle pats, seemed impractical.

Madison's large eyes were wet pools and she held out her hand. Rebecca squeezed it gently, juggling Maggie carefully on her right side. Maggie seemed so delicate, like a doll made of glass, or a baby bird.

Molly gave her some papers to sign, and promised to look after Ethan while Rebecca put the other two to bed.

Rebecca nodded gratefully, signing the papers with a scrawl, not bothering to read them. She kept Maggie nestled in the crook of her arm.

She held Madison's hand as they walked up the stairs, slowly making their way to the third floor. Ethan's angry shouts dimmed and quieted as she closed the nursery door.

She put Maggie in the crib and, on her back, the baby's screams became even louder. Rebecca tried to swallow her panic, her fear that this was too much, that she had made a terrible mistake. Maybe she wouldn't be a good mother after all.

"Just a minute, baby girl," she said anxiously, helping Madison into the rocking chair. She handed her a talking teddy bear.

Rebecca scooped Maggie back up, and put her on the changing table. She pulled off Maggie's full-length onesie. It was ratty and stained.

As Rebecca changed her diaper, Maggie continued to screech, loud and piercing. *What am I doing wrong?* Rebecca thought, trying to hurry.

Dirt was embedded in Maggie's neck and the creases of her bony elbows and the soles of her feet. Rebecca used baby wipe after baby wipe to rub her clean. Tomorrow, she would give them all baths, and she imagined the water turning murky and brown. If only, by some miracle, she could also wash away all the bad things they had endured.

She went to the closet and rummaged through the clothes, keeping her eye on Maggie. Maggie fidgeted uncomfortably, her lips opening and closing in a wave, like she was trying to escape her own skin.

The clothes labeled six months seemed too large so she pulled out white and blue striped pajamas from the three month pile. She managed to fit Maggie's arms and legs in the holes, and zip her up. Her hair was short, barely past her ears, and tangled in dozens of knots.

Propped up on the changing table, Maggie finally stopped whimpering, and she smiled as she reached for Rebecca's cheek. And then, just like that, everything felt different: Rebecca smiled so deeply she could feel it bursting from her fingers. The pads of Maggie's tiny fingers were soft. Rebecca put the pacifier near her mouth and she latched onto it voraciously.

"That's better, then," she said, softly, placing her in the crib, reclined against a soft teddy bear. Her eyes blinked rapidly.

"Hi, sweet girl," Rebecca murmured to Madison, who was waiting against the wall, her hands clasped together. Rebecca lifted her onto the changing table, giving her a pacifier. Madison chewed on the pacifier nervously. Her body stiffened as Rebecca took off her stained t-shirt and shorts and worn shoes. Like her sister, dirt was crusted in the creases of her skin. Rebecca gently wiped her down, humming as she did, trying to suppress her anger. There were faded bruises on Madison's forehead and shoulder and thighs. A dimpled red rash covered her bottom.

Rebecca cleaned the rash, gently, and applied the diaper ointment, feeling rage at whoever had done this to her, whoever who had let her get so bruised and dirty.

Rebecca searched in the closet, and found a beautiful wool pajama suit, all white, and helped Madison into it.

When she turned around, she saw Maggie had fallen asleep in her crib, curled up on her side. Maggie wasn't a particularly good looking baby—her mouth was thin and wide and tilted down at the ends, folds crumpled underneath her eyes —but Rebecca longed to sit near her crib in a chair and watch her sleep.

"Let's go to your room," Rebecca whispered to Madison, taking her small, clammy hand in her own. She flicked off the nursery light and led Madison down the hall.

Madison looked around her room with wide eyes. There was a small dresser, a small table and a toddler bed. There was a stuffed tiger and bear and a set of children's books. Everything smelled new. Rebecca flipped on the nightlight and put Madison in the bed.

"Would you like a story?" she asked.

"Where's my crib?"

"Oh. Do you think you could sleep in this bed?"

"I dunno. Where Than?"

"He's downstairs. He'll be going to bed soon."

"Where Than's bed?"

"It will be on the floor right below. If you need anything, just call out, OK? I'll hear you."

Madison pulled the tiger closer to her body. Rebecca read her a story. Madison was still awake when she finished, and Rebecca patted her on the head and wished her sweet dreams.

"Swee dreams?" Madison repeated, her voice tentative.

Rebecca walked down the stairs, closing the baby gate, feeling a surge of confidence. Molly was standing at the door of the study. She seemed frazzled, her frizzy hair more sprawled than usual, her splotchy skin flushed. Books were strewn everywhere.

"I need to go," she said, tapping her Timex watch. "Will you be OK here?"

Rebecca nodded.

"We'll be in touch. There might be a family member we can move the kids to."

Rebecca nodded again, part of her refusing to entertain the possibility.

Molly pulled her hair in a ponytail. "Either way, we need to keep the three of them together."

"Of course."

Ethan was sitting on the floor in the study, pulling out pages from a book, one after another. Rebecca recognized the magenta cover, embossed with gold stick figures dancing in a circle, their hands connected. She laughed. *The Lost Women of Nobuso* was being torn to shreds.

Molly picked up her canvas bag from the table and headed out the door. "Call if you need anything."

"I will."

"By the way," she said, stopped in the doorway, "remember you can't cut their hair without permission. Sorry."

Then she was gone, and it was just the four of them in the house. For a moment, she thought of another reality, one where Will was here with her, meeting the children for the first time, marveling over the size of Maggie's toes. But then she remembered him in New York, winking, his glamorous girlfriend under his arm, and him being a father to these children seemed ludicrous.

She walked into the study. Ethan did not glance up from his task of demolishing the book.

"I wrote that book."

Ethan looked up at her. "Whatcha mean?"

"All those words in there, I came up with them. It's about a tribe in Africa. I lived with them for years, off and on."

He laughed. "But you are white."

"Some white people live in Africa."

He shook his head, ripping another page out of her book. "Blacks are from Africa."

She sat on the floor near him. "All humans come from Africa, originally."

He glanced at her. "Really?"

"Really."

"Hmm," he said, and returned to the book, ripping out another page. "I didn't know that. The kids at my daycare were mostly white but some black kids too."

"Do you want to go to bed?" she asked gently.

He shook his head. "Nah."

As he said this, he yawned. Rebecca smiled. "How about we go up to your room?"

"My room?"

She nodded seriously. "All yours. Once you get settled in, we can go buy some more things for it."

"A TV?"

"Not a TV, but some toys."

He twisted his mouth, and threw a page at her. "Your book is shit."

She was startled, and didn't know what to say. The words sounded jaded and adult. But he was so clearly a child.

He stood up and threw the book against the wall, kicking the other books he had left on the floor. His small hands were curled in fists. Rebecca wanted to reach out and, somehow, erase his anger.

When he had calmed down, and was tugging on a child lock on a desk drawer, Rebecca scooted over.

"Would you like to see your room?" she asked softly.

He shrugged, giving up on the child lock. Rebecca took his hand. It was warm, and bonier than Madison's. She led him out of the study and up the stairs.

"You have the floor to yourself. If you need anything at night, just call."

The room had pale blue walls, and a large white bureau and a flower armchair. The closet had his new clothes. Cars and trains and books sat in the corner.

He leapt up on the bed, and she leaned down to help him with his shoes. He watched her blankly as she untied his old, scuffed Nikes. An ugly scar ran across the bottom of his foot.

She cringed, angry on his behalf, wondering where it came from, who was responsible.

"What's that?" he asked, pointing to the white baby monitor.

"Oh, it's like a walkie talkie. So I can hear you if you need something."

"Hmm, that's creepy."

She grabbed the Thomas the Tank Engine pajamas out of the cabinet. His eyes lit up, and he whipped off his t-shirt and pants.

"I like trains," he said. "I saw a train show on TV."

"Me too," she said, even though that wasn't particularly true.

He pulled on the pajama top and bottoms, admiring the sleeves with a smile. She knew he needed to be scrubbed, to be cleaned, but she didn't want to push him.

She turned on the nightlight.

"Where are Madison and Maggie?"

"They're sleeping upstairs."

"Maggie don't sleep."

"No? Well, I'll check on her then. Do you want me to read you a story?"

"I need to see the girls first."

Rebecca was touched by his concern, and she led him to their rooms, pointing at their sleeping frames from the doorway. He nodded somberly and allowed her to lead him back to his bedroom.

He climbed underneath the covers of his bed, and curled up in the fetal position, facing the wall. Only his large bush of hair stuck out from the sheets. She grabbed one of the books (*A Day at the Races*) and read very quietly, her voice a raspy whisper. After a while, his breathing became steady, his back rising up and down, and she carefully put the book back in the corner. She reached down to his sleeping form, but she didn't touch him; her hand simply hovered.

"Goodnight, baby boy," she whispered.

Then she stood up and turned out the light and closed the door. Quietly, she went to her bedroom and retrieved the baby monitor. It had been expensive, but it had come with three baby units, so she could have one in each of their rooms. All the rooms were silent.

The study was in disarray. Opened books, papers, pens and a vase were scattered across the floor. She smiled as she shelved the books, and tidied the pens and papers. She threw the ripped pages in the trash. Her eye caught on to one sentence—*The women's historical exchange of goods with other tribes resulted in a linguistic diversity that enabled them to have a social space free of men*—and marveled at how arid, how lifeless, her own words seemed.

The kitchen was clean, and she poured herself a glass of wine and sat at the kitchen table. It was crazy, but she was happy. She could see it wouldn't be easy, but that was OK. She could already see she could love them, that these children could become her children.

PART TWO

Chapter Eight

Brittney

At the first hearing after her children were taken, Brittney yelled at the lawyers and the caseworker and the judge (her own lawyer just stood there, doing nothing), screeching they had no right to do this, they were her children. The faces looked at her with scornful judgment, and the judge remarked, disdainfully, that she might have a mental illness. *Fuck you, asshole!* She had screamed, and the scream had felt funny in her mouth, like a demon trying to get loose.

The judge ruled against her, and then she was in the hall, alone. No one explained how this was even possible. She roamed the city aimlessly, incredulous and angry. She yelled at a homeless man who asked her for money, and as she marched away, she felt like the devil himself had burrowed inside her. When she couldn't walk anymore, she returned to her apartment and slept, refusing to wake up, trying to escape her own fury. When she couldn't sleep anymore and was just tossing and turning, she cried and shouted and broke plates and kicked the trash with her bare feet.

A young woman stopped by unannounced, pushing her way in. She walked through the apartment, not touching anything. She stood near the kitchen table and handed Brittney a bunch of papers. *Sign this if you want your children back*, she said. Brittney signed the papers and then threw them at the woman, and told her to get out.

The woman kneeled down and collected the strewn papers, glancing up at Brittney, her reddish blonde hair framing her face. There was a mixture of pity and repugnance in her raised eyebrows and drawn mouth. Brittney knew she was being childish but she couldn't stop herself. She wanted to kick the woman's horsey white teeth. It wasn't fair, that they could take her children for nothing. The woman shoved half the papers in her leather bag, and stood up, straightening her back and rubbing dust from the arms of her sweater. She put the rest of the papers on the table, glancing at Brittney with lingering condemnation, and maybe a shade of fear. Then she turned on her ugly beige heels and clacked out the door.

Brittney tossed the papers to the floor. She closed her eyes, and tried to contain her outrage that this woman had taken charge of her children, her babies. She had to collect herself, somehow. That was how she would get them back.

She remembered, in high school, smoking weed in the park with her girlfriends, and feeling light and content, and *free*, almost as if she were floating, her anxiety about her mother's drinking, her reckless brothers flaking off and her grandma's death drifting away.

She ran a few blocks over and bought a small bag from a boy she knew from high school, who sold to everyone in the neighborhood. Then she sat in front of the TV and smoked, waiting for the calm.

The smoke settled into the hole in her heart, giving her a dull sense of fulfillment and obscuring the sharpness of her anger. She felt a bit more in control. She collected the papers from the kitchen floor, and read them on the couch. There were names she didn't know, and jargon she didn't understand, but, in the middle, there was a long list of things she needed to do, if she wanted her children back. Clean her apartment. Get a job. Psychological Assessment. Depression counseling. Alcohol counseling (*ridiculous*, she thought, *she barely drank*.) Parenting classes. Visit the children twice a week.

The idea of *visiting* her children broke through her calm,

a sharp pain briefly flaring in her chest. They were her children, for goodness sake, they were part of her body, part of her flesh. They were her, and she was them. How could she visit them?

And what did the assorted list of chores have to do with DHS? They had no right to dictate the trash on her floor and the aches in her heart. That wasn't their business.

She closed her eyes, and let this anger pour out of her like water. She would finish this list of things, no matter how outlandish it was. Even if the caseworker and the lawyers and the judge didn't want her to have her children back, she would get them back.

She reached for her cell phone, grabbing it off the coffee table. She stared at the glowing screen. She wanted to call Trinity, hear her boisterous laugh, her constant reassurances, but a dark billowing resentment prevented her from calling. She wasn't sure she would ever forget, or forgive, Trinity bailing on her that night.

Brittney's finger scrolled through her contacts, searching for someone. There was Dave, but he didn't have children and he wouldn't understand; he would judge her for having left the children alone, even for a few minutes.

She called her mother.

"Who's this?" her mother said.

"Mom, it's me. DHS took my kids."

"What? Why they do that?"

"Because I left 'em here when they were sleeping. My crazy neighbor, the one always complaining about the crying, called the police."

"Sorry, Brittney. That's terrible. Whatcha gonna do?"

"I don't know. All my lawyer said is I got to do all the ridiculous things they say I got to do. It's this long list," she said, wanting her mother to comfort her, to help her out of this.

"Your lawyer is right though. You shouldn't trust DHS. You don't wanna mess around with 'em. Can't Chris go get 'em?"

"Maybe. But I don't know where he's at."

"You gotta find 'em. I can't take 'em. I'm too old and, you

know, with my ...."

Brittney bitterly pictured a bottle of Olde English, her constant companion.

"I'm sorry, Dee. I wish I could ... I wish I wasn't so drunk. But I have been this way as long as I can remember. Ever since I was younger than you. I got my reasons, and they are too dark to share, but I am sorry I can't help you more. I love you and the kids."

"I know you do, Mom."

"Why don't you ask Dave or Will to take 'em?"

Brittney thought of how disappointed her brothers would be in her when they found out. They expected better.

"Angel doesn't like children. You know she doesn't want them," she said, remembering all the times Dave's girlfriend had scrunched her nose at Brittney's children, wiping imaginary germs off the sleeves of her nice clothes if one of them accidentally touched her.

"Yeah, that's true. But maybe this will change her mind. Dave would make a great father. He was always the sweetest of the boys."

"Yeah, maybe."

"You wanna talk to Missy? She did a case with 'em."

"What happened to her kids?"

"She got one of the kids with her still, the other two I don't know. They're gone."

"OK," Brittney said, taking a deep breath. "OK."

"Don't trust DHS. Just do what you got to do to get out."

"Yeah."

Brittney noticed water gathering on her ceiling, a damp heaviness after the cold rain. She suddenly couldn't stand to be on the phone anymore. "I'll talk to you later, Mom," she whispered.

"Call Missy. She dealt with it."

"I will."

Brittney dropped her phone on the floor and walked into the bathroom and threw water on her face. The caseworker had given her the address for where the children were staying, and told her she could come by at 4 p.m. It was still in West Philly, but two or three miles away, and she didn't have any change for the bus.

Outside, the cold air pinched her nose and dried out her eyes, and she huddled in her coat. After walking a while, the sidewalk ran out, and she moved to the shoulder of the road, ignoring the SUVs that zoomed past, honking their horns, displacing the air, blowing it on her face.

It took her almost an hour. She was fifteen minutes late. She stood in front of the house, checking the address again. This didn't seem right. It was a brick mansion with small glass windows and a yard. There was a wood swing on the porch.

She called the caseworker.

"I'm at the address you gave me."

"Hold on a second."

Brittney waited, scraping her sneakers off on the grass. The front door swung open and her caseworker was standing there in a bunchy gray sweater, waving.

Brittney walked up the pathway, and followed her inside the house. It was large and bright. Everything—the furniture, lamps, rugs and paintings—looked ordered out of a fancy catalog. What were her kids doing here, in a place like this? It was like a house from a sitcom on TV.

Ethan and Madison ran over to her, and she kneeled down and hugged them both. They climbed in her lap, and she held them and smelled their necks and kissed their cheeks.

"Oh, I missed you," she whispered. She didn't want to let them go.

There were three women there, and she could see them out of the corner of her eye, watching. One of them offered her a drink. But she refused to look or speak to any of them. She just wanted to be with her children.

"Mom, you takin' us home?" Ethan asked hopefully, and Brittney shook her head.

"I wish I could, baby. They ain't lettin' me yet."

"Why not?"

"I don't know, baby. I don't know. They just ain't."

She could see her caseworker and one of the other women frowning and shaking their heads, but she ignored this. She wasn't going to play nice. Her children should know she would take them right now if she could. That she would never, in a million years, abandon them here in a stranger's house.

Madison began fidgeting in Brittney's arms. She scrambled down, and ran and collected one of her new dolls, holding it up to Brittney, a proud smile on her face. Brittney nodded, grimacing. There were dozens of toy bins. They were buying her children's affection with toys.

"Brittney," Katie said, "try to be more responsive to your daughter. She's asking for your attention."

Brittney closed her eyes, trying to manage her anger, keep it from bubbling over.

"Don't boss my mom," Ethan said, staring defiantly at Katie. He tossed a stuffed teddy bear at her face.

Brittney laughed.

"Brittney," Katie chided, "don't encourage your children to misbehave. That's not good parenting. You need to be an appropriate authority figure, not a friend."

Brittney whispered in Ethan's ear, "That's not good parenting," and he laughed. She stood up, holding Ethan's hand tightly, and went to look at Maggie in her swing. Maggie was fussing uncomfortably, and Brittney laid her left hand on her narrow chest. She was wearing a silk dress and a pink bow in her hair, and Brittney could tell, by the quality of the fabric and the stitching, that it had cost more than any of her own clothes.

Madison handed her another doll—it was a baby with shiny blonde ringlets and long lashes—and Brittney wanted to throw the stupid doll against the wall, shattering its head, but she nodded, pretending to admire it.

Brittney swallowed, and her throat felt dry. For the first time, she looked at the foster woman. She was older, in her late thirties or early forties, and her chestnut-colored hair was thick and straight and poured over her shoulders. She was wearing a cashmere sweater and blue jeans, sipping a glass of water, and watching the children intently. *They ain't your children*, Brittney thought. *You can't just buy my children.*

Brittney turned back to Maggie, patting her chest, wondering why this older wealthy woman wanted her children.

She noticed, then, above the fireplace, a large photograph of six black women, facing a fire. They were tall and dark skinned. Their only clothes were small tan swatches around their waist. She couldn't imagine why the woman would have a photograph like that in her house, and it infuriated her for a reason she couldn't quite discern.

"Mom, don't leave us here," Ethan whispered in her ear, and she pressed him against her body.

"I don't want to baby, but they makin' me. You lookin' out for your sisters?"

He nodded but he was crying, and she wanted to pick him up and run away so they could cry in private. She shifted, shielding him from the three women.

"Why won't they let you take us?" he asked, wiping his own tears with the back of his hand. "It's not fair."

"I don't know. It doesn't make any sense. They gave me all these things I got to do, this long list of things, and said I couldn't get you until I finished it."

"That ain't fair," he protested. "I just wanna go home right now. I don't know this lady or this neighborhood. Everything's different. She's a stranger."

"I know," she said, rubbing the soft spot on the back of his neck.

In what felt like moments later, the caseworker announced the visit was over. Brittney stayed where she was, sitting on the floor, still not believing she had to leave her children. What would happen if she just refused?

Ethan was in her lap, and he didn't move. Madison dropped a toy camera and glanced around anxiously. The caseworker stood in front of Brittney, her young face flushed.

"I'm sorry, but it's time to go," she repeated. "There will be another visit next Tuesday."

Brittney closed her eyes and then stood up. She stroked Maggie's cheek with her finger. Ethan and Madison latched onto her leg, and they were both crying. Brittney leaned down and told them she would be back soon, but her words were garbled. She had to peel them off her leg.

Outside on the street, it was cold and dark. She crossed the street and sat on a porch. The three women came to the door, laughing and talking as they said goodbye. *Of course they'd give the children to her*, Brittney thought, *they're friends.*

Brittney stared at the house's large wood door, thinking she could run inside, punch the foster woman's pale face, shove the other caseworker, and take the children and run away. She knew, even though it was illegal, it would be right. They were her children.

But she had no car, or even money for a bus out of the city. So there would be nowhere to run.

"May I help you? Are you OK?" an older man said. He was standing a few feet away from her.

She looked at him in his tweed jacket and leather briefcase and figured she was sitting on his porch. She shook her head, and pummeled past him.

She needed to go home and smoke. She jogged toward her apartment, the cold air hurting her eyes and nose. She would do her plan, and get her children back, and everything would be OK. Except it wouldn't because her children would be traumatized by the fact that they were taken away from her, and she would never be able to undo that.

~*~

Brittney wondered if the caseworker would find Chris, and he would start working a plan too. They were supposed to be looking for him, but they didn't seem to think he was worth searching for—maybe they thought he was just one father in an ocean of lost fathers.

She left him a note under the welcome mat, and hoped he would show up and do something. She didn't trust him, exactly, but he was better than DHS. Anyone was.

There was a loud knock on the door a week after she left the note, and she opened it, and he was standing there, the note in his hand, a look of disbelief on his face. Even though she was high, she started crying. He put his arms around her, and she laid her head on his chest, and he smelled different than she remembered.

Inside, he took off his coat and they sat on the couch, their knees touching.

"What happened, Brit?" he asked.

His tone was patient, not accusatory, and she told him the whole story, how the neighbor had called DHS when she'd stepped out for a minute because she couldn't stand the sound of Maggie crying.

"What a crazy bitch," Chris cursed.

Brittney had only seen the woman once since her kids had been taken, and she had run over and slapped her in the face. The woman had screamed and scratched Brittney with her long nails. Brittney had shoved her to the floor. Brittney had wanted to punch her, or kick her, but she knew the woman would call the police, and so she had walked away, her fingers trembling.

Chris palmed his forehead. His hair was cut close to his head. "OK, so what's the deal? How do you get 'em back?"

"There's a plan I have to do, but you should come forward. I don't want to fight this by myself."

He sighed and put his head in his hands. His forearms were larger, more muscular than before, and she reached out and held his hand. He squeezed her hand back, and she felt small and protected.

"I can keep giving you some money, but my life right now ain't good for kids. I'm not even staying in one place."

"Chris," she sobbed, yanking her hand away, "you really want some old wealthy lady raisin' our children?"

He glanced over in surprise. "That's who they are with?"

"Yeah."

He raised his eyebrows. "Why?"

"I don't know. They don't tell me nothin'. But we ain't got no family willing to take 'em."

"Did you ask your brothers?"

"Yeah, I did ask Dave and Will," she said, bitterly. The awkward conversations had ended with her brothers asking for her forgiveness: forgive us, we can't. It's too much right now. Maybe later. Maybe Angel would change her mind. Maybe Will's schedule would open up, maybe he would get back with his ex-girlfriend.

"Shit ... my mom can't take all of them. Her back's been killin' her. She can't even work. How long is this plan gonna take?"

She walked over to the cabinet and pulled out the stack of papers and flipped to the list. She handed it to him. He leaned back and read, his face serious and reflective, the way he'd once studied his college textbooks. She suddenly missed him. Or maybe she just missed having another person around. Someone to talk to other than the TV. Someone to touch.

"OK," he said, looking up and rubbing his chin, the papers in his hand, "Maybe six months? I'll help you do all this stuff. Alcohol counseling?"

"Yeah, it don't make any sense. Just because I had one drink at the bar when I was out. I don't even like drinking."

"Damn." He looked around the apartment, noticing it was trashed. "Shit, OK, we can clean this place up together."

She closed her eyes and tried to control the annoyance that was unfurling through her body. "That's it?" Her voice was small and tight.

"Brittney, trust me, they ain't gonna give me the kids. I ain't livin' in the arms of the law here. After I was fired, no security place would hire me. What was I supposed to do? Work at McDonald's?"

"Yeah, maybe. Nothing wrong with that."

"It's not a good job. None of those are. You remember Jimmy?"

Brittney remembered him from some of the house parties, a short man with a silver earring in one ear. He had always seemed aggressive and mean.

"He hooked me up with some work. But it's not exactly legal."

Brittney sat down on the couch again, cursing under her breath, not knowing why she had hoped for better. The Chris she had fallen in love with was long gone.

He leaned over and kissed her on the cheek. "We'll fix this. We'll get them back with you, their mother, where they belong."

She nodded, and pulled his arm around her back. His body was long and hard and the pressure, the weight of another body, even if it was a body that had disappointed her again and again, was somehow reassuring. She closed her eyes, and he stroked the back of her head.

"Look, just stick to the plan, OK? I'll be here helping you out, behind the scenes. I'm sorry I can't do more."

He kissed her on the forehead and pulled away. He slipped on his jacket—it had fur around the collar—and then nodded at her, guilt and regret on his brow. He walked through the kitchen, lowering his head as he slipped out the door. The door clanged against the frame.

Brittney returned to the couch, and lit up another joint. She didn't want to start thinking about how Chris cared more about dealing drugs, or whatever it was he and Jimmy were doing, than rescuing his children. Thinking that way would do no good. She had to take what he was offering.

She sucked hard on the joint, burning her throat, and then, slowly, a feeling of contentment came over her. Chris was going to help her. She would get the children back. It would be OK, or at least what had to pass for OK now.

Chapter Nine

Rebecca

Rebecca felt frayed and tired under the constancy of Maggie's screaming and Ethan's tantrums. She worried she wasn't cut out to be a mother after all, at least not for children like this, but it was a diffuse and untrackable worry because all her thoughts were like strings floating around in her mind, slipping away the moment she tried to reach for them.

Her father's words—*others might be better suited to take care of these children, Rebecca*—haunted her. When her mother called to ask about the children, Rebecca dissembled, brushing her hair out of her eyes, wiping at the stains on her sweater, telling her the children were adjusting, not wanting to admit they weren't.

The court ordered two supervised visits a week for the children's mother, and Rebecca had been curious to meet her, but wary. It seemed wrong you could harm your children, leave them so filthy and bruised, and then still keep seeing them.

Brittney walked into Rebecca's house, led by Katie, the DHS worker, and Ethan and Madison ran over, and clutched at her like they were trying to climb on top of her, or maybe inside her. Brittney seemed young and slightly stunned, like a bunny rabbit caught in a trap. Her clothes were disheveled and her eyes were bloodshot and her hair was in disarray.

Rebecca remembered herself at that age, subsisting on ramen and take-out, pulling all-nighters in the library, and drinking too much at bars, stumbling home with her roommates, laughing as the boys peed behind the bushes. The thought of her taking care of three children, then, was laughable.

Brittney moved over to the armchair, and Ethan sat in her lap, stroking her hand, but Madison wandered away, retrieving toys to show her mother. Brittney nodded, not seeming particularly interested. She whispered something to Ethan, and he laughed. Brittney occasionally wiped her nose with the back of her hand, like a child.

At the end of the visit, Brittney pried Ethan and then Madison off her legs, and slipped out the front door. Then she was gone, and Ethan was throwing toys against the wall, shouting, and Madison was sobbing. Startled by the noise, Maggie began to cry.

Rebecca stood for a moment, paralyzed and overwhelmed. *I can do this*, she reminded herself. *This is what I wanted.*

She scooped Madison up, knowing she would be the easiest one to comfort. Madison buried her face in Rebecca's chest, and clung to her tightly, taking Rebecca's breath away.

"See you later," Katie said, nodding at Nina, the children's caseworker, as she walked out the door. There were so many caseworkers, but none had told her what had happened to the kids.

"Don't worry," Nina assured, her face turned to Rebecca. "The kids will get used to the new situation. It just takes time."

Nina unbuckled Maggie from her swing. "Let's give him some space," she said, nodding at Ethan, who was knocking over the colorful toy bins, kicking the cars and blocks and puzzle pieces, shouting he wanted to go home.

In the kitchen, they sat at the table. Madison had fallen silent, her face pressed against Rebecca's chest, her eyes closed.

"So you're a women's studies professor, right?" Nina asked, juggling Maggie, raising her voice over Maggie's moans.

"Yes, women's studies and anthropology."

"I majored in women's studies and psychology. I miss that

stuff. I still remember reading Susan Bordo for the first time. Blew my mind."

Rebecca gently rubbed Madison's back. "Susan is brilliant."

"What's your research on?"

"My last book was on the Nobuso women in Africa. They live by themselves, apart from the men. I stayed with them for years."

"That's so interesting. What was it like?"

"You know, it wasn't entirely different from an all-girls boarding school. The women were supportive and confident. But there were also defined social hierarchies.

"I can give you a copy of the book if you want."

"Yes, I'd love that. All I read these days is potboilers," she laughed.

Rebecca smiled. She was glad to have someone take an interest in her book, but she was even happier the children's caseworker liked her. It seemed important, somehow.

"How'd you get into casework?"

Nina shrugged. "I like kids. I saw the opening. What else can you do with a psychology or women's studies degree?"

Rebecca was startled, that that really was all it took to be a caseworker, but she just smiled.

That night, Rebecca lay on the floor in Maggie's room, and thought about how utterly exhausted she was. Even her bones felt heavy. She was too old to be up all night. She couldn't imagine working on her journal article edits tomorrow evening, like she'd hoped. The editor had already extended the deadline once.

Maggie's birdlike body was nestled on her stomach, shaking with anger. Maggie had slept for an hour, content, but then she had unfurled, screeching and screaming, her heart beating wildly, her fragile ribs vibrating. Rebecca stared at the white ceiling, her mind fried, and it occurred to her that this —crying all night long—couldn't be normal. Maybe it could be fixed.

In the morning, she took Maggie to the doctor's office the

caseworkers had listed in the papers. It was a rundown clinic. Madison huddled against her side, trying to crawl on her lap, and Ethan kicked his plastic chair, over and over again, mumbling this place was gross, he wanted to go home. Maggie cried in the carrier strapped to her chest.

The TV was blaring, and the room was packed with loud children, and adults with oxygen tanks and wheelchairs and canes. The floor was stained with yellowish streaks. Next to them, a middle aged man coughed, and phlegm splattered to the floor.

Rebecca stood up. She didn't trust this place. She would never have gone there herself. It was too dirty.

At home, she documented the many ways the clinic was substandard, the long waiting time, the Petri dish of illnesses in the lobby, the mysterious stains on the floor, and sent it in an email to Katie and her supervisor, asking to take the children to a private office. After a few days, Katie gave her approval for her to take the children somewhere else, if she wanted to pay for it, as it may not be covered.

One of her bestfriends was a pediatrician, and she was happy to make room for Rebecca on her schedule. Rebecca hadn't seen Erica in over a month, since before the children had arrived, when they'd all gone out to dinner.

When Erica walked into the patient room, she saw Rebecca and Maggie and a brief look of shock fluttered across her mouth and eyes. Then she rolled her stool forward and congratulated Rebecca.

"So how is parenthood?"

Rebecca smiled, tucking her wild hair behind her ear. Her blouse was splotched with baby food, and Maggie's vomit. "It's...."

Rebecca couldn't find the right word. With the long, sleepless nights, and Ethan's tantrums, she felt clunky and run down. But when Maggie was asleep on her chest, her body warm, or Madison was cuddled in her arms, she was happier than she had ever been.

"It's … good," she said finally, because the truth would take too long to explain. "I have three children, siblings."

Erica's eyes grew large. "Three by yourself?" she exclaimed. "It's so funny. Peter and I never even knew you wanted children. We always thought you and Will were like us." As she removed the stethoscope from Maggie's heart, she glanced up. "Do you need anything? I could drop off some food. Isn't that what people do when there is a new baby?"

"Sure, that would be great."

Rebecca had been too tired to cook anything other than pasta or premade chicken nuggets. At least they were organic.

Erica ran her fingers over Maggie's lean belly. "She hasn't gained enough weight since her birth and she's not hitting her milestones," Erica observed, her hand feeling Maggie's back.

Rebecca nodded, worried, for a moment, that Maggie would have special needs after all, and her heart sank.

But Erica diagnosed Maggie with reflux, and prescribed a medication that she predicted would work in a couple weeks. "She'll be like a different baby. If not," she added, "bring her back in. It could be a milk allergy. We'll figure it out."

Rebecca thanked her, grateful, and Erica nodded, an amused, and slightly bewildered expression on her face.

Rebecca smiled as she dressed Maggie in her tiny yellow dress. She figured Erica would tell their other friends in a hushed voice, and they would marvel at what a crazy decision Rebecca had made. But she didn't care. Things like that didn't seem to matter anymore. Maybe they never had.

"Peter and I will bring some food over tomorrow," Erica said.

"Thanks. I appreciate it."

"Just don't fall down the parenting hole."

Rebecca laughed. "Too late."

Maggie screeched louder, and Rebecca stood up, bouncing her on her hip.

Erica walked her out. "Let us know when you're free. There's a new Italian place on South Street, three bells by Craig

LaBan."

"I will," Rebecca called, waving, although going out to dinner, at a nice restaurant, seemed preposterous. She didn't even have a sitter yet.

The reflux medication was a clear liquid, and Maggie resisted taking it. Rebecca had to hold her mouth open with her fingers and pour it in. "Sorry, baby," she mumbled, praying the medicine would work, that she wasn't shoving it down Maggie's throat for nothing.

When it did work, a week and a half later, Rebecca was thrilled. She felt she had passed the first test of motherhood, and this calmed her anxiety, gave her a newfound confidence in what she was doing.

Maggie started sleeping through the whole night, and she woke up happy, laughing and swatting her toys. She flailed her arms eagerly in the air, wanting to be picked up. Rebecca carried her downstairs to the kitchen. For the first time, Maggie reached for her bottle greedily and opened her mouth for spoonfuls of pureed food.

Rebecca weighed her on the scale daily, and the numbers ticked upward quickly. As Maggie learned to roll and scoot, she seemed amazed by her own abilities, by the ease at which she could inhabit the world. And even though Rebecca wasn't directly responsible for this, Maggie latched onto her with ferocity, seeming to believe Rebecca, and Rebecca alone, had saved her from the constant burning in her chest and the resulting stagnation.

As she bumbled around the room, loud and happy, she would look to Rebecca, wherever she was, soliciting her guidance.

Madison collected colorful toys from their baskets and handed them to Maggie. "You're happy baby, now," she announced, stroking Maggie's hair and kissing her cheek. Maggie bounced in response, grinning and waving her hands through the air.

Ethan asked Rebecca how she had fixed Maggie, his eyes

wide with awe. "She used to cry and cry and cry…" he said, more to himself than to her.

"I gave her some medicine. She had a pain in her chest that made it difficult to eat."

Ethan pondered this for a moment, and then asked, "Why didn't my mom give that to her?"

Rebecca didn't know. She knew so little of what had gone on in their lives before they had arrived, filthy and bruised and malnourished. She scrambled for something neutral or reasonable to say, ignoring the anger that rose in her chest whenever she thought about how sick, how bony, Maggie had been.

"I don't know," she said finally, remembering the clinic they had gone to. "Maybe the doctor there didn't know."

He stared at her, his eyes flecked with streaks of amber, skeptical, and then ran off to play with his remote control car.

One day, after Brittney had left, Nina and Rebecca were drinking coffee in the kitchen, discussing Nina's new lawyer boyfriend.

"He wants to take me to Amish country for the weekend. I'm not sure I'm ready for that level of commitment."

"You should go," Rebecca said, feeling generally optimistic, her fingers cupping Madison's head. They could hear Ethan slamming plastic toys against the wood floor, in the living room.

"I just wish I know what happened, before…" Rebecca said, tilting her head to the other room.

Nina blew out a long breath of air, her brown bangs lifting up, briefly. "I don't know the whole story. But Katie told me—" Here, she lowered her voice. "She had a habit of leaving all the children alone, in the apartment, to get D-R-U-N-K at a B-A-R."

"Oh," Rebecca said, and her view of Brittney, which had been tottering back and forth uncertainly, solidified to anger. *They won't be safe with Brittney*, she thought, *they will languish*.

After Nina left, Ethan moved on from the living room, and started ransacking the kitchen. Rebecca didn't really mind. She knew it was a way for him to release his fury. But she didn't want the girls to see it, and she took them to Madison's room, one on each hip.

She leaned up against the wall, and told the girls fairy tales, using her funny voices. "Someone's been eating my porridge," she growled. The girls looked at her and laughed, delighted.

"Someone's been eating my porridge," she said in an English accent.

"And someone's been eating my porridge and they ate it all up!" she exclaimed, in a high-pitched, squeaky voice. The girls squealed and then piled on top of her lap, looking closely at the picture of the three bears.

"There's baby bear," Madison said, pointing.

"Babababababa," Maggie agreed.

Once Rebecca finished the story, and the girls seemed content, she gave them some toys, and told them she would be right back.

"Jack Beanstalk?" Madison asked.

"Of course. In five minutes," she said, ruffling her hair.

Downstairs, toys and books and couch cushions were strewn everywhere. She had cleaned these rooms more times than she could remember, thinking it was Sisyphean, all the cleaning. She'd had to pull her equal pay article, apologizing to the editor, trying to explain she had no time and no attention span, but the editor, whose one child was in college, hadn't understood. She had been annoyed, and told Rebecca she'd never be published in her journal again.

Rebecca sat on the kitchen floor, next to Ethan. He was emptying the kitchen cabinets, and she asked him, softly, if he was OK. Sometimes, he would yell that he hated her and this stupid house with all its stupid rooms. Other times, he would crumple on the floor, and she would offer him chocolate milk, and he would nod slightly.

He looked at her. "I miss my mom," he cried.

"I know," she said, quietly. "I'm sorry." She lifted him up, and carried him to his room, trying not to feel jealous. He sagged against her shoulder. He seemed heavier than Maggie and Madison combined.

She read him Winnie the Pooh, and, to her surprise, he fell asleep, curled up around a stuffed train, his lashes long on his cheeks.

~*~

After an argument with both her department chairs, Rebecca had managed to reduce her teaching load to two classes for the spring semester. She hired Adriana, a college student, to watch the children the fifteen hours she had to be at school. Rebecca had sifted through dozens of applications to find Adriana—a highly-qualified woman willing to undergo a background check for a part-time job.

She invited Yvonne, the woman she had met in foster care training, and her two girls over for a playdate, serving cookies and tea while the children played in the living room. Yvonne sat in the armchair, her teacup resting on her thigh as she stared at the abstract paintings on the wall.

"Those are cool paintings," she commented.

"Thanks," Rebecca said. Will had picked them out, and she had never particularly cared for them, but she had grown accustomed to them. They felt like home. A home Will had generously signed over to her, his guilt likely clouding his judgment. Or maybe it was just optimism, optimism that he would continue to sell books and appear on TV and be appointed to a prestigious chair at Columbia.

Yvonne's girls were five and eight, and they fawned over Madison and Maggie but then got bored. Ethan offered to show them his room, and the three of them ran off like bandits.

Yvonne turned to Rebecca, concern on her face. "Is he safe alone with the girls?"

"Sure. He's great with his sisters. He said it was his job to change Madison's diaper."

Yvonne smiled sadly.

"Is there anything new in your case?" Rebecca asked.

Yvonne shook her head. "Still waiting."

"How long have you had them now?"

"Two and a half years."

"Two and a half years?"

"I know. It's not right. They keep givin' 'em more chances. They're both addicts, in and out of rehab."

Rebecca couldn't imagine having the children for over two years, and then losing them, still. She couldn't believe this was normal. There was a federal law mandating the state terminate the parental rights if the child was in care for fifteen months. Her mind was silently counting down—the first time Maggie had said "mamamamama," her arms stretched up in the air, wanting to be picked up, Rebecca had cried, and thought, only eleven more months, only eleven more months—and she had felt guilty for this, guilty that it was her nose buried in Maggie's soft hair, and her stomach that Maggie's now round belly was pressed against.

"What do you think about the parents?" Rebecca asked.

Yvonne sighed. "I try not to. In the beginning, I felt some pity for them, you know, they're young, they got caught up in bad things. But now I just can't. Not with what they've put the girls through."

Maggie walked along the couch, holding a plastic pink flower, and then made her way to Yvonne's armchair hanging onto the side table. She offered the flower to Yvonne, smiling. Yvonne thanked her.

"Babababa..." Maggie responded, switching to a crawl, moving over to her sister.

"She's going to walk soon," Yvonne noted.

Rebecca nodded proudly. They could hear the children squealing upstairs. They were happy, giddy squeals, but Yvonne put her teacup on the side table and said she was going to investigate. Her steps were quick as she made her way up the stairs.

160

Rebecca got down on the floor, and Maggie crawled into her lap. She tugged at Rebecca's ear, and Rebecca joked, "What are you doing to my ear?" She tickled Maggie and Maggie laughed, her six teeth small in her large, down-turned mouth.

Madison ran over and tugged her other ear, and fell on her lap, and Rebecca tickled them both, and they were all laughing.

Yvonne walked down the stairs purposefully, and the two girls were lagging behind, mumbling about not wanting to leave. Someone had drawn purple mustaches on their faces, and Rebecca couldn't help but smile. Madison and Maggie looked up, and smiled too.

Yvonne seemed unhappy.

"They're washable," Rebecca explained, composing herself. "You can wash it off in the kitchen."

Yvonne nodded, and herded her two snickering daughters into the kitchen. Rebecca looked at the stairs. Ethan wasn't on them, and she shrugged. She would see what he had drawn on himself later. The water was running in the kitchen, and Yvonne snapped at one of the girls, telling her to keep her head down.

Rebecca stuck her tongue out at Maggie and Madison and they both laughed.

"That's silly," Madison said.

"Is it?" Rebecca said, sticking her tongue out again. The girls laughed. She knew she was being indulgent, but after waiting for children so long, she was too happy to be strict.

Yvonne came out of the kitchen with her girls, their faces freshly scrubbed.

"We got to get goin'," she announced, gathering her purse and jacket. The girls obediently put their jackets on.

"Bye babies," the younger one said, waving at Madison and Maggie. "See you later."

Madison waved back, but Maggie was too busy pushing the buttons on a fake camera.

Rebecca stood up to see them out. "Thank you for coming," she said, wondering if Yvonne would keep coming to the house, if she would be able to turn this into a friendship.

They didn't have much in common, other than the children. But that seemed like enough.

Yvonne paused at the door. "We're having a block party next weekend, if you want to bring the kids."

"Thank you. We'd love to come."

The girls had already run down the steps, and Yvonne walked after them, her pace slow and steady. The girls were both tall and skinny and chatty. They seemed happy. She pictured them being sent back to their parents, after all this time. And their parents relapsing.

She remembered how filthy her children were when they arrived—their skin creased and crusted with dirt, Madison and Maggie's butts covered in angry red rashes, their hair matted in knots, their skin bruised green and purple. The second day, she had given them baths in her clawfoot tub. The tub water had become brown and dark beneath the bubbles.

Rebecca had meticulous documentation of these changes —including Erica's monthly notes about Maggie's weight gains —because Nina had told her it might help her case, if it came to that. She had photos and notes in a scrapbook, and sometimes at night, she would flip through it with a glass of wine. It was strange but she found she could miss the girls at night, while they were sleeping. Looking at their photos made her feel content. Madison and Maggie loved being outside, and there was one photo of them sitting in the backyard, shovels in their hand and pails near their feet, and their smiles were radiant.

There were fewer photos of Ethan, because he didn't like to have his photo taken. There was only one where he was truly smiling—she had caught him the moment he had figured out how to rewire the broken remote control car. His face had beamed with pleasure and satisfaction. After she had taken the photo, she had put the camera down and investigated. The car hadn't been working, and now it was. She studied it but couldn't tell how he had fixed it. She was impressed. It wasn't an easy thing to do, and she thought maybe he would be an engineer when he grew up. And then it occurred to her, darkly, the local school he would be sent to at his mother's probably didn't graduate many engineers.

After seeing this innate ability, she decided to enroll Ethan in a Montessori school. When she toured the school, she had been pleased to see the children were all happily occupied with a variety of different activities, some working alone and others in groups.

Ethan had not wanted to attend school, cursing Rebecca and the teachers and then sulking in the corner for the whole five hours. She feared he would destroy their property and get himself kicked out, but the teachers assured her they would work with any child's personality. The second week, he still walked in sullenly, and sulked in his corner, but after lunch, he branched out, shyly exploring the classroom. There were a half-dozen learning stations and hundreds of books. The third week, he shrugged his shoulders and ran to the classroom, quick to return to his favorite station.

The teachers told her he kept to himself, staring at the other children suspiciously. He stayed busy at the motors and pulleys station, learning how to make things run. He also liked the map station, and he was able to draw fairly accurate maps freehand. At snack time, he ate quickly and messily and then tapped his feet, waiting to go back to the stations. He wasn't interested in conversing with anyone but Mr. Sanders. Mr. Sanders was a skinny twenty-something with a bushy beard who loved cars and mechanics. He said "dude" and had a throaty laugh. For him, Ethan proudly displayed his map or latest running car.

Ethan was supposed to start kindergarten in September, and Rebecca registered him for the local public school, to keep his options open. It was the very school she and Will had planned on sending their children to. But filling out the paperwork reminded her that the three children could be gone by then, back with their mother, trapped in their dank apartment. (Nina had told her the apartment was disgusting— rats and roaches and mold crawled over everything.) Mailing in the form was an act of optimism. She longed for them to still be with her, then.

Two days a week, Rebecca picked Ethan up from his Montessori school by herself. Madison and Maggie stayed home with Adriana. She took him out to lunch, to restaurants with large glossy menus and waiters with white aprons and crowded tables. For a long time, he said very little, his eyes glancing around the restaurant suspiciously. It struck her, many times, that he was the only person in the restaurant who wasn't used to nice places, and then she would feel guilty.

She read the menu for him, enunciating clearly as she pointed to the letters. It seemed like he could read, but she wasn't sure how much. He was secretive and he smiled mysteriously when she asked if he knew what a word said. He ate his food—fries and chicken fingers if they had it—quickly and ravenously, as if it might be taken away from him any minute.

She asked him general questions ("How are you doing? How was school? Do you like any of the other kids?") and he ignored her, taking a drink of his milk or wiping his mouth with his napkin. But one day, he started telling her about a toy car he and Mr. Sanders were going to build from scratch, with an engine.

"Wow, that sounds amazing," she enthused, honestly. She was impressed with the school. It was expensive, and she'd had to pull strings to get him in, but she was getting her money's worth.

"Mr. Sanders is lettin' me choose the color and everything."

"Really? What color did you choose?"

He raised his eyebrows, thinking as he took another French fry and dipped it in the ketchup. "I think... silver."

"Silver's a good choice."

"Yeah it will be cool. It's gonna be really cool."

She smiled, happy he was so enthusiastic about something.

"I don't know much about engines. You'll have to explain

164

it to me as you go."

He grinned proudly. "Yeah, OK."

On the way out, he thanked her for lunch—a first—and she squeezed his shoulder, telling him, "You're welcome."

"No, you're welcome," he responded, a clever smile on his face.

"No, you are," she teased, reaching over and pinching his side lightly. He laughed and then chased after her. She squealed as they chased each other back to the car, weaving through the sidewalk crowds.

As she buckled him into his booster seat, she wanted to lean in and kiss his cheek—his sweet, smart, vulnerable cheek —but she didn't because she wasn't sure he would like it. She smiled instead, sticking her tongue out goofily, and he smiled back.

"You're weird," he said, but he said it kindly, like he didn't mind weird.

Chapter Ten

Brittney

After a month of applying for jobs, Brittney got one as a cashier at the Save-A-Lot, and they agreed to schedule her shifts around her visits to the children. It was a step down from the call center, but she was glad to have a job, even if it was boring and the customers stared at her impatiently as she rang up their groceries.

During her shifts, as the red light blinked and she slid item after item under the scanner and stacked them in plastic bags, she would think about her children and how long it was until she could see them again. She would think about their hair, their skin, their smiles, even their cries. These thoughts were distracting—her hands would pause over the plastic bag, incapable of movement—so, sometimes, she would smoke before her shift, to calm her anxiety, and the grocery store became a mindless haze she swam through, smiling blandly at her coworkers and the customers.

She was obsessed with the visits to her children, when she would next be allowed to see them, to smell them, to rumple their hair. Her mind was like a TV stuck on the same show, playing it over and over again. But the morning of the visits, dread would seep into her mind, slowing her down. Because she knew, she *knew*, at the end of the visit, she would be forced to leave them again.

The pain of this—of leaving her children in a stranger's

house, while she walked out into the night—was so bad she took to smoking before the visits. That way her feelings were dulled, and she could walk out the door without weeping.

She still watched the house from across the street, studying its elaborate nooks, wondering which rooms belonged to her children. The living room lights remained on, but she assumed, because it was evening, they would be having dinner in the kitchen.

Once, Ethan gave her a paper card with stick figures of her and the children, in the apartment, their faces smiling, their feet surrounded by trash. She held this crinkled paper in her hands and, encouraged, walked into the backyard, and peered in through the kitchen window, needing to know what her children were doing, what their lives were like inside that massive house.

The foster woman was sitting with the girls at the kitchen table. Madison was smiling and talking as she spooned the food into her mouth; Maggie was laughing as she banged her hands on the highchair. The foster woman was hovering around the girls, touching her hand gently on their backs.

Brittney picked up a stick and threw it at the window as hard as she could. The stick clanked and fell onto the patio.

The woman tilted her head, staring into the darkness, a look of fear on her face.

Brittney ran away. As she was opening the gate, she heard a window slide open. She passed through the gate and cleared the house and then veered right on the sidewalk. She slipped on a puddle of water and slid forward and then caught herself.

She ran for a mile, until her breath was too short and her chest hurt. The foster woman and her daughters had seemed like a happy little family. Maggie had looked joyful. She had changed dramatically since she had been taken. She never seemed to cry anymore, and she had gained weight, her bony features softening. This struck Brittney as a horrible rebuke, a sign she *was* an awful mother. She knew the caseworkers and the lawyers and the therapists and the foster woman were taking notes, judging her, thinking she had been starving Maggie. But the truth was she had tried everything. The doctor had told her there was nothing to do!

Brittney closed her eyes, and then checked her watch. She was supposed to start the evening shift in twenty minutes, but she couldn't stand the idea of dealing with the fluorescent lights and whiny customers and busted produce. She called in sick, and the manager grumbled at her and hung up.

She stopped into a bar, and let an older man buy her drinks. She slammed them down, not even tasting the liquor, just feeling the scalding as it sloshed down her throat and chest. Her mind became a foggy, dark place, and she ranted about the evils of DHS and the foster woman and fake judges and fake lawyers who stood by and did nothing, and the man buying her drinks looked at her like she was crazy and moved to a different stool. Her head was tired and she rested it on the bar and everything went dark.

Eventually, the bartender woke her up, shaking her shoulders. He ushered her out, telling her it was time to go home. She stumbled outside and puked in the nearby bushes. She hated drinking. It made her ill. She wandered around, her hands in her pockets, not feeling like going home. She could go anywhere now, she realized bitterly. She didn't have any children to watch.

She found a token in the bottom of her purse and hopped on the trolley. She stared at the window, but it was dark, so mostly she saw her own reflection. She was struck by how young she looked. She felt like she was a million years old.

"Brittney!"

Brittney turned to see Trinity smiling, a soft leather briefcase slung over her shoulder.

"Where have you been? I've been calling you for ages."

Trinity slipped into the seat next to her, and she smelled like vanilla and baby oil. She was wearing a structured black jacket and pegged pants, things she had probably made herself.

Brittney looked back out the window.

"What's wrong, girl?"

"DHS took the kids."

"Shit, you serious? Why? What happened?"

Brittney sighed, sick of the story. "Because I went out when they were sleepin', to get away from the crying, and my crazy neighbor called 'em. I was only gone for an hour."

"Really? Brittney, that's horrible." Trinity pulled her bag close to her chest. "What can I do?"

Brittney turned toward her, and felt a dim flicker of hope, imagining her cousin with the kids. "You could take the kids. They would let you have them."

Trinity looked startled. Then she blew out a long breath of air, her eyes lowered with guilt.

"I would, Brit. But I've got school and work, and a one-bedroom," she said quietly. "I wouldn't know how …."

Brittney shrugged and turned back toward the window.

"I'm sorry, Brit. What do you have to do to get 'em back?" Trinity's hand was wrapped around Brittney's bicep, pulling her closer. "There has to be something I can do."

There was nothing. Brittney was supposed to go to dozens of appointments and hold down a job at the same time, and there didn't seem to be a way to do both. She had called the Better Parenting Center and asked to schedule her appointments every two weeks, to accommodate her changing work schedule, and the receptionist had laughed at her and said, "Honey, we don't do that. The classes are the same time every week. If you miss one, you have to start the 10-week series over from the beginning."

Brittney rubbed her eyes, reclining into her cousin, feeling the warmth of her arm. She asked Trinity how her boyfriend was.

"Brittney…" Trinity said somberly. "Seriously, how can I help? Do you need money? I have a few hundred saved up. You can borrow it."

"That's not enough," Brittney said brusquely, anger leaking into her tone. It wouldn't hire a real lawyer, or pay her rent for months. "Tell me about Kai."

169

Trinity sighed, leaning her head on Brittney's shoulder. "He's good," she whispered. "He's taking me to New York for my birthday."

Brittney nodded. She wasn't even jealous. It seemed insignificant. Trinity talked about the clothes she was designing for school, and Brittney let her prattle on, nodding her head, not really listening. She didn't care. Trinity stood at her stop, kissing Brittney's cheek, promising she would stop by the apartment.

Brittney was tired, but she still didn't want to go home. She rode the trolley, back and forth, back and forth, through the city.

She knew she had to find a way to get depression and alcohol counseling, and take parenting classes, but the caseworker wouldn't help her—she just kept insisting she find a job with flexible hours, as if it were that easy.

Brittney had gone to three counseling sessions—the therapist prodded her to admit she was addicted to alcohol, and Brittney, stuffing down her pride, agreed she was—but she'd had to call in sick twice to do it. Her work had refused to reschedule her shift for the following week and she couldn't call in sick again without losing her job. So she had to cancel the fourth session. She couldn't make it to the seventh session, either, and, then the therapist refused to see her again, claiming, with all her cancellations, she wasn't "serious about reforming." The caseworker notified Brittney, in a schoolmarm tone, that this "failure to cooperate" would be held against her.

So she had fallen even farther behind, and even though she hated herself for it, it was just easier to get stoned and try not to think about how she was failing, failing, failing, and there was no way out.

She called dozens of numbers, begging people to schedule the counseling sessions around her changing shift schedule, but the receptionists laughed or flatly denied her requests. She applied for overnight jobs, but her resume seemed to disappear into the ether. Only one manager called her for an interview. The hotel was downtown, and she walked into the grand lobby with its crystal chandelier and marble floor, her eyes red from smoking, her black pants scuffed from the subway, and she knew she wouldn't get the job. Even the housekeepers, in such a place, looked a certain way. They were neatly dressed, their straight hair drawn in tight buns.

Chris eventually showed up again, knocking on the door a random Tuesday night. Brittney was sitting on the couch, smoking a joint and watching reality TV. She let him in without a word.

He was carrying a big bag of cleaning supplies, the handle of a mop sticking out. He dropped it on a pile of trash. He pointed to her joint.

"Got another?"

She nodded, and went in the kitchen and rolled him one. Maybe it was because she was stoned, but she was in no hurry. She pinched the edges with her finger, and the paper crinkled loudly. Water dripped from a crack in the ceiling, splashing on the pile of plates. She walked into the living room, handed him the joint, and sat back on the couch.

He lit the joint, and plopped down next to her on the couch.

"How's the case going?" he asked, leaning back.

She closed her eyes and her dry lips stuck to the joint. "There's no way I can do all these fuckin' appointments."

"You got a lawyer?"

"She don't care. She has a hundred other clients, and she just says, 'you have to do your plan.'"

He seemed genuinely aggrieved. "Well, shit, what are we gonna do then?"

"I don't know, Chris."

Her tone was unemotional. She was trapped, and she didn't see a way out so she stoned herself to forget about being trapped.

"Fuck, we gotta think of somethin'."

"Why do you even care?" she lashed. "It ain't like you see the kids anyway."

He looked furious, and cursed under his breath. For a moment, she thought he might hit her. He picked up an empty bag on the coffee table and threw it at the TV.

"Shit, Brittney, I left 'em with their mother, not some crazy old lady!"

Anger ballooned through her complacency, and she stared at him. "Yeah, you left 'em with me to take care of 'em all by myself! That's how we got into this fucking mess!"

They were both breathing heavy, pissed at each other. The TV babbled in the background.

"How was I supposed to do it all alone?" she cried out.

"I don't know. Other moms do."

"Fuck," Chris said, taking a pull of his joint, "forget it. Let's not argue. Let's just clean this shithole up."

He took off his coat—the tan one with the fur collar—and took a few more puffs on the joint and then put it out on the plate Brittney had been using as an ashtray. He put his shirt on top of his coat. She kept smoking her joint, watching him. Her fingers were still trembling with fury. She was vaguely aware of how good he looked in his undershirt, and it annoyed her that she still noticed this.

He took trash bags out and started gathering the empty containers and moldy plates and papers and soda cans, tossing them into the big black bags. Her joint was only a stub and she reluctantly abandoned it on the plate. She grabbed one of the trash bags and started filling it. Fuck Chris, but she would at least clean this place up. That's something she could do.

There were fast food bags and chip bags and newspapers and every time she unearthed a plastic toy, she felt a little weepy, remembering Ethan or Madison playing with it.

Chris changed the channel to MTV, and they cleaned silently. Brittney wanted to ask him what had happened to him, and why, and how, but she didn't because he seemed far away from her. He was clearly still angry, his movements swift and aggressive, even though he had no right to be.

They filled ten bags of trash, and Chris carried them down

to the dumpster, taking two at a time. His steps pounded up and down the stairs. She gathered up the children's toys, tossing them in their baskets. *What happened to you?* She wanted to ask Chris. *How did you become just another deadbeat dad?* After the baskets were filled, she covered them with a yellowed blanket.

The door to the children's room was always closed. The few times she went in there, she sobbed, smelling their dirty clothes and even the old diapers she had never thrown out. One night, she had fallen asleep curled up in Ethan's toddler bed, and when she woke, her legs were stiff and cramped.

She put all the plates and silverware and pots in the kitchen, stacking them on the floor. She found the broom in the back of the closet, dusty and unused, and she swept the living room floor. Chris had finished throwing out the bags, and he nodded at her, sweat on his brow. He retrieved water from the kitchen, and mopped the living room floor, dragging the mop across the wood in wide strokes. She went in the kitchen and fixed herself another joint and sat down on the couch, curling up her legs, watching him finish the floor. The joint tasted bitter and burned her throat. Her throat was always burning.

Chris was intent, and his arms flexed attractively as he moved the mop.

She thought, maybe if he hadn't lost his job, he never would have left, and he would be here, helping her clean on his time off, while the children slept in their rooms.

"Chris...." she said, wondering.

He looked up at her, his hand wrapped around the mop handle, and there was a hardness there that hadn't been there before he'd left.

"Are you OK?" she asked, her voice breaking.

He was surprised, and for a second, there was uncertainty on his face, like maybe he wasn't OK, but then he just nodded, and finished mopping the floor.

He seemed like a stranger, even though he was the father of her children, even though she had once loved him more than herself, and that was the saddest thing, how easily people could break apart. How they could go from everything to practically nothing.

The couch was stained and had crumbs in its cushions, and there was still a vague smell of decay, but other than that, the living room looked as clean as it ever had. It had taken seven hours.

Chris put on his shirt and coat, and then plopped down on the couch, tired.

"You can sleep on the couch," she offered.

He glanced over, and reached out and squeezed her thigh. "Thanks, but I gotta go. We'll do the kitchen later."

She nodded, exhausted. She leaned back and closed her eyes, drifting away from consciousness. She felt him kiss her forehead and then leave. The empty air was stale in his wake, and she thought, *no, I won't fall asleep. I can do all of this. I can stop this from happening.*

She stood up, and brewed a pot of coffee in the kitchen. She wouldn't sleep until the apartment was sparkling. She filled eight more bags of trash, throwing out old cans and bags of takeout, stained dish towels, used diapers and plastic utensils. Then she hauled them all to the dumpster, tossing them in, knowing she looked like a crazy person, her cheeks sweaty and flushed.

It was quiet outside, and she stood still for a moment, and looked up at the handful of stars, thinking about her kids, asleep in their beds. They were only a few miles away but the distance felt like infinity.

She scrubbed the kitchen counters and sink until her fingers were red and raw, two of her nails peeled half off. Downing cups of coffee, she kept cleaning, as if a clean apartment would be enough to undo everything. *This is something I can do*, she told herself. *It's something.* Her biceps and forearms ached. The black mold in the tub wouldn't come off and she threw the sponge in the tub. It was clean enough. She had done it, made the apartment a nice place to live again.

~*~

Brittney was walking home from seeing her kids when she passed a box on the sidewalk, a FREE sign affixed to the side. She rummaged through it. Underneath some flowery dresses, she found a stack of half-used sketchbooks and charcoal pencils. She remembered, before Ethan was born, being curled up in a chair, sketching dresses and pants and skirts and jumpers, her fingers gliding across the page for hours, almost with a will of their own.

She stuffed the pads and pencils in her purse.

At first, her female forms were crude, their faces childish and round, their bodies misshapen. Her hands moved tentatively, and she wondered if she had, somehow, lost her ability to draw, to focus.

But after hundreds of sketches, her hand became quicker and more confident, and the women seemed, not real exactly, but beautiful and curvy. They were women with rounded hips and striking cheekbones. Their clothes were elaborate and sophisticated, the stitches and buttons meticulously detailed on their wool coats, the shine visible on their black boots.

She carried a sketchbook with her to work, and whenever she rode on the trolley, or had to go to an appointment, and she buried her head in the book, shielding herself from the world. The images appeared on the pages, as if from nowhere, and they gave her the feeling that something worthwhile might be etched out of her life.

She loved seeing the woman and her clothes form on the page, piece by piece, their styles and colors developing as she drew. Her mind was pleasantly empty, draining itself into these visions.

The sketchbooks accumulated on the nightstand next to her bed.

The caseworker asked, once, what was in them, and

Brittney crossed her arms and said nothing.

"You need to tell me," the caseworker insisted, her lips narrowing in a thin line.

"Why? What do they have to do with anythin'?"

The caseworker, a stocky woman, moved closer to the side table, as if she might open them herself. "They may go to your state of mind."

"They're just drawings," Brittney warned, positioning herself between the caseworker and the sketchbooks. She didn't want the woman to see what she'd done; she didn't want her to judge her drawings, too. The caseworker would find a way to twist it, to condemn it, and it would become tainted. It was the one thing in her life that wasn't.

The woman paused, and shrugged, as if she really didn't care after all, and went into the bathroom.

"You should clean this," she said. "The toilet is dirty."

Brittney sat on the bed, and spaced out as the caseworker criticized the tub and a smudge on the mirror. She noticed, in the corner of her eye, half a joint left on the windowsill. She dropped a sweater on top of it. The whole apartment smelled like pot.

The caseworker returned from the bathroom, and sighed. Brittney hated her snub nose and her boxy, almost masculine body. She wished she could punch her judgmental face, and, with the fury clenching her stomach, she understood how Chris had gotten into so many fights. How satisfying it would be to break that stubby nose.

"Have you made any progress on your goals?" the caseworker asked, her eyes returning to the sketchbooks.

The anger was so strong in Brittney's chest, she thought if she spoke, she could lash out violently, slamming the caseworker's head against the floor, demanding she return her children. She cursed under her breath, and, then, steadying herself, said, "I told you I need you to find me a therapist that will give me some flexibility. My job won't schedule my shift the same every week."

The caseworker nodded. "But you didn't go to the

appointments I scheduled for you. If you want to be a successful parent, you have to be able to juggle a job and appointments. That's part of life."

Brittney wrapped her fist around the bedspread, until her knuckles were yellow. "Not this many appointments, all at once. They are already letting me schedule around seeing my kids."

"Brittney, I want you to reach your goals. I really do. But I need you to do your part."

Brittney was afraid if she opened her mouth again, vile would spill out, words she couldn't take back.

"Well, I guess I'll be going, then," the caseworker announced, giving Brittney one last look of disappointment before heading out the door.

Brittney couldn't let this woman take her kids. She had to figure out how to beat the system, how to check every last box. She walked to the library, and signed onto a computer. The caseworker had told her about websites that listed jobs, and she searched for overnight ones. It took her twenty minutes to fill out each application. Overnight shift at a nursing home. Overnight shift at Wal-mart. Overnight shift at CVS. Overnight shift at Pancake Delight.

When she had applied for every overnight shift she might be qualified for, she felt better, like had done something. She prayed they would call her back, that she would get one of the gigs.

At home, she lay in her bed, and turned on her small light and pulled out her sketchbook. She drew ugly women that looked like her casework, their lips thin and wrinkled. She clothed them in shiny black jackets, pleated pants, and black boots. They waved briefcases and long pens threateningly. She titled the pieces *DHS caseworker*. Her fingers hurt from pressing down so hard.

Chapter Eleven

Rebecca

Rebecca and the children were waiting in the living room. The girls played happily, oblivious to the passage of time. Ethan sat at his table, drawing an imaginary map, with parking lots and schools and apartment buildings and police stations, asking Rebecca, every five minutes, "Where my mom?" She noticed, in his anger, he dropped apostrophe s's. She had to restrain herself from correcting him, from reminding him that wasn't the proper way to speak.

Madison glanced from her brother to Rebecca, a film of anxiety over her large eyes. Maggie ran around the room, laughing.

After a half an hour, Ethan started throwing toys at the wall, and shouting, "Why my mother ain't here?" looking at Rebecca, as if Rebecca had prevented his mother, somehow, from coming.

Nina called Brittney, her face impatient as the phone rang. "Please inform us if you can't come to a visit, Brittney," she said.

"God, I hate it when they just don't show like this," she said, slipping her phone back in her pocket.

Ethan stared at Nina, his eyes liquid and unreadable, and then he threw his crayons at her head. Nina ducked in surprise, and the crayon skimmed over her thick brown hair and hit the white wall, leaving a thin streak of purple.

Rebecca choked down a laugh—it was ridiculous and sad

and absurd. She wanted to hold Ethan, and tell him it would be OK. But she didn't because he would only shove her away. Annoyance billowed in her chest. Brittney could have at least called to cancel, so he wouldn't be waiting.

Nina shrugged, her mouth tilted down in resignation, as if there was something inevitable about mothers disappointing their children. She waved goodbye to the girls, who were transfixed by Ethan's rampage.

Rebecca heaved Madison on her hip, and walked Nina to the door.

"If she doesn't come to the visits, she's not going to get her kids back," Nina observed.

"Do you know what's going on?"

"You didn't hear it from me, but she's on D-R-U-G-S. Her place smells like pot all the time."

Rebecca's heart fluttered and she closed her eyes briefly. "Oh," was all she could muster. Maybe it was a lost cause, then. Rebecca couldn't pretend that was all bad news, that the thought of keeping the kids wasn't something she would welcome.

Rebecca closed the door and squeezed Madison, kissing her on the neck. *You're safe with me,* she thought. Madison clung to Rebecca's arm tentatively. "Eee-than upset," she said.

Rebecca nodded and rubbed her back. Maggie was pushing her grocery cart around the living room, adding items. It was quiet. Ethan must have run off to his room. Rebecca put Madison on the floor, handed her a beloved doll, and told her she'd be right back.

Madison nodded somberly, watching Maggie bumble around the living room.

"Mama! Mama! Mama!" Maggie squealed, holding up her plastic banana.

"Banana," Rebecca explained.

Maggie nodded, satisfied, and dropped it in her cart.

Ethan's bedroom door was closed and the room was quiet. Rebecca knocked softly. He didn't respond.

She waited a moment, and then entered. The room was

all his now. They had bought a Thomas the Tank Engine dresser and chair, and he was sitting on the floor, looking miserable.

"I need my mom," he pled, staring at the wall. Then he started crying, loud and uncontrollably.

She nestled in behind him, rocking his slender body, kissing his hair. His hair was clipped short, a military cut.

His mother had refused to allow them haircuts for six months, but after the caseworkers informed her that the knots were becoming heavy and painful, she relented. Rebecca took them to a local beauty salon. The stylist shook her head, announcing that the hair was so matted and knotty, it was best to cut off as much as possible. The girls were given short pixie cuts. As she was paying at the counter, Rebecca heard the stylists whispering something about "horrible mother, worst hair ever" but she gave a large tip anyway.

"Can I please have my mom?" Ethan blubbered through his sobs.

"Oh, Ethan," she said, wishing there was something she could do. "I'll try to get her here."

He squeezed her forearms until they hurt. His nails dug into her skin.

She rocked him back and forth more urgently, shushing him.

He let go of her arms, and twisted around, to face her. "You're nice Rebecca and your house is nice but I need my mom."

"I know."

"She's all alone. My dad ain't there anymore. The girls ain't there anymore. It's just her. She needs me."

She nodded, not sure what to say. She didn't want to make promises she couldn't keep. "I understand. I'll see what I can do," she said softly, even though she thought, *what can I do?*

Part of her felt annoyed, like he was interfering with her life with the girls.

He climbed into his bed. "I'm gonna look at some books for a while."

He picked up the book she had gotten him on foster care. It

180

was about mouse children who stayed with another family for a while. The pages were wrinkled from heavy use.

She closed his door, and walked down the stairs, not wanting to leave the girls alone too long.

She looked at the girls, playing happily on the floor, and thought, they are happy and healthy here. She didn't really want their drug-addicted mother coming around.

Maggie ran across the room, and slammed into Rebecca. "Mama, mama," she squealed. Mama was her only word. Her breath was warm and sweet on Rebecca's shin, and, for a moment, Rebecca felt a sharp pang of satisfaction. She was a mother. She was doing it.

Then she thought of Ethan, alone in his room, leafing through his book on foster care, longing for Brittney. The last time Brittney had visited, Brittney had glanced over her shoulder as she was leaving, and her eyes and mouth had been forlorn, her body hunched inward. The expression on her face had felt familiar to Rebecca, and she had almost called out to Brittney to wait. But no words had come out of Rebecca's mouth, and Brittney had closed the door. Rebecca considered Brittney's expression, wondering why it felt so familiar. There had been no anger or irritation on her face. There had only been the sorrow of living in an unbending world, a world that refused you the very thing you were made for.

Rebecca realized she had worn this expression for years, after another futile argument with Will, thinking, despite all her efforts and desires, she would never have a child, at least not with her marriage, that it was one or the other, no matter how much she wanted it to be otherwise.

That night, after she put the children to bed, Rebecca sat on the couch, and called the DHS caseworker, determined to learn something.

"Is there some other way we could get Brittney to come to her visits?" she asked.

Katie crunched on some kind of food. "We could try switching the visits to the office. But I'm not sure that would make her show up more."

Rebecca didn't want to drag the children to a sterile gray office, and have more caseworkers bothering them, questioning them, reminding them they were not normal. And reminding Ethan his mother was supposed to be there, but had chosen not to be.

"Do you know why she isn't coming to the visits?"

"Not really. I encourage her to go."

"OK," Rebecca said. She wished she had Brittney's file, to understand what was happening. She felt like she was in the dark, and without more information, she was grappling blindly, struggling to know what to feel or do. "Can you explain her situation to me?"

"The children seem like they're doing well with you," Katie observed, ignoring Rebecca's question, taking another crunch out of something. "It's good they have you."

"Yes, they are...." *But Ethan*, she thought.

"Great. Call me if you need anything else."

The phone disconnected, and Rebecca stared at it, dissatisfied. DHS was like a black box; she was on one side of it and Brittney was on the other.

~*~

They were eating dinner in the kitchen—spaghetti and meatballs the girls had helped her cook—when the phone rang. Rebecca rose from the table, and picked it up.

"Hello."

"Ethan, please," a raspy, female voice mumbled.

It took Rebecca a moment to place the voice as Brittney's. She sounded stoned, and for a moment, Rebecca was angry at her, for not pulling herself together.

Rebecca glanced over at the children. Madison and Maggie were strapped into highchairs that attached to the table, and Ethan was inhaling his spaghetti.

182

Rebecca walked into the living room.

"Ethan misses you," she said.

There was a long silence, and Rebecca could hear Brittney breathing slowly and heavily.

"He really wants to see you. All the children do," she tried again.

There was no still no response, but Brittney hadn't disconnected.

"Do you need help getting here?"

Brittney laughed, and the laugh seemed malicious, like an indictment. The laugh eventually morphed into something more hopeless. Then the phone was quiet again. Rebecca stared at the pulleys and chains and buckets on Ethan's table. They were part of a kit, and he was building a contraption that would pour water into a cup.

"I want to talk to Ethan," Brittney said, and her voice was trembling.

Rebecca was not sure if Brittney was about to cry, or if she was angry. She searched for the right words *Let me help you I know pain why aren't you visiting anymore what's going on.* But nothing sounded right.

"OK," she said finally.

Ethan was shoveling the last of the spaghetti into his mouth, and Maggie's face and bib were plastered with sauce and tiny pieces of pasta.

Rebecca held the phone out to Ethan. "It's your mom."

"Hi, Mama!" Madison called, happily twirling her pasta on her fork.

Ethan glanced at his sister with annoyance and grabbed the phone, smudging it with tomato sauce. "Hello?"

He leapt off his chair and walked out of the kitchen. The door swung shut behind him. Rebecca leaned over and wiped Maggie's face with a damp washcloth.

"No you can't! You can't! You can't!" Ethan shouted, the volume slightly muffled by the closed door.

Rebecca patted Madison on the head and then walked to

the kitchen door, and opened it a few inches.

Ethan was pacing in the living room, the phone to his ear.

"I wanna go too! I don't wanna stay here! I want you!"

He stood still as he shouted, bouncing on his heels, his free hand flailing in the air. "Why?" he cried into the phone. "Why?"

Abruptly, he threw the phone on the floor, and it bounced underneath the couch. He ran to the front door, and Rebecca ran after him. He jiggled with the child lock, but he was dexterous enough to open it, and he ran outside before she could reach him.

"Ethan!" she shouted.

He didn't turn around, just kept running onto the sidewalk, toward Baltimore Avenue. She wasn't wearing shoes, and she stubbed her toe, howling in pain.

A man on the sidewalk looked at her, and then at Ethan. "Hey, kid, you OK?" he called as Ethan shot by him.

The girls were locked into their highchairs, but she couldn't leave them alone.

"Thanks," she muttered to the man, who was standing there dumbly with his small dog.

She was out of breath and Ethan was still running. *He's only five*, she thought, *how can he be outrunning me?* But then his footsteps slowed down, and he took a right, and darted into an alley. It was lined with garages and he was leaning against one, his chest rising and falling.

"We have to go back," she called, stopping three feet away from him. The blood from her toe was spreading across her white sock.

"No!" he shouted. "I'm goin' to find my mom! I'm goin' home! I'm sick of this."

She pushed her hair back from her face, and she wanted to say, "You're only five! You can't do that." But she took a deep breath and said, because he loved them so, "Your sisters need you."

He closed his eyes and she walked over to him and put her hand on his shoulder. She considered asking him what his mother had told him, but she didn't want him to run off again.

She could feel the tension in his shoulders, his desire to keep running, so she said, even though she knew it was wrong, and maybe illegal, "We'll go see her."

"Now," he emphasized, waiting for her agreement. The amber flecks in his eyes glowed with expectation. His skin was smooth and she touched his cheek and nodded.

They walked back to the house quickly, her hobbling a bit on her foot, him grabbing her hand and tugging. His hand was small and sweaty but it was hard and firm, too. It was a boy's hand, not a baby's. She wished, for a moment, she had received him as a baby, so she could have held him in her arms, and shielded him from all this heartache and loss.

The girls were covered in the rest of their spaghetti and their glasses had been knocked to the floor. Madison's eyes were anxious; Maggie's were antsy, flittering around for something else to do. She was slamming her plate on the table. Rebecca cleaned the girls the best she could, picking the chunks of pasta out of their braids and wiping their faces and hands with a damp washcloth. She was thinking she didn't know where Brittney lived, and Ethan might not either.

"Do you know your mom's address?" she asked Ethan. He was watching her clean the girls, and he paused, his eyebrows raised in concentration.

"Sixty-two and Woodlawn," he said proudly.

She nodded, disappointed. It took her a while to bandage up her foot and buckle the girls in their car seats and Ethan in his booster. The sun was starting to set as she drove southwest, toward Woodlawn. Maggie cried, annoyed at being strapped in her seat. They passed housing projects, and blocks with boarded-up houses and Check Cashing stores and crowded corner stores and nail salons. The humid air seemed to shimmer, and lingering over everything was the possibility of violence.

She glanced in the rearview mirror. Ethan was leaning against the side of his seat, staring out the window, his hand on the glass.

She pulled over near the intersection, and realized, too late, she had forgotten the stroller and the carrier. She managed to heave Maggie on one hip and Madison on the other, her back protesting under the weight. Ethan looked around, confused, and then nodded at a building and started walking toward it. The weather was warm, and people were outside on their porches and in front of the stores, congregating.

Ethan led them to a brick apartment building. It was plain, a big box with cheap windows. The front door buzzer was broken and they walked right in. Madison was too heavy on her right hip, and she was sliding down. As soon as Ethan turned down the fourth floor hallway, she put Madison to the ground, and her arms and shoulders throbbed.

Madison ran to catch her brother. He was knocking on a door, shouting, "Mom! Mom!"

Rebecca walked over to them.

"Brittney!" she called, knocking on the door.

There were no sounds coming from the apartment. Rebecca was relieved. It was easier this way.

Ethan continued pounding on the door with his fists. Rebecca put her hand on his shoulder lightly. He sat down on the frayed welcome mat and rubbed his temples.

"She's not home," he said, and his face was sad and incredulous.

A young woman came down the hall, carrying two grocery bags. She wore tight jeans and a yellow t-shirt with a blue logo on the front. Rebecca nodded at her, and the woman looked away.

She dropped her bags near the door adjacent to Brittney's and rummaged in her purse, pulling out the keys.

"Have you seen Brittney?" Rebecca asked.

The woman sighed and pointed at the girls, running in circles. "Those her kids?"

Rebecca nodded.

"You givin' 'em back?"

Rebecca shook her head. "We're just here to visit."

"Haven't seen her. But like I told the other lady, she's crazy and can't take care of those kids for shit. I even gave that lady a note of Brittney saying so herself, that she couldn't handle it."

"My mom's not crazy!" Ethan shouted, leaping to his feet. His eyebrows were raised in anger and he was panting.

The woman was startled, but then her face settled into understanding, like she expected Brittney's children would be crazy, too.

"She neglected those kids. They were cryin' all the time," the woman said to Rebecca, shaking her head. She grabbed her grocery bags and pulled them inside. The door slammed close.

Rebecca reached out to Ethan, but he yanked away, running to the woman's door.

"You liar!" he shouted, banging his fists against the wood.

"Ethan, I know you're upset, but you cannot use that language."

"Fuck you! I want my mom!"

Rebecca closed her eyes, and she was grateful the girls had drifted down the hall. She thought about the neighbor's confirmation of Brittney's neglect. She shouldn't be here. The other day, she had seen something of herself in Brittney, a glint of recognition, but did she really know what Brittney had done? Or what she was capable of doing?

Madison was running back, her arms outstretched, and Rebecca lifted her up, kissing her on the cheek.

"Ethan," she said, trying to sound calm, even though she felt frazzled and overwhelmed, "your mom isn't here. We should leave."

"No! You can't tell me what to do. You're not my mom!"

He stood in front of her mother's door, his feet planted. "I'm stayin'. You guys go."

Rebecca couldn't physically force him outside. She could call for help from the caseworkers, but she was afraid the caseworkers would take the children away from her. She wasn't supposed to bring the children here. It was a violation of the rules. It might even be illegal.

She sat down across from Ethan, with Madison in her lap, and watched him. He was only five. He would grow bored waiting, or Brittney would come home. The floor was concrete and the lights were fluorescent. *The children had lived here, once*, she thought, running her fingers over the grooves in the concrete, noting the little piles of chipped paint, probably full of lead.

After a while, the girls became restless, kicking the walls and tugging at one another, falling in a giggly heap, and she led them downstairs to play outside. There were a few bushes lining the path, and Rebecca sighed as Maggie picked up an empty beer can, and brought it to her mouth.

"Not in your mouth," she said gently, taking it from her. Maggie laughed and scurried back in the bushes.

Let it go, Rebecca told herself, *let it go. It's only one night.*

The sun had set and the girls needed to go to bed, but there was no sign of Brittney. The neighborhood didn't feel right. Beat up cars drove by with dark windows. Rebecca sat on the steps and cradled her chin.

People came and went into the building, throwing her curious looks. But no one said anything. Maggie waved, and some of them waved back. Madison dug a hole in the mulch, her lovely face steady and intent.

Eventually, Maggie darted to the street, and Rebecca ran after her, grabbing her collar.

"Booboooboo," she screamed, kicking and thrashing. Rebecca scooped her up, stressed by the cries, by the judgmental look of a woman passing by.

She shepherded Madison back inside, Maggie still screaming in her arms, telling the girls it was time to find Ethan. They slowly climbed the steps, Madison taking one step at a time, Maggie swinging her fists at Rebecca's chest.

The fourth floor hall was empty. Rebecca had a moment of wild panic, of fear she had lost Ethan. She walked quickly to Brittney's apartment, her temples aching. Had Brittney come in another way? She couldn't think about how if something had happened to him she would lose everything: him, the girls, her chance to be a mother.

The door was slightly ajar, and she pushed it open, calling, a little desperately, "Ethan!"

The door opened to a yellowed kitchen and it was musty, a gray residue covering all the surfaces. The floor and counters seemed to be wiped clean, but they were cracked and discolored with age. The place smelled of weed, and of something dank.

She remembered how different it had been, at first, living in a hut with the Noboso, the strange smells of the natural oils and the rough textures of the clothes, and she tried to see the apartment, the whole neighborhood that way: just different, not worse.

"Ethan!" she called again.

She ran through the kitchen, and entered the living room. The girls were squealing beside her, laughing, and she tried to smile for their sake. She didn't want to frighten them. A ratty lime green couch faced a large TV. Rebecca opened an interior door. There was a crib and a toddler bed. White paint had peeled off one of the walls, and was littered across the carpet. Madison and Ethan's old room.

Madison and Maggie were pushing the flimsy kitchen chairs into the living room, laughing hysterically in their overtired state. Rebecca opened the other interior door.

Ethan was lying on a queen-sized bed, curled around a pillow.

Thank god, Rebecca thought.

She walked closer—sidestepping a small pile of dirty clothes—and saw his eyes were closed and his chest was rising and falling in a steady rhythm.

"You really scared me," she whispered, lightly touching his back.

Rebecca looked around the bedroom. A stack of sketchbooks and pencils were piled on the bedside table. There was only one photo, in a cheap black frame on the dresser. Rebecca picked it up. The photo showed Brittney and Ethan and

Madison. A man had clearly been cut out—his disembodied arm, long and athletic, was slung over Brittney's shoulder. He had a muscular hand.

Brittney was wearing a tight fuchsia t-shirt and dark jeans. Her face was tilted slightly to the side and she was smiling. She looked happy. Healthy. Ethan was standing, leaning into his mother, and he was flashing a handsome grin. Madison was in Brittney's lap, and her hand was reaching off to her right, to touch the man's leg. She was laughing, her eyes free from anxiety.

What had happened?

Maybe nothing, she realized. Maybe the photo was a kind of fabrication, a projection of how they had wanted things to be. Maybe underneath their clothes, the children were dirty and bruised, and maybe the man had taken off the moment after the photo was taken. How could she know?

She put the photo back on the dresser, and picked up one of the sketchbooks. The sketches took her breath away. Because they were actually good, something one might expect to see from a professional designer. And there were hundreds of them. She couldn't reconcile this with everything else she knew about Brittney.

She found a drawing she especially liked, of a woman wearing a rainbow colored sheath dress, her body strong and curvy. She glanced over her shoulder, and then, very carefully, ripped it out of the book. It seemed important to have, like it was evidence of something. She folded the paper over, and slipped it in her purse. There were frayed edges on the seam of the sketchbook, where the paper had torn, and she pulled them out, one by one.

She put the sketchbook back on the table and turned to Ethan. His mother's pillow was in his grip, and he seemed younger in repose. His hands were still a little chubby. His cheeks were soft. She leaned down and kissed him gently on the cheek and then she walked into the living room. The girls were throwing a small blue ball around the room, and Rebecca knew she should wake Ethan and take them all home, but she was reluctant to disturb him.

She was breaking a dozen rules just being in the apartment, and if Brittney came home and reported her, she could lose the children and her license to foster. So of course it was stupid to stay. But Ethan seemed to need to be here. And the sketches, with their elegance and beauty, calmed some of her fears. Such beauty couldn't come from nothing. Maybe she could form a relationship with Brittney.

"Mama!" Maggie called, throwing the ball at her.

Rebecca caught the ball and smiled softly. She herded the girls into the bedroom. She would let them sleep a few hours. The sheets were dusty, and this gave her pause. Madison jumped on the bed.

"Ethan's bed!" she grinned, rocking back and forth. Then she yawned, her mouth opening wide, her big eyes squinting.

"Let's take a little rest," Rebecca decided, helping Madison into the bed, pulling up the blanket.

"Ethan's bed," she repeated.

"You can use it for tonight."

"I can use it," she agreed, leaning back and closing her eyes.

It was way past their bedtimes. Maggie screeched and ran out of the bedroom, laughing, and Rebecca had to chase her down and corral her into the crib. She had left the diapers in the car, but luckily she found one of Madison's old ones, underneath the crib.

"Bobobobobo," Maggie whined as Rebecca changed her diaper, and then turned out the light.

"Night night," Rebecca whispered, patting her on the back.

Rebecca closed the door, and Maggie cried for a few minutes, but then fell silent.

There was a large screen TV in the living room, but Rebecca felt too antsy to sit still. She looked around at the smudged surfaces and decided to clean.

In the kitchen, there was a sponge and a generic green

cleaner under the sink, and she began scrubbing the kitchen counters. She scrubbed as hard as she could, back and forth, back and forth, but the smudges weren't coming off. They remained there, dark and stubborn, like they were permanent. Still, she kept scrubbing, until sweat dotted her forehead.

Surveying her work, she sighed. It looked the same. The dirt was embedded in the cheap materials. It was the type of surface that would never look clean.

She returned to the cabinets underneath the kitchen sink, to see what other supplies were available. There was a yellow dish liquid and a crusted sponge. That wouldn't do much. She checked the cabinets, and found a few cans of beans and a small bag of marijuana, but no more cleaning supplies.

She moved to the living room, and wiped down the coffee table, and then the top of a cabinet. Nothing came off. After the water dried, it looked exactly the same. Giving up, she washed her hands with the dish soap, until her hands were pink.

She wiped her brow and leaned against the kitchen counter, thinking about the bag of marijuana. She was tempted to throw it out. She had never thought of pot as a bad drug. She had a few colleagues at Penn who smoked regularly, and they were brilliant and prolific writers. But it seemed different with Brittney, like it had impeded her. For Ethan's sake, for all the children's sake, Rebecca wanted Brittney to pull herself together, to put her life in order.

It was after 1 a.m., and she wondered where Brittney was. Maybe she was at a bar, or a boyfriend's.

The couch smelled of stale body odor and marijuana, but Rebecca was tired and it was the only place to lie down. She knew she should leave. But moving three sleeping children to the car by herself, in the darkness of night, seemed like a bad idea. Didn't almost all rapes and muggings occur after the sun had gone down? She couldn't forgive herself if she put the children in danger. They had lived through enough.

So she lay there, too anxious to fall asleep, trying to motivate herself, and time passed and she did nothing. Then the door clattered open, and she panicked. She bolted up. Brittney was standing in the kitchen, rubbing her eyes.

"What the fuck …." she said softly, staring at Rebecca's purse.

Brittney shook her head and walked into the living room.

Brittney stared at Rebecca, her eyes bloodshot.

"What are you doing here?" she asked, her tone tired and flat.

Rebecca straightened, and she thought of Brittney's drawings, how beautiful they had been. "Ethan wanted to see you. He misses you."

Brittney nodded, as if this made sense, and she sat on the floor, against the wall. She folded her hands in her lap.

"He fell asleep in your bed."

Brittney rubbed her eyes with the back of her hands. "OK. I'm going to sleep with him," she announced, pulling herself up. Her motions were slow and heavy. She was wearing a uniform— a blue polo and black pants and a nametag—and she wiped her hands on her pants. Outside the bedroom door, she stopped and stared at Rebecca from across the room.

"You know the children ain't yours, right?"

The sharp tone in her voice bothered Rebecca, and she thought, *why don't you visit them, then?* But she didn't say this because she wasn't supposed to be here, and she didn't want to start an altercation.

Brittney waited a few minutes, rocking on her heels, and Rebecca didn't say anything, because she didn't know what she could say.

"How can you just steal my kids?" Brittney asked, her voice taking on a more abrasive tone.

Rebecca closed her eyes and steadied herself. "I'm not trying to. I'm just taking care of them. I brought them over to see you."

"Yeah to *see* me! They're my fucking kids! I shouldn't have to visit 'em!"

"OK," she said, and she could hear the primness, the

skepticism in her own voice. It wasn't how she wanted to sound. This wasn't what she wanted to talk about. "If you do your family service plan, you'll get the kids back."

Brittney stared at her incredulously and then laughed. She laughed so hard she bent over at the waist. The laugh petered out, becoming bitter, and she walked over to the couch, standing near the arm. "Do you really believe it's like that?"

Rebecca shifted. "That's what Katie and Nina told me."

"The plan's impossible. I'm supposed to hold down a job, but somehow go to parenting classes and therapy and drug counseling and visit my children twice a week. I can't get a job like that. My job schedule changes every two weeks.

"And if I lose my job, I can't keep this apartment for long. I need an apartment to get the kids back."

She started crying, her eyes closed, her chest heaving.

"I'm sorry. I didn't know," Rebecca said, feeling for Brittney, for the desperation in her voice. Maybe what Brittney said was true, maybe the DHS requirements were unrealistic. Rebecca had never found them particularly competent. "Brittney..."

Brittney wiped her nose on her forearm and then turned around and walked into the bedroom, gently closing the door.

Rebecca stared at the closed door, blinking uncertainly. She turned off the lights and walked into the kitchen. She splashed water on her face. A small gray figure darted out from behind the oven, and she jumped backwards.

Before she went to bed, she opened the bedroom door a few inches. Brittney was spooning Ethan, her eyes closed, and he was clutching her hand. His face was content.

Rebecca wondered if Brittney might run off with the children in the middle of the night, boarding them on a bus, but after a half an hour of fretting, she fell asleep on the couch, her arms protectively across her chest.

When she woke up to the sound of the girls jabbering, her shoulders ached slightly. The living room seemed smaller in the pale morning light. Rebecca stretched and then walked into the children's bedroom.

The bedroom smelled musty, but the girls were oblivious, laughing and talking to one another. Madison had given Maggie a bunch of blocks to stack in her crib. Rebecca lifted Maggie out of the crib and put her on the floor, and she realized she didn't have any milk. In her purse, she found organic fruit snacks and she passed them to the girls. They took them eagerly and ran out to the living room.

Ethan and Brittney were sitting next to one another on the couch, both still in their clothes from the night before. Ethan's hand was resting on his mother's thigh.

Madison waved to her mother. "Hi, Mama!"

Brittney waved back, but her face was still. She seemed tired. Rebecca stood awkwardly in front of the couch. They all needed to change their clothes and eat breakfast and Maggie needed her milk and a new diaper.

"We should head back to the house soon. Do you want to come with us?"

Brittney stared blankly ahead, and Rebecca wondered if she had reverted to the silent treatment. "I can't," she finally said, not looking at Rebecca. "I got to work this morning."

She stood up and walked into the kitchen. Ethan chased after her.

"Why can't you come, mom?" Rebecca heard him ask.

"I gotta work," she snapped.

A glass shattered, and then another one. Brittney cursed at Ethan, telling him to knock it off.

"I HATE YOU! YOU'RE ALWAYS GONE!"

Ethan ran out of the kitchen and through the living room and into the bedroom.

Madison started crying, and Rebecca assured her it was OK, Ethan was just upset, and it was OK to get upset. She stroked Madison's head and her back, and then, reluctantly, walked away.

That was the difficulty of having three children; you sometimes had to choose one over the other.

Ethan was sprawled on the bed, his head in the pillow,

crying.

Rebecca sat next to him and rubbed his back, and he rolled over, as if she had touched him with a live wire.

"Just leave!"

"I love you, Ethan," she whispered, as she stood up. Her eyes fell on the pile of sketchbooks. "Your mother loves you, too."

He glared at her skeptically, and she waited for him to soften, but when he didn't, she walked to the edge of the room.

"We love you," she repeated, and then closed the door.

The girls were playing with the blocks from the children's room, and Rebecca walked into the kitchen. The broken plates were in a pile on the floor, and Rebecca stepped carefully to avoid the shards. Brittney was sitting at the table, drinking coffee.

Rebecca sat across from her.

Brittney sighed, and rubbed her forehead. "He don't get it. I have to work at eleven. I can't lose this job."

"He misses you."

"I know," she said, standing up. "I miss him, too." She opened one of the kitchen cabinets, and rummaged around, pulling out a loose piece of paper. She handed it to Rebecca.

"Give this to him, OK?"

It was a sketch of Brittney and Ethan. He was sitting on her lap, and they were both smiling. In the corner, she had written, "I love you, Ethan. Mommy."

"It's beautiful. You're very talented."

Brittney shrugged.

"He's good at drawing, too, you know."

"Yeah, I know." Brittney closed her eyes again, and scratched her face. She looked like she wanted to scream. But her voice, when she spoke, was level. "DHS never wanted to give me the kids back and they ain't going to ...."

She turned away and walked over to the cabinet and started rolling a joint. Her blue polo was untucked and ruffled, and her arms seemed to be trembling slightly. Rebecca wanted to walk over and comfort her, assure her, but she sensed this wouldn't be welcomed and maybe it wasn't even true.

"Look," Brittney said, "even when Ethan is upset, he loves jokes. That's what will get him out of his funk. The cornier, the better."

"OK," Rebecca said, "thank you. I'll try that."

"And Madison, when she's shy with new people, if you tug on her pinkie finger, it usually gets her to open up. I'm not sure why it works, but it does."

"OK. Thank you. Brittney, just call me when you want to come over. It doesn't have to be the assigned times. I can be flexible."

Brittney didn't say anything. She lit her joint with a lighter, and took a puff, still facing the kitchen cabinets. Then she tossed it in the sink and ran the water over it.

"I can come pick you up, too," Rebecca said, brushing her hair back from her face.

Brittney still didn't turn around, but she said, so softly Rebecca could barely hear, "Thank you. That sounds good."

Rebecca walked into the other room and rounded up the children. Madison and Maggie smiled and ran circles around her, happy to go home. Ethan followed her without a word, his eyelids lowered, his mouth drawn.

Madison ran over to her mother and hugged her leg. "Bye, mama," she said.

"Bye, baby girl," Brittney said, rubbing her head. "Bye, Ethan."

Ethan turned away, and Rebecca fought the urge to tell him to say something, to say anything.

Later that night, after the children had gone to bed, Rebecca poured herself a glass of wine and unrolled Brittney's drawing of the woman in the rainbow dress on the kitchen table. It was beautiful, the way the bright colors contrasted, the way the woman's body gently curved. To fill all those sketchbooks, a dozen of them, Brittney had to have been focused and diligent. She had seemed so sincere in her frustration with DHS. Something about the whole situation seemed off, or out of order.

She remembered her mother and Elizabeth's advice—*don't*

get involved with the mother, just take care of the children, that's your job, you don't know the full story—and she folded up the drawing, and slid it in a drawer, reminding herself if Brittney won, she would lose. They couldn't both keep the children.

Chapter Twelve

Brittney

Brittney brought her children presents from the Dollar General, trinkets and balls and action figures and shiny necklaces. The girls would turn them over in their hands, and then put them down, disinterested. Only Ethan appreciated the little gifts, and he clung to them, rubbing them with his fingers, not wanting to let them go. He didn't play with them, though, as far as she could tell. And why would he? The foster woman's house was like a toy store, stocked with complicated gadgets, cars, and construction vehicles.

She wanted to parent her own children—provide for them, teach them—but she wasn't even allowed to be alone with them. How can you parent with women leaning over your shoulder, hectoring you? At one of the visits, she tried to change Maggie's diaper, and Maggie screeched and rolled on the table, refusing to stay still. Brittney could feel the caseworkers and the foster woman judging her, thinking she was incompetent. Katie hovered, her breath on Brittney's neck, "Be gentle with her, Brittney. Try to engage her. Talk to her. Just tell her what you're doing."

But Maggie had never bonded with Brittney. In the apartment, she had tried everything, and, now, she was only allowed to see Maggie four hours a week. How was that enough to make Maggie love her?

She held Maggie's stomach down, shushing her. Maggie

screamed and kicked at her hands. Brittney's face burned in frustration. She couldn't stand the shrieks and the feel of Katie pressing against her arm, not giving her any space. She lifted Maggie and put her back on the floor.

"Don't just give up," Katie said. "She needs a new diaper. You can do this."

Brittney sat on the floor near Madison. She was building a zoo with stuffed animals, and Brittney picked up the horse.

"Neigh," she said, lifting her nose in the air.

Madison laughed. "Oink, oink," Madison said, wiggling the pink pig.

The foster woman scooped Maggie up, and Maggie played with a board book, content, as the foster woman changed her diaper. Brittney was mortified; she felt like a terrible, incapable mother.

She had to get away. She crawled into a large pink teepee, another new toy. Ethan scrambled in after her, holding a book about cars. He sat in her lap, his long legs sprawled. Quietly, she read to him.

"Mama!" she heard Maggie squeal. "Mama!"

Brittney knew she was referring to the foster woman, not her, and the air she was breathing felt thin and sharp in her chest. Ethan turned to face her, and she forced a contorted smile.

"It doesn't mean anything," he whispered. "She's just a baby. She doesn't know any better."

Brittney stroked his scalp. His hair was short and prickly. "Oh, Ethan," she said wistfully. "You're so smart, you know, that?"

He pulled her arms tighter around his stomach. "Keep reading," he urged.

She smiled, and turned the page, reading about different types of cars, and their engines. It felt good to have the weight of his small body against her own, to have his hair tickling her chin, his hands resting on her forearms.

"Mom," Ethan interrupted, turning back to her, "When are we gonna be able to go home?"

"I don't know, baby. They won't tell me anything."

Katie stuck her broad, pale face into the teepee. "It's six o'clock."

Brittney didn't want to leave. Why couldn't she just stay here, in the teepee, reading to her son?

"The visit's over for today," Katie said, her tone striving for neutrality, but sounding annoyed.

Brittney kissed Ethan, and then crawled out. Madison ran over and squeezed her legs.

"I love you, baby," Brittney whispered in her ear, and then she released her. She walked out the door, not bothering to say a word to the caseworker.

She rushed home to smoke, wanting to numb herself, to erase the pain of having to leave the children in another woman's house, again.

She put the photo of her children face down on the dresser. She couldn't stand the reminder. She went outside, and hopped on the bus downtown, sitting in the window seat. She sketched and looked out the window. Neighborhoods passed by: downtown skyscrapers, tall and blue, circled by people in business suits; in Old City, brick townhomes lined cobblestone streets; loud crowds stumbled out of the South Street bars, their motorcycles roaring. There were so many different types of people and places, and as she stared, she thought, *why am I me? why couldn't I have been someone else?*

She got off the bus miles from her apartment, determined to trudge back across the city. The steady movements of her arms and legs felt good, almost purposeful.

She stopped at Rittenhouse Square, drawn to the green grass, and sat on a wood bench. Sycamore and oak trees lined the pathway, their leaves rustling in the wind.

The roofs of the residential buildings surrounding the Square mingled with the dark sky. Some of the windows were lit up, like glowing boxes. The restaurants on the ground floor were packed with people, and when the doors opened, the sound of dozens of people talking and laughing drifted into the night air.

The chatter was gentle, welcoming almost, but as Brittney's high wore off, the sound became mocking, reminding her how other people were congregating in the warm light, eating expensive food, and she was sitting on a bench in the dark, all alone. A homeless man was loitering nearby, rummaging in the trash can. The back of her ankles were sore.

She reached in her purse for another joint, and lit it. She walked away from the Square, inhaling deeply, not wanting to run into a cop. It was a quiet night, and she stayed close to the buildings on Walnut Street, scanning the people coming toward her. Her throat stung but she kept inhaling. She could not stand to be sober. *Maybe*, she thought, *I should quit my job and see a therapist.* But she couldn't really see herself sharing everything with someone she didn't even know, telling them the truth. Because it wasn't their business, and she could never say it aloud. *It's my fault the children are gone and never coming back. All my fault.*

She knew the months were passing, and the children were becoming other children, and she was accomplishing nothing. But she was paralyzed. The caseworker had made her plan impossible, and if she went through the motions, she would still lose the children, but then she'd lose her dignity, too. The therapists and caseworkers would smile patronizingly as she shared her thoughts, divulged all her failures, and then tell her, sorry, it still wasn't enough. She wasn't enough.

Because how could she keep the apartment without a job?

She was sick of having the same conversation in her head, over and over. It was like a maze with no way out. She hurried onto the Walnut Street Bridge, and the open air was cool on her cheeks. She stopped at the railing. The river was wide and dark. She dropped the joint over the side. The slender white roll evanesced in the black sky.

The water was barely moving, the waves lapping gently against one another. Cars zoomed by on the freeway, their lights bright yellow. Brittney thought about jumping. She imagined her head slicing through the surface, and swimming underwater, kicking and thrashing, until she reached the ocean. She had never been to the ocean, and, in her mind, the ocean was salty and blue, and she could float on her back, staring up at the stars. It was a kind of freedom, an escape.

She closed her eyes, and leaned against the railing, her toes lifting, thinking how easy it would be. How good it would feel for everything to be over. But then she thought of Ethan, his serious face waiting for her, expecting her.

She lowered her feet.

If it wasn't for Ethan, she could just vanish. Madison loved her, but she was happy at the foster woman's house. She reveled in all *the things*: the elaborate toys, the hardback books, the sprawling backyard she could run through barefoot. And her vocabulary had exploded. Sometimes, she used words Brittney didn't know, like cygnet or farrier. Brittney just nodded, glad her little girl was learning, even if she was leaving her behind.

Maggie, of course, didn't even know Brittney was her mother.

Brittney wanted her girls back, but the more time that whipped by, like a strong wind shaping everything it touched, the less she could see it happening. The foster woman spoiled the children, and Brittney didn't think she could stand their unhappiness at being returned to a cramped apartment, and a chaotic daycare, and an overworked mother.

But she would never get over losing them, either. The joint hadn't worked very well. Her throat burned and she felt spacey and anxious. A bus was coming and she jogged to the corner. She hopped on, and found a seat by the window.

She sketched more women, this time with ballerina inspired dresses, made of tulle and satin. They wore ballet flats. The women in her sketches seemed happy, and, for some reason, this provided a small comfort, even as she was crying, wondering what she was going to do.

She stopped answering the caseworker's calls. She couldn't think straight with the caseworkers orbiting her, watching her every move, telling her what to do. Instead of showing up for her official visits with the children, she called the foster woman and asked if she could stop by in the evening, after her shift ended at the grocery store. The foster woman agreed, but when Brittney showed up, she seemed nervous, her arms crossed, her once perfectly styled hair skewing in different directions.

"I have to work on a paper I'm writing. Do you want to watch the children out here?" she asked, gesturing to the living room.

Brittney nodded. It would be the first time she'd been alone with the children since they'd been taken. The foster woman disappeared into her office, to do her work, whatever it was.

Maggie looked at Brittney skeptically, and then toddled to the foster woman's office and banged on the door with her little fists, shouting, "Mama! Mama!" The door opened, and the foster woman, who seemed distracted and slightly annoyed, reluctantly let her in.

Brittney turned to Ethan and Madison. "Do you guys want me to read you a story?"

"Yeah," Ethan said, and he walked over to the bookshelf, and picked out a book. He handed it to her. *Charlotte's Web.* "It's kind of sad."

"OK," she said, sitting on the couch. Madison crawled into her lap, and Ethan snuck under her left arm. She started reading, and it didn't seem sad, yet, just the story of a girl on a farm, raising a baby pig.

As she read, Brittney almost forgot she wasn't in her own house, raising her own kids. The little pig moved away from the girl, to her uncle's farm, and he was lonely.

"Poor Wilbur," Ethan said, shaking his head.

"Poor Wilbur," Brittney agreed.

But soon the pig had a great friend, a spider named Charlotte.

"Doesn't he still miss Fern?" Ethan asked.

"Probably," Brittney agreed. "I would think so."

"It's after eight."

Brittney looked up. The foster woman was standing near the upstairs railing. "I already put Maggie down," she said. "Do you want to put them down?"

"Sure," Brittney said, surprised to see Madison had already fallen asleep, curled up in her lap.

"Can you show me Madison's crib?" Brittney asked Ethan, and he nodded somberly.

"She's got a bed now," he explained.

Madison had her own large room. It was nicely decorated, with purple butterflies on the bedspread and flying across the wall. Brittney tucked her into the bed, leaving her in her clothes. She didn't wake up.

After she put Ethan down, reading him two more chapters, she walked back downstairs. The living room was empty. The foster woman's office door was open, and Brittney stood in the doorway. The foster woman was typing on a large computer, her hair in a bun, an empty glass of wine next to her keyboard.

She turned around. "You leaving?"

Brittney nodded, suddenly curious about what she did. "What are you writing?"

"Oh, I'm writing an article on child rearing among early Mormons. When a man married multiple women, the women would often raise the children together. It interests me, this idea of a bunch of women raising children together."

"Weren't they jealous of each other?"

"Mostly, no. It seems to have worked out. Maybe because they were expecting it to be that way."

"I guess I know a lot of people whose moms are helping them out. Maybe that ain't so different."

The foster woman smiled. "You're right. That isn't so different. Maybe that will be my next paper."

"You a writer?"

"Writer, and teacher. I teach at the college."

"That sounds like a good job."

"I like it."

Brittney nodded, thinking maybe the foster woman could help her kids get good jobs like that, so they wouldn't have to worry about money. So they could buy a nice house like this.

"Thanks for letting me come over."

"Anytime."

Brittney walked back through the living room, and out the front door. It was quiet on the street. She turned back to the house, the downstairs lit up, and felt the same terrible ache of separation she always did. She wanted to live with her children, be there when they woke up. Standing on the dark street, knowing her children were inside, tucked in the foster woman's beds, made her feel invisible, like she was slowly fading to nothing.

~.~

Brittney needed a break from her sadness, and for a few weeks, she worked, smoked, slept and sketched, and didn't permit herself to think about the children. When she was tempted, she pushed her nails into her palms until they bled. She tried to stay on autopilot, because it was easier than caring.

She met Trinity for dinner one night, at a local diner. Trinity was in a booth, wearing an angular navy jacket and an elastic black dress.

"Hey, how are things going?"

The waitress dropped off glasses of water, and they both ordered burgers and fries.

"I'm surviving," Brittney said. She was no longer mad at her cousin. She'd come to feel, somehow, what she'd always known: that Trinity couldn't be faulted for not babysitting that night.

"How's the case goin'?"

"It's not good. I try not to think about it. I don't think they're going to give me the children back."

Trinity's mouth opened in surprise. "But that's ridiculous.

You're a good mom."

No one had said that to her in a long time. She didn't believe it anymore.

"The caseworker doesn't like me. She thinks the kids would be better off with the old lady. She's really rich and she has a good job."

"Isn't there anything you can do?"

"I don't know. I'm just worn out from fightin' 'em and the girls seem happy there."

Trinity reached over and squeezed her hand. The waiter dropped their plates on the table, and Brittney looked away, embarrassed, until the waitress left.

"What about Ethan?"

"He wants to come home."

"Fuck. I'm sorry."

Brittney shook her head. "Even my lawyer, one of those public pretender types, says family law ain't like other law. You don't get innocent until proven guilty. And the plan, the so-called 'family service plan,' it's impossible ..."

They both took bites of their burgers, and ate for a while, silently.

Sick of ruminating, sick of problems she couldn't solve, Brittney asked her cousin, "So what's going on with you?"

Trinity smiled coyly. "I been meanin' to tell you. I'm movin' to New York."

Brittney was surprised, and then sad. Trinity had been her best friend for as long as she could remember. Philadelphia wouldn't be the same without her. "How come?"

"Kai got a job in Manhattan. He wants me to come with him."

"Oh," Brittney said. She had met Kai, once, and he was slender and quiet. He wore clear glasses and polo shirts. He was into computers and science fiction. She wouldn't have expected Trinity to fall for someone so nerdy, but the affection between them had been real. They touched each other's arms and legs, and goaded each other about their divergent interests.

"You know I've always dreamed of moving there," Trinity said, softly, "the fashion center of the universe. But without Kai, I don't think I'd have the guts. Promise me you'll come visit."

"Of course," Brittney agreed, although her future seemed like an empty pit, and she couldn't see anything good happening to her, ever again.

As she rummaged in her purse for her cash, she put a sketchbook on the table, and Trinity grabbed it.

"What's this?" she asked, opening it before Brittney could stop her.

Brittney sighed, shaking her head. "Nothing."

Trinity flipped the pages, studying the women and clothes carefully. Her eyebrows were raised, and her mouth was slightly parted. "Brittney, these are really good. Do you have others?"

Brittney nodded, thinking of the dozen books in her bedroom.

"OK, why don't I set up a meeting with one of my professors? You could enroll next year."

Brittney shrugged. "Maybe."

"Let me keep this. I'll ask."

Brittney shrugged again, and stood up, laying down the cash for her burger. Trinity slipped the sketchbook into her leather satchel. They kissed goodbye on the street, and Brittney walked home slowly. The weather was warm, but not hot, and the breeze felt good on her bare arms. She thought about moving to New York with Trinity, trying to enroll in fashion design school. She was only twenty-three. She could start over again.

The caseworker was standing in her hall, knocking on her door. DHS stopped by whenever they wanted, expecting you to let them in. Brittney turned around, headed back down the stairs. But the caseworker saw her, and called out.

Brittney stopped.

"Where have you been?" the caseworker accused, her white nose wrinkled.

Brittney ignored her, unlocking the apartment door.

The caseworker followed Brittney in, her steps loud and

persistent. Brittney coughed on her flowery perfume.

"Will you sign these papers authorizing Rebecca to take the children to New York? She'd like to take them for her mother's birthday party."

Brittney closed her eyes, and she pushed her nails into the palm of her hands, feeling the half-moons of pain. She didn't want her children going to New York without her, having a whole other life without her. They should be visiting *her* mother, not the foster woman's mother. She couldn't stop everything, but she could stop this.

"No," she said flatly.

The caseworker looked at her impatiently. "You know, Brittney, if you keep missing your visits, you won't get your children returned," she said, her eyebrows raised and her lips parted.

Brittney closed her eyes.

The caseworker sighed, and left, the door rattling loudly behind her.

If Brittney kept making her visits, she wouldn't get her children back either. She ran her fingers through her hair, and strands tangled between her fingers. Her hair had been falling out from stress; clumps circled the drain in the shower and littered her pillow. She picked up the scissors from the kitchen drawer and went into the bathroom.

She held a thick rope of hair out and cut it off. The hair fell in the sink and on the floor. She lifted another clump and cut it. The foster woman had already cut the children's hair. Their hair now barely covered their ears. Brittney would chop hers off in solidarity.

After she finished, she stuffed the twelve-inch strands in the trash. She smoothed the hair down against her scalp. It was patchy and uneven.

The following week, after a double shift at the grocery store, she showed up at the foster woman's house unannounced. The foster woman let her in, concern on her face.

"How have you been?"

Madison and Ethan hugged her, and she hugged them back, kissing their warm cheeks.

"Fine," she said to the foster woman, not wanting to talk, knowing the foster woman, with her easy life, could never understand.

Ethan clung to her in the chair, but then he yelled at her, asking how she could do this to him, why she wasn't fighting harder.

"I'm sorry," she said, her voice cracking. She was sorry.

Ethan shouted at her and ran away, stomping up the stairs. She watched him go but didn't chase him down. He was right. She was failing him.

Madison walked out of the pink teepee, and her eyes flittered anxiously.

"Mama Becky, where Ethan?" she asked.

Brittney sobbed, once—how could Madison be calling another woman mom so quickly? For two years, Brittney had mothered her, and all that had slipped away, been erased. Brittney's scalp itched, and she couldn't be there anymore.

She ran out of the house and down the street, hating this neighborhood with its beautiful mansions and clean sidewalks. The foster woman shouted her name, and this enraged her even further. Her children weren't enough? She had to bother Brittney, too? Brittney didn't stop running. She looked over her shoulder, once, shaking her head at the foster woman, thinking, *you've stolen my children, and I hate you.*

~*~

Trinity's professor was an elegant black woman in her forties. She wore a turquoise wrap dress and red heels, and sat at the edge of her desk as she flipped through Brittney's sketchbooks. "These are excellent," she announced, handing them back to Brittney. "I will write you a recommendation for fashion design school. You'll have a lot to learn, but this is certainly a good start."

Brittney nodded; she was so flustered she barely remembered to thank her as she gathered up her books, and shoved them in her duffel bag.

After the meeting, Brittney found herself daydreaming, imagining herself going to school, learning how to do things properly. Maybe this would be her chance to build a new life. Maybe she could make good, build herself up, and come back for her children as someone they could be proud of.

She was spending a lot of money on weed, over seventy dollars a week. She thought about stopping so she could purchase material, and sew one of her designs by hand. It had been so long since she had constructed anything.

But her shifts at the grocery store dragged on, the scanner beeping, the customers complaining about the prices and the waits, and it was just easier to keep smoking. She kept working, saving money, and sketching. It was like she was waiting for something to happen. Sometimes, she dreamt about the old Chris, and him rescuing the children and bringing them home, and the five of them being a happy family. She could hear the children's laughter; the feel of their small bodies pressed against her chest, and see Chris's charismatic smile and his lips against her cheek. Then she woke up, alone in her dank apartment.

She passed a storefront church on her way to work one morning, and heard the choir singing. Their voices were light and uplifting. People were stomping their feet. She paused outside the double wood doors, listening for a moment. The last time she had been to church was with her Grandma Frances, when she had been eight or nine.

God Loves You, Come Home, the sign read.

How could that be true? She wondered.

But she opened the door, and stood in the back row. People were wearing their Sunday finery, and they glanced at her black slacks and blue polo and nametag. She nodded, and they nodded back, welcoming.

She clapped her hands and stomped her feet, losing

herself in the music. It felt good to forget who she was, to be connected to a power higher than herself.

When the song ended, everyone exhaled, and took their seats. The minister stood up, and thanked the glorious choir. He was middle aged and handsome. His voice bellowed as he warned against crass materialism, and superficial pursuits, and the sins of the body. Brittney closed her eyes, wishing she could live in the surety of his voice. *Someone like him could save me*, she thought. *Save me.*

She opened her eyes, reassured by the adamancy of his gestures, the certainty in his tone. She glimpsed three children near the front, two boys and a girl, their slender frames sitting obediently between their nicely-dressed parents. And then her mood plummeted, back to earth, and she couldn't stop looking at them, thinking, that will never be me, my three children will never stand in a church by my side.

She snuck out the back. She called in sick to work, and walked home. She flipped through the papers the caseworker had given her months ago, searching for the name of a therapist. She picked one at random, and called and left her number on the voice mail. *I will fix this*, she thought, *I will get my children back.*

The therapist returned her call on Monday, while she was working, and she returned the call on Tuesday morning. The first opening was in a month, at 11 a.m. She took it, even though part of her thought, *what's the point?* A month felt like eternity.

The caseworker left more messages on her phone, telling her she was falling farther behind, and she'd better get her act together. There were no solutions offered, though; it was just chiding that had begun to sound rote and mechanical.

One afternoon, as she was about to leave for work, the caseworker knocked on the door, her heavy leather bag on her shoulder.

"You aren't doing your plan."

Brittney excused herself, saying she was on the way to work. As she walked to the stairs, the caseworker called her name. Brittney paused, waiting.

"If that's your attitude, you should just sign your rights over now. You aren't going to get your children returned. As you drag out your plan, they're bonding with the foster mother. The judge is going to see that and say maybe it's in their best interest to stay with her."

Brittney squeezed her fists, and told herself not to punch the woman in the face, like she wanted to. She turned around and the woman looked self-righteous and also a little afraid.

The woman bit her bottom lip, and shifted her bag in front of her body. "Look, it might not seem like it, but I *am* trying to help you. I am telling you the truth about how these things work. You have to find a way to get yourself to your appointments and visits. You need to finish the parent classes, and the drug and alcohol counseling. You just have to do it."

"I got an appointment for counseling."

"OK, that's a good start. But you can't just go once. You'll have to finish all the appointments. It says here you missed your last drug test."

"Fine. I will quit my job and just go to the appointments. Happy?"

The caseworker glanced at the wall, and blew out a bilious breath of air. "Maybe that's for the best. Eventually, you'll have to get another job and keep an apartment. The children can't be returned to you if you don't have anywhere for them to live."

Brittney stared at her, incredulous.

"Look, this is all part of your family service plan. It's for the children's own good. The plan you signed, remember? Do you want them to be homeless?"

Brittney laughed, and ran down the stairs. How could things be so impossible? She thought being outside, in the warm air, would make her feel better. But it didn't. She ran to work as fast as she could. She didn't want to think anymore.

During her break, she walked in the parking lot and called Ethan. She needed to hear his voice.

"Mom," he said, "where you been?"

"I'm sorry, baby, I've been working a lot. But I got a new

joke for you. Knock knock."

"Who's there?" he said, reluctantly.

"Doughnut."

"Doughnut who?"

"Doughnut open the door."

He chuckled. "Not bad. I got a new one, too. Rebecca bought me a joke book."

Brittney ignored the jealousy that shot up her spine, the knowledge that she could never afford to buy new books, not if she wanted to have any savings. "Tell me," she said, forcing cheer into her voice.

"A prisoner gets out of jail. 'I'm free! I'm free!' he yells. A little kid looks at him and says, 'So what? I'm four.'"

She laughed, even though it was corny. "How's school going?"

"Mr. Sanders is cool. He lets me build real motors."

"That's really neat, baby."

"Did you know Formula One cars can go 186 miles per hour? I want to be a driver when I grow up."

"I bet you'd be good at it."

She heard a woman's voice calling in the background.

"Mom, I got to go. We're having dinner. Pizza."

"OK, I love you. Take care of your sisters."

"Come see us, Mom."

She paused, and before she could say anything, he had hung up. Talking to him was like digging inside an open wound. She wiped the tears from her face, and went back inside to ring up more customers.

On her way home, it was dark and quiet. The sidewalks were empty. She debated whether to go through the motions of counseling sessions and parenting classes.

Her scalp itched, and she pulled at her short hair. It was growing out slowly. The manager had laughed when she'd come in with the homemade cut, shaking his head in disbelief. But it suited the ugliness she felt inside.

She opened the door to her apartment, and was surprised

to see the kitchen trash had been emptied, and there was an envelope of money on the counter. She must have left the door unlocked again. She didn't really care that she had missed Chris. He only reminded her of all that she was losing.

She pulled her weed out of the cabinet. She slowly rolled a joint. The effects had dulled with her heavy usage, and she knew she should stop, but it was a habit she had gotten used to. The ritual was reliable, and that was satisfying, when everything else in her life seemed out of her control.

She sat on the floor, against the wall, and she inhaled the smoke, pressing it between her fingers.

Oh how much she missed Ethan! Her son who still loved her, no matter what. Brittney blew smoke and rubbed her eye with her other hand, remembering the foster woman's offer to come over, anytime. She put her joint out on the floor, and found the woman's number, on a scrap of paper.

"This is Rebecca," the woman answered.

"Could you bring the kids over?"

The foster woman said nothing, and Brittney thought about hanging up. She had been lying; she didn't really want Brittney to see her kids.

"Right now?"

"Yes," Brittney said.

"Oh. OK. We can't stay long. It's their bedtime."

"OK."

Brittney tidied up the living room, dumping her old joints, putting a sweater in the laundry basket, and then she took a long shower. The water burned her neck.

There was a gentle knock on the door, and then Maggie ran in, laughing. The foster woman stepped in tentatively, smiling.

Brittney wiped her nose on her forearm and then hugged Madison and Ethan. Ethan tugged her hand, bringing her over to the couch.

"Come see my maps, mom," he said, pulling a sketchpad out of his backpack. Brittney studied them carefully. They were very detailed, with houses and buildings and roads.

"These are great," she said, rubbing his head. His hair had grown out a little, and it curled softly against her fingers.

"There's our house, me, you and the girls," he said, pointing to a starred building. "There's daddy's. There's grandma's. There's Rebecca's."

She nodded, trying to smile, not to dwell on the impossibility of it. She wished the foster woman would see he belonged here. She picked a piece of lint off his shirt, and then hugged him close to her chest. He smelled vaguely of soap and laundry detergent and himself.

"Ethan, you're such a good boy," she whispered.

She took deep breaths, feeling her son's skin against her own. Madison and Maggie were running around the apartment, chasing each other. Brittney was exhausted, and she wished she could sit here, forever, her son's warm, small body entangled with her own.

He looked at her and smiled.

She rubbed his shoulders, feeling how much he had grown.

"Come on," she said. "I want to show you something."

She led him into her bedroom. He sat next to her on the bed. She passed him one of her sketchbooks. He thumbed through it, looking at all the women carefully.

"These are really good, Mom," he said. "I wish I could draw people like that. My people look funny."

"You will, one day."

"Can you draw another picture of us? With dad and the girls, too?"

"Sure, Ethan," she said, though the prospect made her sad. She remembered sketching Ethan. Tears had run down her face as she had drawn; she had been simultaneously happy, and devastated, as his sweet face had appeared on the page.

"Can I sleep here tonight?" he asked, kicking off his shoes and laying back on the bed.

"Sure," she said, thinking about how nice that would be. But then she remembered she had picked up an extra shift in the morning. At minimum wage, it took forever to save any money. "Not tonight, though," she said, "I have to leave for work at five a.m."

"Oh," he said, disappointed. He seemed to collapse into himself.

Madison and Maggie ran into the bedroom, the foster woman trailing behind them. Madison squeezed Brittney's knee, and rubbed her cheek on Brittney's thigh.

"Hi, Mama," she sang.

Brittney smiled and stroked Madison's head. Her hair was still so short and boyish. She hoped it would grow out quickly. If only everything could be undone as easy as a bad haircut. Madison turned to Maggie.

"Catch me!" she proclaimed, and then ran out of the room. Maggie giggled and darted after her.

The foster woman stood awkwardly at the end of the bed, her left hand clasping her right elbow.

"The girls should go to bed soon," she said softly. "Do you want to come back to the house with us?"

Brittney reached over and put her hand on Ethan's, not wanting to let him go. Couldn't he stay with her, at least?

"I can't. I have to get to work early."

"Mom," Ethan protested, his voice low and hard. "You just don't care." He scrambled off the bed, and ran into the other room. The door to the bedroom slammed shut.

"It's not that simple," she said, to herself.

The foster woman seemed stricken. There was something gentle and thoughtful about the woman, the way she moved and spoke. Maybe they weren't as different as they seemed.

"It's just…" Brittney started, then stopped.

"I know," the foster woman said, tucking her hair behind her ear. "I'll check on him."

Brittney nodded, and reached out for a piece of charcoal. She held it tightly in her hand. She heard Ethan exclaim, "You don't get it!" but this didn't make her feel any better, that he was angry with the foster woman, too.

Minutes passed, and then she heard the woman walk into the other room, and call the girls.

Brittney rose out of her bed, and found Ethan sitting in the kitchen, his head on the table. She put her hand on his back.

"I'm sorry, baby. I got to keep this job. To pay rent. I can come by tomorrow."

"I don't care," he said listlessly, not raising his head. "You just keep disappearing. You don't want us."

The breath left her lungs, and she leaned against the chair. "Ethan... I do..."

The foster woman and the girls came into the kitchen, and the woman looked at Brittney with a tentative intimacy, like she was hoping Brittney would reach out to her, or be her friend. For a moment, Brittney stared back at her. *Help me fix this*, she thought, madly.

But then she remembered the woman laughing with the children's caseworker, their faces flushed in pleasure. She was stupid to trust her.

Brittney leaned down and nuzzled Ethan's ear with her nose, like she had done when he had been a toddler, when he was all chubby cheeks and baby powder. He jerked his head away.

"Goodbye, Mama," Madison called. Brittney lifted her chin, and waved, trying to smile, her lips not quite reaching up.

Ethan abruptly stood, knocking over his chair. He followed the foster woman to the door, dragging his feet.

"I love you, Ethan," Brittney said, her voice urgent. "I do want you."

He didn't respond, just tilted his head further away.

The foster woman smiled apologetically, her cheeks flushed. "Call us," she said, and then she and the children were out of the apartment. The kitchen door rattled shut, and there seemed to be something definitive and final about it.

Ethan was right. She would never be able to see them enough. It was always stolen hours, here and there. The children would be better off without her. It was too hard on them, all this back and forth, this instability.

She would let them go. The foster woman was old and rich but she was OK. She did care about the children, Brittney could see that. And she gave them all *the things* they could ever need. More things than Brittney could ever give them.

She would have to leave Philadelphia. She couldn't stand the constant reminders of the children, and the life she used to have. She would move to New York, with Trinity. She would start over there, and once she had her stuff together, once she was successful, she would come back and see the children. She would become someone strong, someone worth loving.

She stood up and gathered her bag of weed and her rolling papers, and took it into the bathroom. She flushed it all down the toilet.

She scrubbed her face clean. She dug out her old powder and eye shadow. She applied it carefully, watching her face become more attractive. The yellowness in her skin faded; her eyes looked softer. She tied the turquoise scarf around her head, and it put her features back in perspective.

She would get a second job and she would save even more money, enough for a new life. She would stop talking to the caseworkers. They had won. For now.

Chapter Thirteen

As the months passed, Rebecca could see the children losing touch with their mother. They were small children; they didn't have long memories. Maggie, in particular, seemed to have forgotten she had ever had another mother.

Ethan withdrew further into himself, and never mentioned his mother or his old neighborhood, as he used to. He started referring to Rebecca's house as "home," at first shyly, but then reflexively.

Madison made Rebecca promise she would "never go away." Rebecca knew she had no right to promise that, but she did because Madison was too young to understand the whimsies of child services, and she deserved stability. Or at least the appearance of it.

Rebecca and the children were busy with school and playdates and caseworker appointments and work. In the summer, she bought a membership to a local pool, and, on the weekends, they whittled away long afternoons, laughing and splashing and drinking cold juice and eating peanut butter and jelly sandwiches. Ethan sat in a lawn chair, wearing a large straw hat, drawing maps of imaginary cities.

In late August, they picked apples in Lancaster, and visited the children's museum. Rebecca wasn't allowed to take the children out of state so her sister promised she would come down Labor Day weekend with her children and the nanny.

Elizabeth arrived Saturday afternoon, driving her new Mercedes. She parked it in the driveway and when she stepped out of the car, she was wearing large sunglasses and a tight-fitting Burberry jacket over a pink polo and she looked at the house with a bewildered expression. Emmy, who was eight, climbed out of the passenger seat. She was wearing a Burberry jacket and dark jeans and a red polo and large sunglasses like her mother. Her white-blonde hair was halfway down her back.

The nanny opened the rear door and walked around to the other side, and opened Sophie's door. Then she leaned in and lifted Rachel out and held her on her hip. Rebecca watched them from the window—the girls were still all shiny blonde hair and straight noses and blue eyes and naturally tanned skin. She called out and told them to use the backdoor, it was open.

The children were playing in the living room, and Rebecca hugged her sister, who looked older once she had taken off her sunglasses.

"Thanks for coming."

"Of course. I wish I could have come earlier. It's tough with work."

They walked into the living room, and the nanny returned to the car for the bags.

Elizabeth sat down on the couch and stared at Ethan, Madison and Maggie, appraising them as if they were bottles of wine or a legal document.

"Hi," she said, loudly. "I'm your Aunt Elizabeth."

Madison walked over, and leaned on Elizabeth's knee. "Hi!"

"Hi," Elizabeth repeated. "How are you?"

"Good," she said, and then she laughed and ran away.

Elizabeth leaned over, her face near Rebecca's.

"Do they have the same father?" she whispered.

"Yes."

"She's so beautiful."

Rebecca shrugged. Maybe they didn't really have the same father. It was another thing she would never really know about them. "Do you want something to drink?" she asked her sister.

221

"Sure, I'll have a glass of wine."

The nanny was in the kitchen, stacking the bags on the floor. Elizabeth picked up a large white bag and handed it to Rebecca.

"Presents for the children."

Rebecca smiled, and looked inside. There were a dozen packages, wrapped in shiny silver paper. "Thank you."

Rebecca pulled down a bottle of white wine, and opened it. She poured two glasses and handed one to Elizabeth. Elizabeth took one sip and sputtered.

"What is this?"

Rebecca handed her the bottle.

"How much was it?"

"Probably ten bucks."

Elizabeth laughed. "Figures."

They returned to their seats on the couch. The older girls were watching Ethan work on one of his homemade cars, their mouths slightly parted. Rachel was chasing Madison and Maggie around, laughing.

"They seem like good kids," Elizabeth announced. "When will you know if you can adopt them?"

"In January, they might change the goal to adoption."

"That would be better for everyone."

Rebecca flinched at her sister's harshness.

Elizabeth smiled and shook her head, like Rebecca was a lost cause. "Sure you don't need money for a lawyer?"

"I'm sure."

"If you're sure," she said. "So what's there to do around here?"

"We could go to Clark Park."

Elizabeth smiled. "Why don't we let Maricel watch the children and go get manicures?"

"All six of them?"

"Sure, why not? She's a pro."

The older girls suddenly laughed loudly, and Ethan stared at them accusingly. "Leave me alone," he told them.

"You're stupid," Emmy said, a superior look on her face. "You talk wrong!"

The nanny rushed over, and reprimanded Emmy, telling her to take a time out.

"You can't make me, you're not my mom."

"Emmy, be nice," Elizabeth said.

Emmy stuck her tongue out at the nanny and Ethan, and then retreated to the corner of the living room. She pulled a phone out of her purse and started playing on it. Sophie laughed and then followed her older sister, pulling another phone out of her own purse. The nanny shook her head and clucked her tongue.

So much for getting along. Rebecca was nervous about leaving the children alone with someone they didn't know, especially since she wasn't even allowed to, legally. But she had so rarely been out by herself, except to work, since they'd arrived, and Maricel seemed competent. She nodded at her sister.

"OK, let's go."

Elizabeth smiled and stood up, stretching her skinny arms. "Maricel, we'll be back in a couple hours."

"I want to come, too," Emmy said. She held out her fingers. "I need a manicure."

Sophie glanced over, her large blue eyes expectant.

Elizabeth shrugged, and the girls smiled, gathering their leather purses and coats and pulling on their sunglasses.

Rebecca stared at Ethan. He had his head bent in concentration. "Ethan, do you want to come?" she asked.

After he finished attaching a wheel to a base, he glanced up. "Come where?"

"To the nail salon."

He laughed and shook his head.

"Mama, I want to come," Madison said, tugging on her pant legs.

Rebecca crouched down, and hugged her. "It's only for big kids. We'll be back soon, OK? Maricel will take care of you."

Madison looked at Maricel and nodded cautiously. "You promise you coming back, Mama Becky?"

"Yes, I'll be back soon. I promise."

"It'll be fine," Elizabeth assured, smiling at Rebecca knowingly.

Elizabeth drove, and they circled around Rittenhouse Square, searching for a parking space. An art show was running in the square, and the sidewalks were packed with pedestrians and vans. Elizabeth swerved and honked, shaking her head.

"Terrible drivers around here," she said.

She zipped into a barely open spot, and then they walked over to the salon. The next available appointments weren't for an hour, and the woman offered them champagne while they waited. The girls settled into the cushy leather chairs, and tapped away on their phones. Rebecca watched her nieces, their blonde hair falling in front of their faces. They were incredibly lucky, how easy their lives had been.

Elizabeth checked her own phone, and sent a few messages, and then picked up a glossy magazine.

"So," she said, flipping the pages, "Madison really is a beautiful child."

"True," Rebecca agreed.

"It will help."

"Probably." Though there were dangers, too, the dangers of letting others take care of you, and the dangers of boys, and then men, wanting you for only one reason.

"Speaking of beauty, when are you going to start dating?"

Rebecca laughed incredulously. "I'm too busy with the children and work. I barely have the energy to think about Will anymore, who still texts me, trying to chat. It's almost pathologically persistent. I texted him a photo of the kids, once, and he liked it with an emoji and then that silenced him for about a month."

Elizabeth laughed. "Oh, Will. You know dating will only get harder, the older you get."

"Thanks, Mom."

"Mom loves the fact that you're a single mother. Gives her feminist street cred she wishes she had."

"True. Dad, on the other hand, still seems a little skeptical. When he was here, he seemed continually surprised by Ethan's intelligence."

"Sounds like dad. I think he secretly looks down on people living in poverty."

Rebecca glanced around, as if there might be someone to offend in this fancy salon. Of course, there wasn't.

"Anyway," Elizabeth said, "he's old. He'll get over it. The other day, I overheard mom telling some colleague, proudly, she had foster grandchildren."

"Why?"

"Who knows. Maybe she felt like it gives her free reign to comment on class issues."

Rebecca smiled. Her mother called frequently to talk about the children, even though when she visited, she only seemed to relate to Ethan, who was old enough to have a proper conversation. It had been the same with Elizabeth's children. Neither of Rebecca's parents enjoyed small children, who they seemed to view as irrational and noisy little adults.

Rebecca sipped her champagne and tried to relax. Her phone rang and she grabbed it out of her purse. It was Brittney. She paused—it wasn't a good time, but she hadn't heard from her in five weeks.

"Hi," she said, deciding to answer.

"Could you pick me up tonight?"

Rebecca looked at her sister. She was reading a magazine, rolling her eyes at an article on the "Five Best Sex Positions for His Pleasure."

"OK. But my sister's in town with her children."

Even as she said it, she knew it was a bad idea. The visit would only be more awkward if Elizabeth was there, judging. But the children hadn't seen Brittney for over a month. She had been visiting the children regularly, in the evenings, but then she had vanished, never explaining why.

"That's OK," Brittney said, and then disconnected.

Elizabeth was staring at her with curiosity.

"It's Brittney, their mother, she wants to come over tonight."

"Is that normal? She just calls and you go pick her up?"

"It's not the protocol, no."

"Then why do it?"

"Because she's their mother. And she seems OK."

Elizabeth raised her eyebrow. "Rebecca, this could bite you in the ass."

Rebecca nodded. "I know, but I'm trying to do what's best for the children."

"But what if they take them away from you and then they don't have you or their mother?"

Rebecca closed her eyes and shook her head. "You're right, but I don't know what else to do."

"You should follow the official procedures. Let her come to the visits at the assigned time."

The woman called them back for their manicures, and Rebecca tensed as the woman rubbed her hands with natural oils. Elizabeth was right, she knew she was, but she also couldn't bring herself to turn Brittney away.

The girls were surprisingly still as their nails were painted, holding their hands out, watching the women work. Rebecca was antsy, and she looked over at her sister, thinking of how different their lives had turned out, how much simpler Elizabeth's seemed.

"How is work?" she asked, a subject they rarely discussed even though it seemed to occupy 95% of Elizabeth's waking hours.

Elizabeth smiled proudly. "Good. I brought in a new enterprise client."

"That's impressive," Rebecca noted, even though she wasn't sure what her sister aimed for. Maybe only dozens of enterprises would be enough. Rebecca's own work on the childrearing practices of 19th century Mormons had stalled out.

She was spending all her work time on administrative meetings and committees, putting in face time so her department chair wouldn't get disgruntled. In the fall, she would have to return to a full teaching load, and she wasn't looking forward to it. She wasn't ready to spend less time with the children.

"How's Phil's work?"

She shrugged, "He's making a killing."

"But?"

"Seems unstable to me. The prices are ridiculous."

Rebecca nodded. She hadn't been reading magazines or the paper lately. After the children went to bed, and she'd finished her work, she just wanted to relax. She felt uninformed, but she didn't care. It would only be for a few years of her life, before they were older and had their own friends and activities, and she didn't want to miss any of it.

After their nails finished drying, Elizabeth paid the bill, and they headed outside. The girls ran ahead, laughing. Rebecca called Brittney and told her they were on their way.

Rebecca put her phone back in her purse. Elizabeth jangled her keys.

"You sure you want to do this?"

"Yes, I'm sorry to impose, but I just don't know when she'll come over again. It could be two months."

"I don't mind. I'm curious, actually, but those children are in state custody, and you don't want to interfere with the state. It's like poking a sleeping giant."

Rebecca was suddenly annoyed. *I know, I get it!* she wanted to scream, but she didn't because it was rude and she barely saw her sister these days. She had always been the one to visit, and with the kids, it had been impossible to leave Philadelphia. She reached out and squeezed her sister's shoulder, and she remembered when they were little like Elizabeth's girls, laughing and giggling in the closet as their mother searched for them, yelling it was time for bed.

"It will be OK."

Elizabeth shrugged and slid into the driver's seat. The

drive back to West Philadelphia was slow and congested, and the girls started arguing in the backseat. Elizabeth turned up the radio. She had it on the hit station, and a teenage girl was singing about lost love, but even her lamentations seemed light and airy.

Brittney's block was bustling with young men, and Elizabeth raised her eyebrows. She pulled over in front of the building.

Rebecca called Brittney and told her to come down. She took Rachel's seat out of the rear row and put it in the trunk, and then sat in the backseat so Brittney could have the front. The girls looked at her as if she had invaded their space, and then returned to their phones.

An elderly black man pushing a cart of trash bags knocked on the front window.

"Nice car, man," he said.

Elizabeth ignored him, and he laughed and kept walking.

"Mom, that man was gross," Emmy said, looking out the window for the first time. "Look at all that trash. And those men's pants are hanging down! I can see their underwear."

"It's just a different style, Emmy," Elizabeth said, leaning against the window. "Relax."

Rebecca realized Brittney was standing at the corner, scanning the cars. Rebecca opened the door and called her name. Brittney turned in their direction, and seeing Rebecca and the Mercedes, paused. Then she gathered herself and walked forward. Tentatively, she opened the passenger door and sat in the front seat.

She was wearing a new uniform—a rumpled red polo and black pants—and had a small black purse in her hand.

"Hi, Brittney," Rebecca said.

Elizabeth smiled and nodded and drove into traffic, making the first U-turn.

"Who are you?" Emmy asked rudely, leaning forward.

"She's Ethan, Madison and Maggie's mother," Rebecca said quickly.

"Well, if those are her kids, then why aren't they with

her?"

Rebecca leaned forward in her seat. "Elizabeth, make a left here," she said, hoping to change the subject.

Elizabeth nodded and put on her blinker.

"Hello!" Emmy called. "Answer me!"

"Emmy, it's complicated. Please play on your phone," Elizabeth said brusquely, her eyes on the road.

Brittney was leaning against her own window, her face turned to the side. Her arm lay tensely on her lap.

Elizabeth turned up the radio, and Rebecca leaned against her window, and told Elizabeth where to turn. The pop music was loud, but the car still had the feel of an awkward silence.

When they pulled into the driveway, Rebecca eagerly stepped out of the car. The sky was streaked with pink, and the air was warm. Elizabeth raised her eyebrows at Rebecca and smiled slightly, and Rebecca smiled back to indicate she knew this was absurd, but there was nothing else to do. Brittney followed them inside, her expression wary, as if she were thinking about bolting.

In the living room, Madison and Rachel were playing with the plastic kitchen, and Maggie was riding around on her two-wheeler. Maricel was sitting on the couch.

"Where's Ethan?" Rebecca asked.

Maricel glanced over. "He went to room."

Rebecca nodded. "Let's go in the backyard. I'll order some Chinese."

"Out! Out! Out!" Maggie called, tumbling off the two-wheeler and running for the backdoor. Rachel dropped her plastic pot and chased after Maggie.

Madison waved at her mother. "Hi, Mama!"

Brittney smiled and held out her arms. Madison ran to her, and gave her a hug. Then she scrambled down, and held her mother's hand.

"Want to go out?" she asked.

Brittney chewed her lower lip, and nodded.

"Their shoes are next to the door," Rebecca told Brittney,

and then turned to her sister. "I'm going to get Ethan and order Chinese for everyone. Help yourself to some wine."

Elizabeth nodded, and retreated to the kitchen. The older girls plopped down on the couch.

"Can we watch TV?" Emmy asked.

"Ask your mother," Rebecca said, hoping she would give her approval. She walked upstairs and found Ethan in his bed, reading a *Frog and Toad* book. She climbed in next to him.

"I love that one," she said.

He smiled and rested his head on her chest. She stroked his forehead.

"Your mother's here."

He stiffened and closed the book. "Are those girls gone?"

Rebecca shook her head. "They're leaving tomorrow."

He frowned, and scooted to the edge of the bed, his legs dangling to the floor. "I don't like them. They were mean."

He looked at the floor.

"They're not always mean. Maybe we'll go visit them in New York, and they can show you all their toys."

"What's going to happen to me?"

She reached over and hugged him. Her arm looked so pale, almost white, next to the natural tanness of his skin, and she was acutely aware he had a whole life outside of hers, that he carried with him a whole family and culture she did not know.

But then she wasn't, and he was just Ethan, a boy she loved. She wanted to give him stability, but she couldn't promise anything. It was out of her control.

"We can't be sure. But I will always love you, no matter what happens."

"Yeah right."

"I will."

"Everybody leaves me."

She kissed his forehead. "Sometimes people leave, but they still love you … I had a husband I left, and I still love him. In fact, I love him so much, it's easier not to talk to him."

"Why's that easier?"

"I don't know. I guess because if I talk to him, I miss him more. I remember why I love him."

"That don't make sense. I don't want them to leave anyway. I'm sick of everybody leaving me."

"I know, I would be, too. You've been brave."

He nodded, lost in thought. "Will you keep us, though?"

"I'll try. The state gets to decide where you go, and I can only tell them I want you."

"What's the state?"

"The caseworkers and a judge."

"The judges on TV are OK."

"Judges are OK," she agreed.

He stood up. "I want to see my mom."

Rebecca squeezed his hand and then they walked downstairs. The older girls were watching TV with Maricel, and Rebecca and Ethan walked past them silently. Rebecca stopped in the kitchen and told Ethan his mother was in the backyard. He pulled his hoodie off the peg and slipped it on.

She flipped through the takeout menus, and called the nearest Chinese place and ordered a great deal of food. She poured herself a glass of wine, slipped her clogs on, and walked out the back door.

Madison and Maggie and Rachel were running and kicking the soccer ball, laughing. Elizabeth was drinking a glass of wine and messaging on her phone, her fingers flying across the tiny keypad. Brittney was sitting still, her mouth drawn in an unhappy line, her arm around Ethan's waist. He was fidgeting.

"Do you want a glass of wine, Brittney?" Rebecca asked.

Brittney glanced over at her, and then looked back at the girls, without indicating yes or no. Rebecca swallowed a large gulp of wine, and put the glass down on the table. Elizabeth smirked, and she smiled back, shrugging. She joined the girls, kicking the soccer ball as they all chased it, squealing. Even though Maggie was two years younger she had no trouble keeping up. She had started walking at ten months. She pushed her sister and Rachel out of the way so she could punt the ball with her foot.

Rebecca kicked the ball again, and the girls chased after it, running near the fence. They played this game for a while, until Madison and Rachel lost interest, and they disappeared inside the wood playhouse, laughing. Maggie grinned at Rebecca. "Bobo!" she called, flapping her arms. "Bobo!"

Rebecca kicked the ball as hard as she could, and it bounced off the far fence. Maggie ran after it, her arms almost straight by her side, her braids flapping. Rebecca retrieved her wine, and took another gulp, trying to quell her nerves. She felt responsible for hosting her sister and Brittney, and they were sitting there silently. Well, Elizabeth was busy, typing away on her phone, so maybe she was happy. Work was what she did; maybe she was glad for the excuse to return to it. But Brittney looked fatigued and miserable, like she was barely enduring this visit.

Rebecca chased after the ball, holding her wine glass out, and kicked it again. Ethan kissed his mother on the cheek and then hopped off her lap, running after the ball.

"I want to play," he called, kicking it to his sister.

Maggie smiled and chased after it.

Brittney leaned forward in her chair, her head in her chin. Rebecca walked over, finishing her glass of wine.

"I'm going to check on the food. Do you want to come?" she asked Brittney, thinking she might want something to do.

Brittney nodded slightly and followed her inside.

Once they were in the kitchen, Brittney asked for a glass of wine, and Rebecca poured her a large glass and refilled her own. Brittney sat at the stool and cupped her wine glass, slowly sipping it.

"How are things?" Rebecca asked.

Brittney let out a hollow laugh. "The children … they're really changing."

Rebecca brushed her hair out of her face and closed her eyes and wondered what to say. She reluctantly opened her eyes —Brittney was leaning over her glass, staring into the wine. Her short hair was greasy, the skin circling her eyes was puffy, and her mouth was turned down.

"Brittney ...." she started, unsure.

"Stop," Brittney interrupted, her voice surprisingly firm. "You don't get it. But it doesn't matter. It's too late. The new caseworker told me that."

"She did?" Rebecca tried to keep her voice neutral, above the rush of conflicting emotions—joy because oh how badly she wanted to keep the children, and guilt because the children weren't hers to keep, not really.

Brittney nodded and stepped off the stool. She glanced over Rebecca's shoulder, and frowned, and then turned back to Rebecca.

"I came here to tell you I won't really be around for a while. I'm moving to New York with my cousin. It's for the best. It's too hard on them, me coming and going, me in and out. They need stability. I can't ... but promise me you're going to ... love them. Really love them," she said, and tears were running down her cheek. She didn't bother to wipe them away.

"Of course I will. I do. But Brittney, you're always welcome here. You know that, right?"

Brittney nodded slightly, her chin jutted forward. "Maybe. Maggie don't even know who I am anymore."

Then she turned away, and walked into the living room, and Rebecca heard the front door close.

"Wow," Elizabeth said, from the corner.

Rebecca turned, surprised to see her sister.

"She seems really depressed."

Rebecca could feel Elizabeth's judgment of Brittney—what a loser, her facial expression clearly said. There was no understanding, or pity even. The doorbell rang, and Rebecca excused herself, and rushed out of the kitchen. Maricel and the girls were still watching TV. She hoped it was Brittney, coming back, to stay longer.

She swung open the door, and there was a Chinese man in a white t-shirt, giant plastic bags of food dangling from his hands.

Rebecca invited him in, and located her purse, and paid him cash. She brought the bags back into the kitchen. Elizabeth was pouring another glass of wine.

"Seriously, Rebecca, I think she's clinically depressed."

"Wouldn't you be?" Rebecca snapped, untying the plastic bags.

Elizabeth shook her head. "No, I'd be angry, and I sure as hell wouldn't be sitting around wasting time. But look, it sounds like you're going to keep the kids. That's something to celebrate."

She held up her glass of wine, and Rebecca ignored this, setting out the boxes of food on the kitchen table.

"It's not that simple, Elizabeth. Yes, I love the children, and want to keep them, but not because … she was bulldozed."

Elizabeth slid into one of the chairs, watching Rebecca arrange all the food.

"It's just an excuse. But there's nothing you can do about it, anyway, right?"

"I know," she snapped, annoyed, opening the rice boxes and dumping them in a large bowl.

"I know," she repeated, more calmly. "You're right, I guess. It was never my decision to make."

She realized the children were outside alone, and she excused herself to gather them. It was dark outside, and the porch light made a half-circle on the lawn. She couldn't see the children, and she called out to them.

They came running out of the playhouse. Rachel had dirt smudged on her face, like a beard. As they came closer, she realized they all did, and she laughed, shaking her head.

"Inside, everyone," she called, waving her hands toward the door. Ethan opened the door and held it for his sisters and Rachel.

Rebecca could hear her sister's light laugh and Maricel telling the children to clean up their faces. Rebecca sat on the edge of the patio. She had talked to the new caseworker once— a woman in her late thirties who insisted on being called *Miss*

Delevan. Ms. Delevan had been clipped and to the point. She hadn't shared her opinions on the situation, or told Rebecca what was likely to happen.

Rebecca took off her clogs and rubbed her toes in the grass, digging. A cool breeze passed over her and she shivered. She hated the uncertainty of everything. She loved the children, and even though she sympathized with Brittney, the truth was she couldn't bear the thought of losing them at this point. It had almost been a year and even though a year was not long in the scheme of things, it was long enough to gestate and birth a baby, and it was long enough for her not to be able to imagine her life without the children.

So, she was sorry for Brittney, and maybe it was wrong, but she was glad to keep the children.

She stood up, carrying her clogs, and walked back into the house barefoot. Ethan and Madison were clean, and sitting at the table, eating their food with Elizabeth and her girls.

Maggie was running around the kitchen, in circles, defying Maricel's order to clean her face. Rebecca laughed and scooped Maggie up, and brought her to the faucet.

"Got to clean up," she said, smiling.

"No, no, no, Mommy," Maggie protested, "Mommy, Mommy, Mommy," and Rebecca kissed the soft spot on her neck, and rubbed the water over the dirt on her face, scrubbing it away. Maggie squirmed, but let her do it, and once she'd finished, Rebecca hugged her hard, almost aggressively.

Rebecca put her in the highchair and served her rice and chicken and broccoli and she dug right in. She had a good appetite. Rebecca kissed all her children's heads, and Elizabeth smiled at her as she did so, as if to say, *I told you so, you're happy, they're going to be yours.*

Chapter Fourteen

Brittney

Brittney was near the end of a double shift, on autopilot, checking out a customer. There was a white woman in the back of her line. The woman was middle aged and stiff. She had a pale upturned nose, her tan coat buttoned to her neck, and a vague look as she stood empty-handed.

Brittney returned her attention to her current customer, a young black man.

"Thirteen twenty-two," she said, and he swiped his card, pulling up his jeans at the same time.

Brittney processed the transaction, and thought about the woman. No one like that shopped at the Save-A-Lot. The woman had to be with DHS. The new caseworker had called her on the phone and told her she needed to report to the office, to discuss the case. It didn't look good, she had announced officiously. Brittney had gone in for the appointment, but she had stood outside the sterile gray building, paralyzed, finding herself unable to open the front doors and walk past the security guard and squalling children and the office workers in their cheap, ill-fitting suits and hear the awful things the new caseworker had to say.

She glanced at the woman, as she ran an older woman's items over the scanner. The woman was holding her purse against her chest, staring at Brittney with a stolid expression.

"Fifty-seven eighty-two," she announced, turning to bag

the groceries and drop them in the woman's cart.

The older woman rummaged in her pocketbook, and handed her the exact change. Brittney took it and printed out her receipt.

The woman was at the front of the line. Brittney took a deep breath.

The woman clutched her purse and said she was Brittney's new caseworker.

"Not a good time," Brittney responded, impatiently. "I'm workin'."

The caseworker smiled and didn't move.

Brittney looked over her shoulder, searching for her manager.

The caseworker declared that she had read Brittney's file, and Brittney might as well sign over her parental rights. The customers in line guffawed and shook their heads.

Brittney stormed off, ignoring the customers cursing at the delay and the caseworker instructing her not to walk away. The store was crowded, and the lines were long so she hurried to the front office.

The manager was typing something into his computer.

"Kymire," she said, "some DHS lady is harassing me. Can you get rid of her?"

He looked up, confused, and then nodded, following her back to her register. The line was empty. The woman had left a letter on top of her register. She shrugged, and folded the letter and put it in her pocket, and announced she was open. The manager turned back to the office without a word.

The letter's weight in her pocket annoyed her. She could feel it every time she moved her hips. It was a reminder DHS would find her anywhere.

After she clocked out, she walked home. She had worked ten hours straight, and she was exhausted. She fell on her bed and pulled the letter out of her pocket. It was a detailed account of all the ways she had failed—not completing drug counseling, not completing depression counseling, not completing parenting classes, not completing alcohol counseling, missing visits. It asked her to consider voluntarily relinquishing her parental rights.

She ripped the letter up and tossed the pieces in the toilet, watching the fragments swirl and then vanish into the sewer.

She went into her closet and pulled her legs up to her chest. The black pant legs brushed against her cheek, and the shoes poked underneath her butt. She picked up her tattered shoebox and opened it.

The box was filled with twenties, all the money she had saved. She fingered the cash. It was her way to New York, and the Fashion Institute of Technology. She could sleep on Trinity's couch, as long as she needed. But even without rent, there would be food, books, and tuition, and materials for her clothes.

She was saving money from extra shifts at her two jobs and the money Chris occasionally dropped off. Sometimes, she felt guilty about this, knowing he intended it for the children, but she figured he owed her a debt much larger than money. This was the least he could do.

Not seeing the children was difficult, and sometimes, her desire to stop by, or ask the foster woman to bring them over, was overwhelming. She longed for Ethan's somber, pleading face, and Madison's sweet smile, and even Maggie's hyper energy, her little body zooming across the room like a shooting star.

Instead of calling, she reached for a rusted kitchen knife she kept in her bedside drawer. It was old and dull and she felt the weight of it in her hand. The knife was light, but it seemed powerful. She dragged it across her inner thigh. The delicate skin broke in a ragged line. She gasped in pain. Bright red blood oozed out, and she closed her eyes, letting the pain and endorphins obliterate the thoughts of her children.

This was for the best. She knew it was. She didn't want to confuse the children, or herself. The caseworkers would never return the children to her and she wanted the children to be happy without her. Stopping by would just upset them.

But one evening, the cutting wasn't enough. She needed

to see her babies. She placed two band aids on the deep cut on her thigh, and took the bus to the foster woman's house. The neighborhood was filled with well-dressed people riding their bikes and walking their dogs and playing with their children. She hadn't seen the house in months, since she'd told the foster woman she was leaving, and she had forgotten how beautiful and imposing it was. How it belonged to a different world than the one she lived in.

The front windows were open, letting in the cold breeze, but she couldn't see anyone in the living room. She walked into the backyard. There was a wood playhouse—as tall as her—in the rear, underneath an oak tree. Blue and pink scooters leaned against the fence. More toys. *Her children would have everything*, she thought bitterly.

But she wanted her children to have everything, she reminded herself. Even if she wasn't the one giving it.

She walked onto the wood patio and looked in through the open kitchen window. The four of them were eating dinner, and music was playing. Rich people music. There were no words and the instruments were faint and ordered. Ethan was shoveling the pasta into his mouth, and drinking large gulps of milk. Madison was eating carefully, and she stopped between spoonfuls to smile at the foster woman, or talk to Maggie. Maggie was a mess, her bib covered in sauce, her arms and legs swinging wildly in her highchair. She laughed as she threw her food to the floor.

Ethan finished his food, wiping his mouth with the back of his hand. Then he ran from the table and opened the backdoor. Brittney froze. He ran right past her, to the rear of the yard, behind a large oak tree. She could hear him hammering.

She knew she should go home—the children were happy and healthy, that should be enough—but she walked toward Ethan, her firstborn, her only son. The grass in the yard was verdant, overgrown. It scratched her ankles. Self-consciously, she straightened her coat and flattened down her wisps of hair. He was working at a small table, his face intent, as he banged a screw into a metal cage.

"Ethan," she whispered, wishing suddenly for the impossible: that she could replace the foster woman in this beautiful house, with the money for all these things, and raise her son, as she was supposed to.

He looked up in surprise. "Mom."

His expression was happy, and she thought, *oh, Ethan, how much I love you.* But then he seemed confused and angry. The expressions on his face were different than she had seen before—the lift of his mouth higher, the narrowing of his eyes, the wrinkling of his nose, it was all off—and she wondered, was it because of the foster woman, or just because he was getting older?

She was sorry she had bothered him, causing the turmoil on his face. But she wasn't, because she loved him so much. He was still her son.

She walked over and kneeled down in front of him. She hugged his body, smelling his neck and hair and chest. He smelled like lavender soap, but also himself.

"I miss you," she whispered into his thin chest. A streak of blood was visible on the thigh of her green tights, and she closed her legs, so he wouldn't see it.

He looked down at her, and his mouth was open expectantly. "Where you been?"

How could she explain it to him? "They ain't going to give you back to me, baby."

"Why not?"

"It's hard to explain, baby. But I love you, OK?"

He sat down on the mulch, and rubbed his forehead. "That don't make any sense. I don't believe you."

She reached over and grabbed his hand. It was warm. "It's true, baby. They didn't think I was good enough for you. Are you OK here?"

"It's OK. The girls are OK."

"Good," she said, even though her heart sank. It was good, though. She wanted them to be happy. She leaned over and kissed him on the cheek. "You're a good boy, you know that?"

She stood up. She asked him to show her what he was working on. He stood, too, wiping off his pants, and walked over to the table. He was building a toy car, and his voice was clear and proud as he showed her how all the pieces connected.

"That's great, baby," she enthused. And it was.

The sky was pink, turning purple. The backdoor opened and she could hear the girls running across the lawn, squealing with laughter. Brittney sat against the fence, blocked by the oak tree, and hugged her knees. She held her finger up to her lip, and Ethan nodded.

The foster woman was walking toward them, her steps crunching against the twigs and fallen leaves. Ethan leaned down and kissed Brittney on the cheek, his breath warm and oniony, and then he ran out to meet the foster woman. Brittney could hear them talking. The foster woman's voice was gentle. She wanted to see what Ethan was working on, but he led her away, asking her to kick the ball around.

Brittney huddled closer to the fence, touched by Ethan's protection. He had always been older than his years. She listened to the sounds of her children playing happily with another woman. She closed her eyes.

The sky was darkening. Her girls were laughing, and it was a light, chirpy sound. Maggie was shooting back and forth across the yard, her squeals trailing her as she kicked a ball around. Madison was tending to her baby doll in the playhouse, and her voice was quiet and loving.

They were doing good, Brittney thought, digging at the cut on her thigh, wanting to feel some kind of pain. More blood seeped out onto her tights.

The sun's light dimmed to a gray sky, and the foster woman called out to the children, saying it was time for bed. Maggie whined and protested, trying to run away, but the foster woman cajoled her inside. The door closed with a dull thud.

The backyard was silent, and Brittney was cold in her green tights. The bark on the tree was peeling and she ripped off a piece and threw it to the ground. The large red splotch on her thigh looked like a headless man. She took her keys out, and carved a B in the trunk. *I was here. I love you.*

She stood up, and fingered Ethan's tools and metal pieces. *Maybe he would be a mechanic one day*, she thought.

She left the backyard, peering up at the lit windows on the second floor. She couldn't see anyone. But she sensed they were warm and cozy, hearing stories in their beds. Only she was outside in the cold, with nowhere to be and no one to be with.

~*~

In December, she walked through her apartment for the last time. She wouldn't miss the ratty old couch or the plywood cabinets or the piles of trash and the smell of dank mold. The children's room was musty, and she fingered their t-shirts and shorts and dresses, and pressed Madison's favorite teddy bear against her cheek, and she missed what briefly was, and might have been.

She had run into Chris on the street, and he had been laughing with buddies, but his eyes had looked fatigued. "I'm moving to New York," she told him, and his face collapsed, but his buddies had been watching so he simply nodded. "The kids?" he asked. She shook her head slowly.

"Good luck, then," he had said, his buddies pulling him along, down the street. She noticed his fist balled in anger, and she wondered if, later, he had punched someone else, since he couldn't punch her or himself.

She locked her apartment door, and mailed the keys to the landlord. He would have to deal with the furniture. She lugged her two bags to the trolley and rode it to 30th Street Station. She boarded the Bolt Bus to New York.

She felt lighter, with just her bags. She had brought clothes and her sketchbooks and one photo of the children, buried at the bottom of her bag. Nicely dressed twentysomethings were sitting around her on the bus, and they talked loudly about bands and books she had never heard of. She leaned her head against the window, and watched the passing fields.

So this is what is outside of Philadelphia, she thought.

They passed empty fields, and industrial landscapes, large metal structures emitting puffs of steam, and small subdivisions, and then things got denser. They went through a long, dark tunnel, and when they drove out, there was suddenly a looming city with skyscrapers and honking cars and constant streams of people. The people were mostly white, but as they drove farther into the city, they were black and brown and yellow, too.

The bus pulled over near Penn Station, and dumped them on the sidewalk. Brittney stood there with her two suitcases, stunned by the noise and the smells and sound of thousands of people talking. She let the crowd open and close around her, wondering what she would do if Trinity didn't show up. She didn't know anyone else in the city.

But then she realized Trinity was standing in front of her, smiling. She was wearing a black leather jacket and black leather pants and thigh-high black boots. Her hair was cut in a straight bob.

They hugged, and Brittney could feel her cousin's ribcage.

"Everyone's skinny here," she explained.

Trinity and her boyfriend had started smoking cigarettes, and their apartment reeked of smoke. It was a small one-bedroom, and they had cleared out a living room cabinet and put folded sheets on the couch. Brittney arranged her clothes and scuffed shoes in the cabinet, burying the photo of her children underneath her sweaters. She rolled up her empty duffel bags and slipped them under the couch.

She looked out the window, at the constant swarms of people and the impossibly tall buildings jutting up in every direction. This was a place she could start over. It was hard for her to believe, as she felt like she had lived and lost a whole life.

But she could still begin again.

She tagged along with Trinity to her fashion design classes, and Trinity persuaded her professors to look at Brittney's sketches. They nodded, and flipped through her books quickly, impressed but busy. The only woman professor lingered on the sketches a bit longer, and finally said she would help Brittney enroll in a community college that offered fashion design classes in the spring. Next fall, she would help her apply to the institute.

Brittney applied for jobs, to save more money. An old diner in the East Village hired her to wait tables. Their walls were covered with photographs from the seventies and eighties. Artists and musicians smiled in the booths, looking like they owned the world. It gave her strength to imagine herself connected to these people. In the corner, near the back, she noticed a photo of a young woman who looked a bit like her, the same dishwater hair and wide mouth, a cigarette dangling from her mouth. Sometimes, when she was on the way back to the kitchen, this photo would catch Brittney's eye, and her heart would skip a beat.

She waited tables during the day, and after her shift ended, she rode the subway for hours, working on her sketches. The clothes she saw in New York—people wore wild things—leaked into her drawings, and they became zanier, more urban, more sophisticated.

Her hair had grown out to her ears, and Trinity styled it in the kitchen, cutting it in a diagonal from the front to the back. She looked young and stylish, and, sometimes, when she was waiting tables or riding the subway, she felt that way, too. Another waiter at the restaurant, an aspiring actor, flirted with her when he came in at the end of her shift, asking her where she was from, and who she wanted to be. She laughed, and told him a fashion designer. "Good," he said, "because I don't date fellow thespians. Can I take you to dinner?"

She wasn't sure what a thespian was, but she smiled and agreed to dinner. He took her to an Ethiopian place, and they ate with their fingers. He was a slender man, not much taller than her, but he had a booming voice and a masculine face.

"What's your story?" he asked.

"My story?"

"Sure, everyone in New York has a story."

"I want to be a fashion designer," she shrugged, returning to her food. She wasn't going to tell him her story. She tried not to tell it to herself.

She went back to his place after the third date, and it was a small studio, not far from the restaurant. There were paintings of the ocean and sailboats on the walls.

"I love the ocean," he explained, putting his hand underneath her shirt and squeezing her breast.

She closed her eyes. She didn't love this man, but she wanted to be loved again, even if only for a while.

They kissed, and then he gently disrobed her, running his hands over her body with his slender fingers. She was self-conscious, and pulled his body on top of hers.

"A condom?" she whispered.

He smiled and pulled one out of his nightstand. He slipped it on. His penis was so small she could barely feel him. She suddenly wished she were somewhere else. He was grinding on top her, grunting, oblivious. *Please hurry*, she thought, staring up at the blue ocean on the wall, wishing she could float away in the waves.

He came with a satisfied moan. She was relieved it was over, and pulled his silk sheets up to her chest.

He tied off the condom and tossed it in the trash and then lit a cigarette. He held the pack out to her. She took one, having grown accustomed to the smell, and leaned back on the pillows, lightly inhaling.

"So, you have a child?" he asked.

She turned to him as if he had slapped her. He pointed to her stomach, which had a half dozen stretch marks around her belly button. She was mortified, and angry. She put out the cigarette and pulled on her tight black pants and turquoise tank and low brown boots.

"I don't mind if you do," he offered, blowing out smoke, watching her with a dull, satiated look in his eyes. "I don't judge."

She grabbed her purse and ran out the door. She rode the subway all night, not wanting to go home. It was a good lesson for her. Turning to men for comfort was never a good idea. Where had it ever gotten her?

When she saw him at the restaurant, after that, she ducked her head, and walked away, as if she had some urgent matter to attend to. He smiled at her, a vague, knowing look on his face, but he let her go.

In January, her two classes at the community college started, and she was intimidated by the other students. There were students who had worked at Vogue and Chanel and spoke in industry terms she didn't understand. But she worked hard, studying old design books, staying in the studio late into the night. Her fingers became raw from sketching and sewing and pinning and tugging. She owed it to her children to make her life right. She wanted to go back to them, and have them be proud of who she had become.

She and Trinity spent a lot of time together, studying on the couch, and brainstorming design ideas, and planning their futures. They would start a company together as soon as they had the money, they decided. It would have a Philadelphia edge, be a little gritty. Brittney was struck by how they had dreamed of that very thing when they were girls, and now it seemed like it might be possible. This made her weepy because she sensed the whole life that had come between then and now.

Chapter Fifteen

Rebecca

In February, Rebecca celebrated the fifteenth-month anniversary of the children coming to her home. She could have called Yvonne—who was *still* waiting to adopt her girls—or Martha or Natalie, as they were all part of the process, and would have understood the celebration, but she thought if she shared the celebration with anyone, it might jinx it and the children would be taken away. So she poured herself a glass of champagne and sat on the carpet and flipped through her book of memories, flabbergasted at the old photographs of Maggie, who had once been so boney and fragile.

She laughed at the later photographs of Maggie and Madison being silly, sticking their tongues out or walking in Rebecca's running shoes or dancing with their hands in the air. She traced the many faces of Ethan: mostly dark and somber, almost turned into himself. He did not ham for the camera. But there were photographs where he was working on his toy cars, and his expression was studious and proud, and others where he had his arm over Madison's shoulder, and there was a strange mix of fraternal and paternal love lighting up his eyes.

After drinking two glasses of champagne and finishing the memory book, she thought of Brittney, who had birthed the children, if nothing else. The rest was unclear—how bad things had been, why she had disappeared from their lives. She picked up her phone and dialed her number. No one answered. It made her sad, this inability to find Brittney. But it also made her life easier. Simpler. She would be lying to herself if she had said there wasn't a part of her that was glad.

Earlier, she had asked Ms. Delevan, the new DHS caseworker, if Brittney had changed her number, and she had responded with an imperious stare and a clipped, "That's not your concern." Ms. Delevan's formality was chilling—she was obviously a bureaucrat, carrying around a notepad she made marks in, neutrally studying the children, as if they were pieces of fruit she'd been sent to examine. Rebecca spoke to her as little as possible, fearing she would observe something Rebecca was doing wrong, and use it against her. It seemed like anything could happen in the system. Yvonne's girls had been in her care for four years, and still, she could not adopt them. The parents were fighting hard, filing appeal after appeal. Martha, in contrast, had adopted Dyod after twelve months.

The week before the fifteenth-month permanency hearing, Ms. Delevan requested Rebecca provide any records she had kept on the children, and Rebecca handed over her large memory book, with their photographs and doctor's appointments and school reports and notes about their progress. Ms. Delevan flipped through it, and as a bureaucrat, was impressed with the detail. She announced she would return it later, after the hearing. Rebecca didn't want to let it go—it had all their memories—but she did because Ms. Delevan wore her authority like a heavy winter coat, and a firm look on her face dared anyone to try to take it away.

Rebecca drove to the Save-A-Lot, where Brittney worked, and asked about her. The manager said she'd quit, and gave her the address he'd forwarded her last check to. It was in New York. Rebecca paid a service she found on the Internet to acquire the phone number for the address, and when she called the number, a young man answered.

"Is Brittney there?"

"Brittney, yeah, hold on."

She could hear him hand over a phone, and Rebecca wondered if he was her boyfriend.

"Hello?" Brittney said, softly.

"Brittney, it's me, Rebecca. The fifteenth-month hearing is in a few days. You should be here."

"Why?"

"If you don't do anything, they'll probably terminate your parental rights."

She breathed in and out softly, but didn't say anything. Rebecca remembered something Nina had told her.

"Maybe you should sign over your rights. That way they won't bother you later."

"What do you mean?"

"Nina told me if they terminate your rights, they will investigate you if you ever have another child."

"Oh."

There was a long silence. Rebecca didn't know what else to say. She wanted to know how Brittney was doing, but she wasn't sure this question would be welcomed.

"How are the kids doing?"

"They're doing really well. Ethan is learning so much science in kindergarten. Things I have long forgotten. Madison loves preschool. There's one girl she calls her best friend, and whenever she gets to school, she runs up and holds her hand. It's very sweet. Maggie started daycare, she seems to like it. She's started to talk a little more. She's not a big talker. She can climb anything, though."

Brittney let out a large breath, and it sounded like sadness and relief. "Thank you," she said finally, and then disconnected.

Rebecca hoped Brittney would call the caseworker. She wasn't going to tell anyone about the call. Ms. Delevan was a stickler for the rules, and Rebecca knew it wasn't her job to track Brittney down.

At the hearing, she sat in a row behind Ms. Delevan and the DHS lawyer and watched the door, wondering if Brittney would walk in. The hearing began, and the judge, an older white man with a bald head, asked Brittney's lawyer where she was. The lawyer, a slender woman in an ill-fitting button-up shirt, shrugged.

"I'm really not sure."

"When's the last time you spoke with her?" the judge asked.

The lawyer sighed and rummaged through her stacks of paper. "Not for a while ... two or three months or so."

The judge turned to DHS.

"Have you been able to reach her?"

The DHS lawyer was a young man and he consulted the papers and shook his head. "Not for two months. DHS caseworker Ms. Delevan visited her address and called her numerous times but was unable to make contact."

The judge sighed, and rubbed his forehead. "Now remind me, has anyone been able to reach the father?"

Rebecca had a moment of panic, imagining the father waltzing in and demanding custody of his children.

"No, your honor. We've never been able to reach him."

He asked for DHS's recommendation on how to proceed.

Ms. Delevan coughed and sat up primly in her seat. "We recommend terminating the parental rights and changing the goal to adoption by the foster mother, your honor. It has been fifteen months, and the mother hasn't made any progress on her plan. She's failed multiple drug tests. The circumstances that led to the children's dependency have not altered. In addition, the children are flourishing with the foster mother."

"The foster mother is a Penn professor?"

"That's correct, your honor."

The judge nodded, impressed, and he stroked his chin. For the first time, Rebecca felt like it was a real possibility, that the children would be hers, legally. That she could cut their hair and visit New York without court permission. That she could tell them they would never have to leave.

The judge turned to the children's lawyer, a young woman who had barely seen the children. "What do you think?"

"I agree with DHS. I think the children would be best served now by moving to adoption."

The judge nodded and turned to Brittney's lawyer. "Do you

have anything to add?"

The lawyer blushed, and played with her papers. "I have to advocate that the mother should be given more time."

Ms. Delevan bristled from the other side.

"Your honor," she said, "The mother has shown no interest in her children. The children were bruised, filthy, and the youngest child was a failure to thrive when taken into custody. In addition, the children were found alone in a hazardous apartment while the mother was drinking in a bar, hooking up with strange men. The mother also has an untreated drug addiction."

The judge nodded, and looked at Brittney's lawyer expectantly.

The woman shifted in her seat, and tucked her hair behind her ear. She looked like she was going to say something, but then she just closed her mouth and turned away.

"OK," the judge concluded, shuffling his papers, "I am going to enter an order following DHS's recommendation to change the goal to adoption and schedule a TPR trial."

Brittney's lawyer flushed, and gathered her papers. The DHS lawyer conferred with Ms. Delevan, and then she pulled on her wool coat, and walked out of the courtroom.

The DHS lawyer and the judge seemed to be preparing for the next case, and Rebecca gathered her coat and purse and left. In the hallway, she scanned the faces, still incredulous Brittney had not shown up. She had expected her to rush in at the last minute, her clothes disheveled, her eyes red.

Outside in the cold, she allowed herself to feel excited. It was happening. Only a few more months and it would be over. Of course she knew the adoption could still veer off track. A new judge or lawyer could intervene. Brittney or the father could abruptly return, and object to the termination of their rights. Anything could happen in family court, it seemed. But the adoption felt inevitable.

Chapter Sixteen

Brittney

Kai blew into the apartment at odd hours, enthused about a local political campaign. He was volunteering after work, coding for the campaign website. He covered the apartment's walls in posters. Trinity rolled her eyes, thinking it looked lowbrow. Brittney smiled agreeably, but secretly she found it endearing he was so passionate about something. And if he could work on a political campaign, she could become a fashion designer.

At the end of the spring semester, she presented her final project, an ankle-length aquamarine dress she had carefully designed and constructed. It billowed at the breasts and thighs and calves. She knew her evening gown was strange, but she thought it was beautiful. The professors studied the dress, tugging at the materials, feeling the curves, walking around the mannequin. Brittney's palms were sweaty. She was an imposter and she imagined the dress unraveling, falling to a heap on the floor.

The professors conferred with one another, and she tried to interpret their expressions. They seemed neutral, but maybe it was disdain, or pity. Maybe they knew who she was, what a terrible person she was. How she had lost her own children.

One of them smiled slightly, and they walked over to her, all three of them.

They praised the dress's originality, remarking on how the silkiness of the material contradicted its formal shape, creating something unexpected that was also lovely. She took deep breaths as they spoke, and thought, *OK. Maybe I will be OK.*

In June, she rode the Bolt Bus back to Philadelphia, her cheek pressed against the window. She was wearing a purple shift dress she had sewn herself, and black tights and silver ballet flats. Her hair was curly and styled. Her makeup was on. She had looked at herself in the mirror, and she liked what she had seen. A stylish New Yorker. Better than Philadelphia. But the way she looked was small compensation for how terrible she felt.

She was going back to Philadelphia to sign over her parental rights. The foster woman, and then the caseworker, had told her, if she didn't, they would be taken away involuntarily, and then DHS would investigate her if she ever had another child. She didn't think she could ever have another child—it would be a betrayal to the three she had lost—but she was only twenty-four, and she couldn't be sure. And she knew she never wanted to speak with DHS again. They were a nightmare.

So signing her rights over was the best option. But still, she didn't want to voluntarily sign her rights over. There was nothing voluntary about it. Her children had been stolen, and the rest of it—the pretense she could ever have won them back —was a farce. She wanted to spit in the caseworkers and lawyers and judges faces, tell them, even though they had gotten away with the kidnapping, they would be judged by a higher power.

She was too nauseous to eat or drink anything. The courthouse was packed with people, and she kept her head down, drifting through the crowd. She puked in the bathroom. Her lawyer, who she vaguely recognized, was waiting for her outside the courtroom in a cheap gray suit.

"You look good," the lawyer remarked, surprise in her voice.

Brittney stared back at her, this dishrag who had stood by as DHS had gotten its way. She was angry that the lawyer who had been so useless to her would make such a frivolous comment. Who cared what she looked like? What did that have to do with anything?

"Anyway," the lawyer said, shuffling her feet and heaving her bag up on her shoulder, "are you ready to sign over your rights?"

Brittney nodded.

"OK." The lawyer's face was blank, as if she didn't really remember the details of the case and didn't care either way. They walked into the courtroom.

The judge was an old white man, and his eyes flittered over Brittney. After everyone sat down, the lawyers and the judge started discussing her case, and Brittney dug her nails into her palms, and tried not to think of her children. She reminded herself they were OK, and the foster woman was giving them opportunities she never could have. Maybe they would even become doctors, or lawyers.

The judge shook his head, as if he were annoyed with the whole proceedings. He spoke directly to Brittney. His voice seemed high-pitched. He reprimanded her for failing her children, and she wanted to shout, *No, you failed my children!* But she didn't. Because she knew yelling wouldn't help.

He asked her questions—did she understand this was permanent? Was she doing this of her own free will? Was she sure she wanted this? His tone was listless, and his head was down, focused on his papers. He was checking off little boxes as she answered: a barely audible "yes," which really meant "no!" But he seemed satisfied to check his boxes, and remove the case from his docket. The lawyers, too, seemed satisfied at the closing of the case.

Brittney walked out of the courthouse alone, tossing the papers, the proof of her renunciation, in a green trash bin. She stood on the street, and the summer sun burned her eyes. She was disoriented. Tourists and lawyers and families were walking past her on the sidewalk, talking, but they seemed far away. Everything seemed far away.

She had a strong desire to go see her children, to know they were OK. They were only a few miles away. But they weren't her children anymore. Not really. On the way back to the bus stop, she walked into a bar, and drank two shots of whiskey. She wiped her mouth and asked for the bill. Incredible, she thought. It was twenty-two dollars. As much as the round trip bus tickets. She threw down two tens and a five, and walked back outside.

She boarded the next bus back to New York, taking the last seat available. It was in the back row, and the toilet smelled of urine and bleach. No one—not Trinity, not Chris, not her mother—knew what she had done today. She leaned her head against the window, and stared at the flat yellow fields. They seemed barren.

She picked up her cell phone, and called the foster woman.

"How are the kids doing?" she asked, her voice cracking.

The foster woman enthused about Ethan's projects in school, and Madison's friends in preschool, and Maggie's climbing the art museum stairs all by herself, all the way to the top.

"Like Rocky," the foster woman laughed.

Brittney smiled, wiping the tears with the back of her hands. "Thank you," she said, and slipped the phone back in her purse.

"You coming or going?"

It took a moment, but Brittney realized he was talking to her. She looked at the young man sitting next to her. He was dressed in khaki pants and a dress shirt. A little nerdy, like Kai.

"I live in New York," she said, and finally, it felt true. She didn't feel like she was just visiting anymore.

"Me, too. I was interviewing at Wharton. The business school."

She nodded. "How'd it go?"

"Good. At least I think so," he said, laughing. His teeth were straight and white. "You never know, right?"

"No, I guess not." She turned back to the window. She didn't feel like talking.

"Nice dress," he noted.

She smiled, despite herself. "I designed it."

He looked at it more closely, and nodded, impressed. "You in school for design?"

She nodded, and it struck her that this didn't feel like a lie either. She was a design student living in New York, as hard as it was to believe.

When they got off the bus, he asked for her number, and she recited it to him. She wasn't sure if she would go out with him. But it felt good to know there were possibilities. She might love someone again, someday. And her children would be OK. Once she had made something of herself, she would go back to them, and they would know her again.

Chapter Seventeen

Rebecca

The case dragged into the hot summer, but, finally, near the end of August, the adoptions were finalized. Rebecca celebrated by driving with the children to New York—without court permission—and visiting her sister and parents. They rode to the top of the Empire State building, and took a ferry across the river. Ethan loved the boat, and asked what kind of engine it had. The captain was happy to talk to him, pointing out all the buttons and levers.

They visited Brittney, who was living near 14th Street with her cousin and her cousin's boyfriend. She seemed healthy. Her eyes were clear and her hair had grown out, and it curled past her ears. She was wearing a blue jumper she had sewn herself. The girls marveled at it.

Brittney showed them her sketches of women's clothes, and Ethan was impressed. He pulled the map he had drawn in the car ride up out of his pocket. Brittney studied it carefully, tracing the streets with her finger.

They went out to lunch, and Maggie made a mess of the table. Brittney asked Ethan and Madison about school, and they both talked for a while, and she seemed proud of them. She nodded at Rebecca, and there was gratitude in her eyes, and maybe a little sadness.

The children were playing with paper straws, twisting them and launching into the air.

"Miss Rebecca," Ethan said, "can we go play over there?" He

pointed to a corner with arcade games and a bouncy horse.

"Sure," Rebecca said, reaching in her purse. She gave him a handful of quarters. She stood up, and helped Maggie down from the booster seat. The children ran off.

Brittney watched them, and smiled as Ethan heaved Madison up on the bouncy horse.

For a moment, they sat in silence. Brittney was running her finger around the perimeter of her plate, and her hand seemed long and delicate. It wasn't surprising she could draw so beautifully.

"Brittney..." she said, wanting to reach out to her, but not quite knowing how. "You know, for as long as I can remember, I always wanted children."

Brittney's eyes widened, and anger, briefly, flared.

"That's not what I meant," Rebecca stumbled. "What I'm trying to say is I was married for over a decade. My husband kept telling me we would have children later. And I waited, growing older and older, because I loved him.

"But later never came. Before I knew it, I was almost forty, with no children."

Brittney's eyes were still wary, but they had softened.

"I still loved him. But I couldn't see my life without ever having children. So I left him.

"And I was too old to start over with someone else. I had to do it alone.

"What I'm trying to say is maybe... maybe I wanted children too badly. I ... might have approached this whole thing the wrong way."

Brittney seemed surprised, and guarded, like she wasn't sure she wanted to hear this.

"The truth is," Rebecca continued, struggling to unearth the right words, "I don't trust DHS either. I know they can be arbitrary and bureaucratic. I was selfish to not ... I don't know, do something.

"I'm sorry I wasn't ... braver."

Rebecca had said these things because she was free to now

—legally, the children were hers—and she knew that this, too, was cowardly. But maybe it was better than nothing.

Brittney was picking at the pizza crust on her plate, tearing it into pieces. "They might have listened to you, a wealthy woman with a degree."

"Maybe," Rebecca acknowledged. "They might have."

Brittney closed her eyes, and ripples of frustration ran over her face. "It's like they didn't see that I was there, day after day, night after night, taking care of my kids, all by myself."

Brittney went quiet, closing her eyes, as if she had said more than she meant to. Rebecca remembered her first month with the children, before Maggie had been treated for reflux. She had felt clunky and exhausted, and that had only been a few weeks. It was easy to see how after six months of constant crying, with no help, things would have begun to fall apart.

Rebecca reached over and wrapped her fingers around Brittney's hand. Brittney's hand was roughly the same size as her own. But her fingers were calloused.

Brittney squeezed her eyes shut, and her face was perfectly still, and Rebecca could see Madison's sharp cheekbones.

Brittney straightened her back, and pulled her hand away.

"Well," she said lightly, "at least we never have to see DHS again."

Rebecca smiled, raising her glass of water. "Here's to neither of us having to deal with them ever again."

Brittney raised her glass, and they clacked against each other, water sliding over the edges.

Rebecca paid for lunch, leaving a generous tip for Maggie's food littering, and they both herded the children outside, walking the few blocks to Brittney's apartment. Brittney promised to call and visit, when she had a break from school. Her voice was clear and confident, but subdued.

"Please do," Rebecca urged. She wanted her children to have their mother in their life.

Brittney stared at the four of them for a moment, and then

wiped her eyes with the back of her hands. She leaned down and whispered something into Ethan's ear. He nodded, and hugged her hips tightly.

On the way back to Elizabeth's, Madison and Maggie laughed and skipped on the street. Ethan held Rebecca's hand.

"My mom's doing pretty good now," he said, looking up at Rebecca.

"She is. I think she's going to be OK."

Ethan nodded, and there was a small smile on his face. He was quiet for a moment.

"The judge said you would never leave, right?"

"That's right. The judge said you're mine forever." She grinned. "Whether you like it or not."

He smiled and then ran after his sisters. He grabbed one of Madison's braids and she squealed and chased after him. Maggie ran ahead, her hands a V in the air.

Rebecca watched them, and she was happy.

There would be no more court appointments or caseworkers popping by or lawyers asking questions. But there was still Brittney. Seeing Brittney in her stylish jumper, her eyes clear and ambitious, she wondered if, one day, Brittney would come back for the children, and she would be young and hip and fun, and the children would be drawn to her. Rebecca would seem boring, and she would lose the children back to her. Not legally, but in their hearts.

It was possible.

Maggie circled back and grabbed Rebecca's hand.

"Up, Mommy! Up!"

Rebecca crouched down, and Maggie scrambled onto her shoulders, looping her legs around her neck and holding onto her head. She laughed as Rebecca stood. Madison and Ethan waved at Maggie, smiling, and Rebecca smiled back, her heart expanding.

Maybe the more people who loved them, the better. Love wasn't a zero sum game. Maybe, one day, they could have an old bookish mother and a young hip mother.

Stranger things had happened.

Chapter Eighteen

Brittney

"Are you sure you don't want to come to Kai's parents' house? There's plenty of room," Trinity said, as Kai grabbed their suitcases from underneath the bus.

Brittney smiled and shook her head. "Thanks, but I want to see the kids."

Trinity nodded, concern on her brows. "OK. Call if …." Her voice trailed off. "We can come pick you up anytime."

"It's no problem," Kai agreed. He pointed to a silver BMW. "There's my dad."

Trinity wrapped her arms around Brittney, lingering. She smelled like tea tree oil.

"I'll be fine," Brittney assured, ignoring the nervous sway of her stomach.

Kai heaved his and Trinity's suitcases in the trunk, and then held the door open for Trinity. Kai's father was wearing wire-rimmed glasses, and he turned his head, and said something to Trinity in the backseat. Trinity laughed.

Brittney watched them drive away. Kai's parents lived on the main line, in a large house with a pool. She searched the cars for a silver station wagon. Brand new. She fiddled with the top of her suitcase, wondering if this was a mistake. The foster woman had invited her to Thanksgiving, and after thinking about it for a few weeks, she had agreed.

The station wagon double parked in front of another car, and the foster woman waved at Brittney, her cheeks flushed.

"Sorry I'm late. Maggie pooped her underwear right when

we were about to leave."

Brittney smiled, and the foster woman took her suitcase, and lifted it into the trunk. Brittney sat in the passenger seat.

"Hi, mom," Ethan said, reaching for her hand.

"Guess what? I made stuffing!" Madison announced proudly. "With raisins and celery."

"Neat," Brittney said, swallowing a lump of sadness in her throat, imagining Madison in the kitchen, helping to stir and pour, a serious look on her face.

The foster woman glanced at Brittney, taking her eyes off the road.

"How's school going?" she asked warmly, and for a surreal moment, it felt like the foster woman was her mother, and she was home from college for the first time.

"Good," Brittney said. "It's really good actually."

"Do you make that?"

Brittney fingered her wool dress, the color of the sky on a clear summer day. It had a scoop neck, and long sleeves, and it was tight, almost like an embrace. "Trinity made it for me."

"It's beautiful."

"I think so."

Brittney fingered Ethan's hand, feeling the muscles and the bones. It seemed so much larger than the last time she had seen him, a few months ago.

Brittney wondered if her family would show up. Her mother, Dave and Angel, and William had all promised to come, but they had seemed to think the invitation was strange. She had told them, her voice shrill, this was the only way for her children to see them, and that had silenced them. They judged her for losing the kids, she knew they did. But they understood she still loved them.

"I made a few things, but I mostly ordered prepared food from Whole Foods," the foster woman rambled. Her shirt was untucked, but her hair seemed stylish again, like she had it professionally done. "I've never been much of a cook," she shrugged.

"It's OK," Brittney said. She didn't care about the food.

The foster woman's house, with its sprawling yard and trees that seemed to reach the sky, seemed bucolic. Brittney had grown used to Manhattan, with its miles of skyscrapers, its wide streets, its constant streams of cars. Brittney got out of the car and watched as Ethan unbuckled himself, smiling shyly at her. The foster woman unstrapped the girls. The children shrugged on their winter coats, and then ran into the backyard.

"Mom, come look at what I built!" Ethan called.

"Go ahead," the foster woman urged. "I'll put your suitcase in the guest room."

"Thanks," Brittney said, her low-heeled boots digging into the soft ground, as she followed Ethan to his work table. She was glad it was in the same place as before, just as she had been picturing it. Every night, right before she fell asleep, she thought of her children in the backyard. She always pictured them happy: Madison smiling, rocking a baby doll in her arms, Maggie running across the grass, laughing, and Ethan building at his table, his head bent, his eyes intent.

Ethan was working on a train track, screwing the rails together. He waved the train at her.

"Once I am done, it will actually run."

"Cool," she said, running her finger over one of the tracks. It was silver and smooth. Expensive. It all looked expensive.

Madison ran out of the playhouse.

"Come play dolls with me," she urged.

"OK," she said, squeezing Ethan's shoulder. "I'll be back."

"OK," he said, not looking up from his tracks.

Madison wanted Brittney to be the Prince, and she obliged, holding the doll as Madison's Princess brushed her hair in the mirror.

"OK," Brittney said. "Should we run away together?"

Madison's doll leaned over and kissed Brittney's, and she giggled. "Let's get married. You're my own true love."

Brittney laughed. "Your one true love?"

"No, my *own* true love. All mine."

"Oh, OK," Brittney smiled.

The foster woman appeared in the doorway. "Dinner will be ready soon," she said.

Brittney nodded, and put the doll down.

"No, bring him inside. Prince Charming is coming, too."

"OK," Brittney said, picking him up, and holding Madison's hand as they walked across the lawn. The trees, shorn of their leaves, seemed spindly and bare. She realized Madison had stopped calling her mama and, for a moment, she froze. But then she walked forward, swallowing this loss, focusing on the warmth of her daughter's hand.

The house smelled like pumpkin pie and turkey. Brittney curled up in the armchair, holding the Prince, and smiling at the children as they brought her books and toys. The foster woman was tinkering with the dishes on the dining room table. Brittney glanced at her watch, afraid her family wouldn't show up, and the foster woman would think something must be deeply wrong with her, after all, that her own family would stand her up on Thanksgiving.

The doorbell rang, loud and clear, and the children stampeded to answer it. Ethan pulled the door open.

Dave and Angel and her mother were standing there, looking slightly uncomfortable.

"Grandma! Uncle Dave!" Ethan said, smiling, reaching for their hands. He pulled them inside.

Madison's head was tilted in confusion, like she was trying to place them. "Grandma?" she repeated, uncertain.

Maggie had already run back to the toys.

Brittney's mother whistled. "Nice place they got here," she said.

Angel had walked inside, and was inspecting the furniture.

Dave let go of Ethan's hand, and reached over and embraced Brittney. He still smelled like the outdoors, ruddy and masculine.

"You look good, baby sis. You look good."

"Thank you for coming," Brittney whispered in his ear, feeling like the whole thing was suddenly less strange.

The foster woman rushed into the living room, smiling, and everyone introduced themselves. She offered them drinks, and Brittney's heart plunged a little when her mother requested "a large one," winking at the foster woman.

Ethan tugged Dave over to his homemade circuits, showing him how to light them up.

"Well, look at that," Brittney heard Dave say.

Angel was perched on the edge of the couch, staring up at the photograph of six black women, nearly naked.

"What is *that*?" she asked.

Brittney had always wondered the same thing. The foster woman had returned with a tray of drinks, and a blush crept up her neck, like a flower blooming.

"It's a tribe in Africa, the Nobuso. It's a tribe of all women. I stayed with them, on and off, for years."

"Huh," Angel said. "Why did you do that?"

"Oh," the foster woman said, handing out tall glasses of red wine. "I wanted to study a society of all women, see what it was like."

"Huh," Angel repeated, taking a sip of her wine.

"What was it like?" Brittney asked, curious.

The foster woman put the tray on the coffee table, and looked up at Brittney. "It was mostly lovely. There was freedom and contentment in the way they were."

"How'd they have kids, then?" Brittney's mother asked.

The foster woman laughed. "When it was the right time, they visited the men, or even other tribes. The men were happy to comply."

"I'm sure they were," Angel said, snorting.

"What happened to the boys, when they grew up?" Brittney asked.

"At puberty, they left to join the men. I thought this would be devastating, but the mothers seemed OK. Every couple months, they had celebrations with the men, and the mothers always found their boys first, to make sure they were OK."

Brittney nodded. She liked that story, how unconventional their lives were. She sipped the wine, and it warmed her.

At dinner, the children sat at their own table, laughing and squealing. Maggie darted around the table in circles, not wanting to sit still.

Brittney sat between her mother and her brother. For a while, they ate silently, watching Maggie run around the room.

Brittney's mother reached over, and patted her thigh.

"You look healthy," she said, loudly. Her breath smelled of wine. She had already drunk four glasses, only pecking at her food like a bird.

"Thank you, mom," Brittney said, hoping she wouldn't make a scene, yell at the foster woman for stealing her grandbabies. She didn't want her mother to ruin this—whatever this was.

Her mother smiled, and turned back to the table. "You infertile?" she asked the foster woman.

"Mom," Dave chided. Angel laughed.

The foster woman smiled, embarrassed. "I don't know. I never tried. My husband didn't want children."

"You married?"

"I was. We divorced."

"Pretty woman like you, you could have found someone else," Brittney's mother said, skeptically. "Didn't need to take someone else's children."

"Mom," Brittney said softly, resting her hand on her mother's. It felt bony and fragile. Her mother looked at her.

"What? It's true."

Ethan was suddenly at the table, tugging at her mother's hand.

"Grandma, you want to come see my room?"

She smiled at him. "Sure, I do, Ethan. You lead the way."

Dave winked at Brittney. Brittney leaned against his bicep, feeling the hard warmth of it, holding onto his hand.

"This was delicious," Dave said, politely, pointing to his empty plate.

"Oh, thanks. I can't take any credit. Most of it came from Whole Foods," the foster woman explained, smiling.

Dave smiled back at her, and Angel watched him silently, her eyes narrowing. She stood up, her heels clacking on the wood floors, and wrapped her arms around his neck, possessively. Brittney let go off his arm. Madison was sitting by herself, eating pumpkin pie, and Brittney rose out of her chair, to join her.

"How is it?"

"It's very good," Madison said, nodding her head as she took another bite. "You want a bite?"

Brittney smiled and opened her mouth. "Thanks," she said.

Brittney's mother came down the stairs. "Sure is large in here," she said, loudly. "More space than anyone could need."

Brittney agreed with this, but she didn't say anything.

"Does anybody want dessert?" the foster woman asked, rising from her seat.

"I'll take some," Dave said.

"I'll take another glass of wine," Brittney's mother commented. Ethan tugged her hand. "Read me a book, grandma," he urged.

"Let me get my wine first," she said, pouring herself a glass, and bringing it with her into the living room.

Brittney noticed one of Madison's braids coming undone, the hairs unraveling near the end, and she pulled her over.

"Let me fix that braid for you."

"OK."

She undid the hair, letting it fall loosely, and then braided it more tightly, her fingers working quickly.

"Can you teach me to do it like that?"

"Sure, baby, when you're a little older."

"OK," she said, fingering her braid, twirling it.

Dave and Angel were eating their pie, and Brittney could

see their feet touching, underneath the table. It was strange that Angel didn't want children, and because of this, her brother might never have a child. Dave looked at her and Madison.

Madison moved shyly behind Brittney's arm, peeking out at Dave.

"Madison, you remind me of your mother at that age," he told her. "She was sweet and shy, too."

"Mama?" she asked, perplexed. Brittney felt her heart drop.

"Your mom," he said, pointing to Brittney.

"Oh," she said, and her small fingers curled more tightly around Brittney's bicep, but her eyes were confused.

Dave ate his last bite of pie, and then leaned back from the table. "Thank you for having us," he said to the foster woman. Angel flicked her wrist at Dave, and mouthed *time to go*. Dave smiled warmly and stood up.

"Yeah, thanks," Angel said, glancing at the foster woman, a territorial expression on her face, as if the foster woman might be interested in Dave.

"My pleasure," the foster woman said.

In the living room, they slid their coats on, and helped her mother into hers.

"Goodbye, Ethan," Dave said. Ethan ran over and hugged him. Dave clapped his back.

"Come visit us anytime."

"OK, I will," Ethan said, nodding somberly.

The foster woman nodded. "I could drop him off ..." she said.

Brittney remembered how, after Chris left, Ethan had looked at men differently, with more longing. Maybe he still wanted a father. That was one thing the foster woman couldn't give him either.

Brittney walked her family to the door.

"Happy Thanksgiving," she said.

"You want to come home?" her mother asked.

Brittney considered it. Home seemed safe, but she wanted

to wake up with her children, spend the day with them.

"No," she said, finally. "I will be OK here."

Dave kissed her on the cheek, his two-day beard scuffing her chin.

Brittney rummaged in her purse, for her phone. There was a message from William, apologizing for missing the dinner. His ex-girlfriend had dropped the children off, at the last minute. Next time, he promised.

Brittney led Ethan and Madison to their bedrooms, and helped them into their pajamas. They piled onto Madison's little bed, and she sat in the middle, their warm bodies pressed against her.

She read book after book, until her voice began to falter. "Last one," she said, stroking Ethan's hair, and they mumbled agreeably. When she finished, she tucked Madison in, kissing her smooth forehead, running her fingers over her hair.

"See you in the morning," she said.

"See you in the morning," Madison repeated, as she rolled onto her side, her arms wrapped around a teddy bear. She had always been a good sleeper.

Brittney walked down the stairs, with Ethan's hand in hers. She turned on his nightlight and he climbed into his bed. She sat on the edge. He reached up and played with her hair, and his fingers were light as snow falling.

"I'm glad you came home, mom," he said.

"Me, too," she said, pressing her cheek next to his cheek, ignoring the wrench in her heart. This house *was* his home. "I will see you in the morning."

"Promise?"

"Promise."

He expelled a breath of relief. She could feel the steady rhythm of his breathing, and the beat of his heart. She lifted her head. His eyes were closed, and he seemed peaceful and content.

"Goodnight, baby boy," she whispered.

Back downstairs, the foster woman had finished cleaning the kitchen. She brought out two glasses of wine, and handed one to Brittney. She put hers down, and then turned on the fire.

"It's gas," she explained.

Brittney nodded, and curled up in the armchair, and watched the orange flames flicker. The foster woman had her legs tucked under her, and she was also staring at the fire, her cheeks pink. There were wrinkles flanking her eyes, as delicate as spider webs, that hadn't been there before.

"Thank you for doing this," Brittney said, abruptly. "For having me and my family over."

The foster woman glanced over. "I know this will never be easy, but I hope ...."

Brittney waited a minute, but the foster woman didn't finish her thought. It didn't matter. Brittney knew what she meant, knew the general shape of the airy, happy thing she was reaching for. "I do, too," she acknowledged. And then, more softly, she said, "Rebecca."

The name felt strange in her mouth, like cotton candy, and her resentment and anger briefly gathered. But she swallowed it. She had seen all you could lose if you didn't swallow your anger. It was time for something else, something more forgiving.

"Rebecca," she repeated, staring up at the beautiful women, the women who lived without men.

She looked over at Rebecca, and Rebecca looked back at her, smiling tentatively. Brittney was unsure, maybe even afraid. But she smiled back, and, slowly, a feeling of hope spread, until it seemed larger than her, larger than all of them.

BOOKS BY THIS AUTHOR

Peyton And Isabelle

"A terrible secret transforms a young couple's life ... this is a thoughtful, affecting tale. A powerful, involving drama," Kirkus Reviews

"The relationship between Peyton and Isabelle is intense, moves with lightning speed, and will keep readers turning the pages as Yearwood's story spans the course of these lovers' lives," Booklife Review

Peyton is born to a teen mom in the hollers of West Virginia. After he lands a football scholarship to a Boston prep school, he knows this is his chance to climb out of backbreaking poverty.

Determined to make something of himself, he excels on the field and in school. No one can stop him. He falls in love with Isabelle, a fellow student, and feels like he can do anything. Surrounded by kids who are destined to rule society, he starts to see a life where he never has to want again.

But senior year, he and his prep school friends set off fireworks that spark a fire in a nearby building. Their decision to flee and cover up their involvement, even after they realize the fire killed multiple people, weighs on him.

Peyton begins to realize that all the success in the world may not make up for losing himself. As the decades pass, he and Isabelle remain at odds about his decision, and they try to hold on to one another as guilt, ambition, and fear cast shadows across their lives.

BOOKS BY THIS AUTHOR

Peyton And Isabelle

"A terrible secret transforms a young couple's life ... this is a thoughtful, affecting tale. A powerful, involving drama," Kirkus Reviews

"The relationship between Peyton and Isabelle is intense, moves with lightning speed, and will keep readers turning the pages as Yearwood's story spans the course of these lovers' lives," Booklife Review

Peyton is born to a teen mom in the hollers of West Virginia. After he lands a football scholarship to a Boston prep school, he knows this is his chance to climb out of backbreaking poverty.

Determined to make something of himself, he excels on the field and in school. No one can stop him. He falls in love with Isabelle, a fellow student, and feels like he can do anything. Surrounded by kids who are destined to rule society, he starts to see a life where he never has to want again.

But senior year, he and his prep school friends set off fireworks that spark a fire in a nearby building. Their decision to flee and cover up their involvement, even after they realize the fire killed multiple people, weighs on him.

Peyton begins to realize that all the success in the world may not make up for losing himself. As the decades pass, he and Isabelle remain at odds about his decision, and they try to hold on to one another as guilt, ambition, and fear cast shadows across their lives.

BOOK CLUB QUESTIONS

1. Was Will a good partner to Rebecca? Should he have made a decision about not wanting children earlier?

2. What are the biggest factors that led to DHS coming to Brittney's apartment?

3. Should DHS have taken Brittney's children when they were called?

4. Should Rebecca have done anything differently to help Brittney?

5. How should DHS have treated Brittney once her children were in their custody?

6. Did Brittney make the best choices she could have given the circumstances?

7. How do you think Rebecca and Brittney's relationship will develop in the future?

8. Are there any elements of American cultural norms that impacted both Brittney and Rebecca's struggles?

9. How do women's relationships with children differ to men's relationships with children in America today? How much has this evolved in the last fifty years?

10. How would the children's lives turned out differently if they had never left Brittney's custody?

11. Should the foster care system and family law system be reformed? Why hasn't it been?

Made in the USA
Las Vegas, NV
23 December 2024

15221107R00166